T0129253

Murder by the Sea

The By the Sea Mystery Series by Kathleen Bridge

Murder by the Sea

A By the Sea Mystery

Kathleen Bridge

LYRICAL UNDERGROUND
Kensington Publishing Corp.
www.kensingtonbooks.com

I dedicate this book to my friend and mentor, author Elaine Wolf. If it wasn't for your guidance and inspiration, I wouldn't have written this or any other book.

"The heart of a man is very much like the sea, it has its storms, it has its tides and in its depths it has its pearls too."

—*Vincent van Gogh*

Chapter 1

"Dear Miss Marple, it's so wonderful you've taken time away from your knitting and sleuthing to share a few moments with me. Shall I refresh your beverage?"

"Thank you, Mr. Holmes."

He bowed and took his pipe out of his mouth. "Please, call me Sherlock. What libation may I procure for you?"

"A corpse reviver or a zombie would be perfect."

Liz laughed. "I don't think the vicar of St. Mary Meade would be too happy if he heard one of his favorite parishioners ordering something so untoward."

Eighty-three-year-old Betty Lawson, author of 1960s teenage mysteries, who'd recently scored a contract for a new series set in Sherlockian London, looked the perfect Miss Marple in her wire-framed spectacles. Her gray hair was in a French twist punctuated with crisscrossed knitting needles.

"Miss Marple is always full of surprises," Betty said, handing the debonair Captain Netherton, aka Sherlock Holmes, her empty glass. "In case they don't know how to make a corpse reviver, it's cognac, calvados, and sweet vermouth."

"And a zombie?" the debonair captain asked.

"Apricot brandy, lime, and pineapple juice. Or a glass of white wine would also be fine," she said with a laugh.

"Back in a flash, Milady Jane." As he walked away, Liz heard him mutter, "Corpse reviver?"

Atticus Finch joined Betty and Liz. He wore a white rumpled dress shirt and a striped buttoned-up vest. His shirtsleeves were rolled above the elbows of his long arms, his tie loosened around his neck. Under the crook of his arm, he carried a worn leather Alabama law book. "Daughter," he said, peering at her from behind tortoiseshell-framed eyeglasses. "I mean, Miss Eyre. I think Miss Havisham is having a wardrobe malfunction and needs your assistance." Liz's father, Fenton Holt, couldn't have chosen a more perfect character from the novel *To Kill a Mockingbird* for the New Year's Literary Masquerade Ball. He was a former public defender who now took on small cases from his law office at the back of their family-run hotel. "She texted me from her sitting room," he added.

"Aunt Amelia, texting! Will wonders never cease?" Liz straightened the lace collar on her serviceable, long black wool dress and tucked in a section of strawberry blond hair that escaped her brown wig. She'd unearthed the wig from a trunk in her great-aunt's wardrobe closet. Aunt Amelia had worn the wig when she'd played the Collins family's maid on the set of the '60s television daytime soap drama *Dark Shadows,* featuring a campy vampire named Barnabas Collins. As Aunt Amelia explained it, *Dark Shadows* came along decades before the *Twilight* books.

"I better run," Liz said to her father. "I don't want Miss Havisham to miss a minute of the ball. Hey, where's your fiancée? I'm dyin' to see what fictional character she chose." Her father and Charlotte, also known as Agent Pearson, chief homicide detective on the Brevard County Sheriff's Department, had gotten engaged under the mistletoe on Christmas Eve. Liz and Charlotte had butted heads on more than one occasion, and things had gotten a little dicey when Liz helped Charlotte solve not one but two murders after she'd been told to lay off. But lately, Charlotte and Liz had put aside their differences because they both cared about the same man.

"Charlotte's due to arrive any minute and she wouldn't tell me who she's coming as," he said. "You better hurry. Your great-aunt sounded frantic."

"Okay. Save a dance for me," Liz said, kissing him on his smooth cheek.

She parted her way through the noisy crowd. Every New Year's Eve, the gala moved from venue to venue and was sponsored by the Melbourne Beach and Vero Beach library systems. This year, the charity event was taking place in the center courtyard of the Indialantic by the Sea Hotel, located on a barrier island on the central east coast of Florida. The hotel had recently received historical landmark status and had been in Liz's family since 1926.

The ball kicked off a week-long New Year's Writers' Festival. Liz's great-aunt had talked her into teaching a five-day workshop on the Importance of Setting in Fiction. "It's for charity, Lizzy dear," Aunt Amelia had said. "The same library system that has a copy, or should I say *copies*, of your own novel."

The workshop was scheduled for Monday in the lush gardens of St. Benedict's Abbey, a former monastery. The building and the five acres of land it sat on had been deeded to the state and was being used as a writers' retreat for unpublished authors hoping to get their writing juices flowing. Their only muse was the view of the Atlantic out the abbey's window.

Liz knew all about the importance of setting. Her first novel, *Let the Wind Roar*, took place during World War I at fictional Penrose Castle in Cornwall, England. Her second, unpublished, novel, *An American in Cornwall*, was set during World War II at the same castle. However, that was where the similarity ended. Each book was a stand-alone, the only things tying them together were Penrose Castle and the surrounding countryside. Her great-grandmother had grown up in a castle in Cornwall called Isle Tor and had immigrated to Melbourne Beach to marry Liz's great-grandfather. When Liz was a teen, she'd found a satchel in the hotel's luggage room filled with her great-grandmother's diaries. The descriptions of the moors and the sea had sparked her interest in the wilds of Cornwall and had never left her writer's imagination.

Liz brushed aside her worry about the class. Plus, Betty, her biggest supporter and mentor, would be in the classroom next to her. Aunt Amelia had also commandeered a class for Betty to teach: Writing the Teenage Mystery Novel.

Liz glanced around the packed crowd as she made her way toward the doors leading into the interior of the hotel. Most of the ball's attendees were dressed as their favorite character from literature. There were four Alices, two White Rabbits, a slew of Mad Hatters, and a large representation of characters from *The Lord of the Rings*. She saw an abundance of empire-waisted ankle-length gowns and beribboned, upswept hair and recognized a few Emmas, Janes, Elizabeths, and Fannys stepping off the pages of Jane Austen.

She made her way out of the courtyard's French doors and stepped into the Indialantic's lobby, which appeared frozen in time from when the resort first opened, almost a hundred years ago. It was filled with bamboo furniture, tropical-print cushions, and numerous potted palms. Even the antique glass ornaments on the ten-foot Douglas fir Christmas tree held true to the hotel's inception. Most of the ornaments were brought from England by Liz's great-grandmother Maeve.

Liz took the spiral staircase up to the second floor. When she reached the end of the long hallway of suites, she heard her great-aunt squeal, "Ouch!" She ran inside and found Katniss Everdeen from *The Hunger Games* with a bow and arrow slung across her back. She was trying to zip up Miss Havisham's dingy-white wedding dress. Katniss, also known as Kate, Liz's best friend since childhood, said, "Sorry, Aunt Amelia, but this dress seems to have shrunk since I laundered it." Kate had always called Liz's great-aunt Aunt Amelia. They weren't related by blood, but the ties were just as strong.

Aunt Amelia had her back to Liz. "That's so kind of you, Katie, to make excuses for the dress not fitting properly. We both know my voluptuous physique is more to blame. It's impossible to believe I was once a size eight. However, that was almost sixty years ago."

Liz glanced over at a photo on the dressing room wall that showed a svelte Amelia Eden Holt arm-in-arm with the actor Adam West, who starred in the '60s television series *Batman*. In the photo, unbeknownst to Mr. West, fiery, red-haired Amelia was giving the actor bunny ears. With over fifty television roles to her credit, Liz's great-aunt was known as a prolific character actress in the 1960s and early 1970s. In the many star photos Liz had viewed over the years, she could tell Aunt Amelia had been a "character" both on and off the screen. And she still was. Since taking over the running of the Indialantic by the Sea Hotel, Aunt Amelia had turned to local theater to quench her passion for the spotlight. Her current role in the Melbourne Beach Theatre Company's production of Agatha Christie's *The Mousetrap* was as Mollie Ralston, proprietor of Monkswell Manor. The role was originally meant for a newlywed in her twenties, not an eighty-year-old woman. Rest assured, Aunt Amelia would make the part her very own.

Liz walked up to Kate and grabbed one side of the dress's zipper. Kate held the other side. "No problem, Auntie. Kate and I will get it closed. On the count of three, tug. One. Two. Three!"

They both stretched their sides of the yellowed-satin material to meet the center of Aunt Amelia's back.

"Take a deep breath, Auntie," Liz said, tugging harder. They closed the zipper, but the sound of ripping fabric soon followed.

Aunt Amelia put her hand over her right hip, hiding a three-inch tear.

"Oops," Kate said.

"'Please don't squeeze the Charmin!'" Barnacle Bob belted out. Aunt Amelia's macaw, who liked to repeat '60s television commercial jingles, many of which Aunt Amelia had starred in, was perched on the back of a velvet slipper chair.

"Hush, BB," Liz said with a grin. At least he hadn't used one of his curse words. She and Barnacle Bob had a joking relationship. At least she thought they did. However, she'd never let him sit on her shoulder as did her great-aunt. The one time he had, he'd ripped a gold hoop from her earlobe, drawing blood.

Aunt Amelia turned and faced them. Liz couldn't help but burst out laughing. Her great-aunt's usually brightly made-up face was a powdery white. Her trademarked frosted blue eyeshadow and thick black eyeliner had been replaced with smudged charcoal shadow that circled both her eyes raccoon style, giving her a ghoulish appearance. She wore only one shoe, as depicted in the Dickens novel *Great Expectations*, showing that when Miss Havisham received the news of her canceled wedding, she was in the midst of dressing.

"No worries, my avian pet. I'm fine," Aunt Amelia said, tickling Barnacle Bob under the beak. "The girls had no choice but to squeeze me inside the dress like sausage into its casing. Reminds me of the time I had to wear a corset on the set of *The Wild Wild West*. I'm not too worried about the ripped seam. Miss Havisham's tattered wedding dress would have looked very similar."

Barnacle Bob whistled. "Va-va-voom!"

"What a charmer," Aunt Amelia said. "But I think it's time for you to get your eyes tested, BB."

"Brownnoser," Liz said to the bald-headed parrot. "Auntie, you look the perfect, insane, jilted bride-to-be. We'd better hurry downstairs so you can judge the best costume contest. Seems you have another Indialantic by the Sea success on your hands."

Aunt Amelia clapped her hands in excitement. "You're right, darling. I don't want to miss a thing." After appraising herself in the full-length mirror, satisfied she looked her best—or, in this case, her worst—she exited the lavishly decorated bedroom. Liz and Kate followed behind, holding on to the long train of the wedding gown. They looked like two bridesmaids—one from the nineteenth century, the other from the postapocalyptic future.

When they entered the sitting room, Liz glanced out the French doors that opened to a wide balcony that overlooked the ocean. The moon was bright. They couldn't ask for a more perfect night for the ball. The temperatures at the end of December in Florida could be on the cool side, but nothing like last December, when Liz still lived in Manhattan. That had been one record snowfall after another, which made the city a perfect backdrop for the holiday season. However, Liz didn't miss the tree at Rockefeller Center or the shop windows on Fifth Avenue because this Christmas they'd celebrated in the Indialantic's grand library, surrounded by thousands of books and a roaring fire in the fireplace her great-grandfather had commissioned in 1926, hoping his new bride would miss Cornwall a little less.

Aunt Amelia insisted that the Indialantic have three live, ten-foot-tall Christmas trees. Soon, the trees would be recycled into garden mulch. Her great-aunt, an avid gardener and environmentalist, made sure the tree farm in North Carolina from which the trees were shipped would plant new saplings in their place. Most islanders were eco-conscious.

"Oh, I feel like I've forgotten something, Lizzy," Aunt Amelia said, opening the door to the hallway.

A horrendous squawking came from behind the closed door of her great-aunt's bedroom.

They all laughed.

Kate said, "Let me rescue the little brat. You go on ahead."

"You heard her, Auntie." Liz grabbed her great-aunt's elbow and steered her out of the suite. On the way out the door, Aunt Amelia grabbed a small mantel clock off the credenza. The clock's face was frozen at twenty minutes to nine.

"Nice touch, Miss Havisham," Liz said, referring to the clock.

As they scurried down the hallway, Aunt Amelia said, "Yes, the exact time I received the letter canceling my wedding. Oh, Lizzy, has the band arrived?"

"Yes. I heard them start up as I was leaving the courtyard to find you." Liz stopped for a moment, gasping for breath. She was sure her great-aunt could beat her in a relay race.

Kate caught up to them just as Barnacle Bob whizzed by, the edges of his peacock-blue wings brushing against Liz's cheek. She opened her mouth to chastise him only to inhale a pin-feather. The parrot latched onto Aunt Amelia's right shoulder and belted out, "Wheaties, breakfast of champions," then held on for dear life.

"You need your Wheaties, BB," Liz said, "just to keep up with your mother. Don't know if BB goes with your costume, Auntie."

"Have no worries. He'll be relegated to his cage in the butler's pantry. The last time he was in public, it didn't turn out too well."

"That's an understatement," Liz replied.

"Are you going to sing any Broadway favorites tonight, Aunt Amelia?" Kate asked as they took a breather at the top of the spiral staircase leading downstairs. The sound of jazz filtered up to greet them.

"In answer to your question, Katie, I'll sing with the band if prodded."

Liz knew it wouldn't take much prodding.

"I think the song 'I Feel Pretty' from the musical *West Side Story* would fit in nicely with the theme of the ball," Aunt Amelia continued.

Liz wasn't sure an elderly, macabre bride singing "I Feel Pretty" would go over too well with the literary purists. The musical was based on Shakespeare's *Romeo and Juliet*, so her great-aunt was right on that account. But she knew one thing: it didn't matter. When Amelia Eden Holt made up her mind, nothing could hold her back.

Chapter 2

"Care for a glass of bubbly, ma petite?" Hercule Poirot asked Liz, nodding toward the ice sculpture of Ernest Hemingway. Papa Hemingway's mouth spouted a geyser of champagne.

"Would love one, Grand-Pierre." Liz called the hotel's eighty-one-year-old chef "Grand-Pierre," a play on the French word grand-père, which translates in English to grandfather, because that was how she thought of him. Pierre Montague had been at the Indialantic from before Liz arrived with her father twenty-three years ago at the age of five. Chef Pierre resembled Agatha Christie's Poirot 24-7, with his waxed and curled mustache. Only instead of the homburg he wore now, you could usually find him in his white chef's toque from dawn to dusk. She said, "Of course you would come as none other than your favorite character from fiction. Love your dandy ascot, gold-handled cane, and patent-leather boots. Are you sure Dame Christie never met you before you came to America?"

"*Mon Dieu!*" he said, tapping his cane on the courtyard's terracotta tile. "I'm not that ancient, Lizzy dear. Monsieur Poirot made his first appearance in 1920 in *The Mysterious Affair at Styles*. I wasn't even born yet. Plus, Poirot is Belgian. I'm French."

"But of course," Liz said. "May I have this dance, Grand-Pierre?"

"I'm afraid my dance card is full. Feeling a little light-headed. I think I only have one dance in me this evening and I promised it to…" He looked toward the French doors leading to the dining room. "There she is now."

Liz followed his gaze. Greta Kimball, the Indialantic's housekeeper, came toward them. She wore a long, navy brocade dress with a hat and a veil. In her hand was an oversize apothecary bottle with the word ARSENIC written in antique script. Liz smiled at Greta's ingenuity. If it wasn't for the arsenic bottle, she would've never figured out that Greta's costume was that of Flaubert's Emma Bovary. Liz had always suspected Greta and Pierre had become more than friends. The grin on both their faces confirmed it. "Go meet her, Grand-Pierre. She can't see you through all the Mad Hatters' haberdashery. Promise to take it easy and rest. You're a precious commodity around here." He didn't hear her last words. He was already hurrying toward Greta. Liz worried about him. They all did. He'd been their rock for decades. She was happy Pierre hadn't had to plan or prepare the menu for the evening's festivities. A swanky party planner from Vero Beach had been hired to make sure the night went off flawlessly. The task may have been too much for the Indialantic's chef after he'd recently been diagnosed with a form of memory loss. His periods of confusion had caught them all off guard. Now it was their turn to step up to the plate. Liz had been taught to be a gourmet cook by Pierre. Her first lesson was at age five, standing on a stool in the Indialantic's huge kitchen with a wooden spoon in her hand. Recently, either she or Greta helped the chef prepare the hotel's meals.

Luckily, the Indialantic by the Sea was more of a boardinghouse than a full-service hotel. Most of their meals were taken at the kitchen's long farm table. The second-floor hotel suites housed Clyde B. Netherton, retired US Coast Guard captain, and his Great Dane, Killer; Betty Lawson, mystery writer, and her feline, Caroline Keene, nicknamed Caro; Greta Kimball, housekeeper, and her sphinx cat, Venus, and, finally, Aunt Amelia, proprietor of the Indialantic hotel and shopping emporium, and her macaw, Barnacle Bob. Chef Pierre Montague and self-proclaimed hotel manager Susannah Shay also had their own suites on the second floor. Both were petless, along with Liz's father, who lived on the first floor in a three-room apartment next to his law office. Their animal-free status could change at any moment if Aunt Amelia had anything to say about it. Which she usually did. Liz lived in a beach house on the property that had once been the Indialantic's old bathing pavilion with her new kitten, Brontë—thrilled the pet pressure was off.

Starting with the literary ball, Aunt Amelia was taking the Indialantic by the Sea Hotel in a new direction. The money from the rent of the emporium shops covered most of the bills, and now that the hotel had been deemed a local landmark by the Barrier Island Historical Society, the plans were to offer events to be hosted inside the hotel, focusing on weddings and conferences. Running a hotel on a daily basis had been too much for Aunt Amelia, especially after last April, when someone had been murdered in one of the hotel's suites. Liz's great-aunt already had a booking for a weekend wedding in the spring. It was to be a small, intimate affair, the bride a famous psychic and the groom a warlock. Liz knew a recipe for disaster when she saw it. But one thing she loved: living with Aunt Amelia was always an adventure and Liz planned on making up for the ten years she'd missed while living in Manhattan.

Over the din of the raucous crowd, Liz heard her great-aunt's contagious laughter. Aunt Amelia was in the corner near the five-piece band, holding court to her minions. As Liz knew from helping her father and great-aunt with the running of the hotel and emporium, a lot of work went into an event this size. She was happy Aunt Amelia had handed over the reins of the literary ball to a party planner. Liz was on deadline, only pages away from completing her second draft of *An American in Cornwall*. Her fingers were just itching to type "The End." Each night, as she drifted off to sleep, the final scene played over and over in her head. The ending had been a revelation. She hadn't seen it coming. As often happened, an author's best-laid plans went by the wayside when the story's characters took over. But until next Saturday when the Literary Festival activities came to a close, her writing had been relegated to the back burner.

"Miss Eyre, where'd you disappear to?" An exceedingly handsome, raven-haired man stuffed a wild mushroom canape into her mouth. He wore a dark green double-breasted frock coat with oversize lapels that fit snugly to his muscular, six-foot-three frame.

Liz had a mind to swoon. She and Aunt Amelia had tried to talk Ryan into dressing as Fitzwilliam Darcy, Heathcliff, or Edward Rochester, but he'd refused, saying those were characters from women's romance novels that no man could live up to. Of course, he hadn't read *Pride and Prejudice*, *Wuthering Heights*, or *Jane Eyre*, so who was he to judge their male appeal? Liz thought real-life Ryan was all three rolled into one, and she kissed his rough cheek. Ryan was her father's part-time private investigator, who also helped his grandfather at the Indialantic emporium's café and gourmet grocery, Deli-casies by the Sea. Ryan rented the caretaker's cottage on the hotel's grounds and lived with his newly adopted puppy, Blackbeard. He was also Liz's boyfriend. There. She'd said it. *Boyfriend.*

"Am I supposed to guess who you are?" she asked, glancing at the bag he held in his right hand. "What's in the flour sack?"

He pulled out a pair of ornate silver candlesticks.

"Well, if it isn't Jean Valjean from *Les Misérables*. Thought for sure you'd come as Dashiell Hammett's shamus, Sam Spade. Or Mickey Spillane's Mike Hammer."

"I do enjoy reading other genres," he said. He took two glasses of champagne off the tray of a passing waiter and handed one to Liz. "To us! And to Jean Valjean and other heroes and heroines of literature. 'He lay back with his head turned to the sky, and the light from the two candlesticks fell upon his face.'"

Liz clinked her glass against his. "Nice quote. Proving Jean Valjean led a true and honorable life. Well done, Mr. Stone."

"Thank you, Ms. Holt."

The band stopped playing and they heard someone onstage tapping at the microphone. "Attention, everyone," Aunt Amelia said. "It's an hour before the new year. Shortly, I'll announce when we should move outdoors for the countdown and smooches, followed by a dazzling display of fireworks over the Indian River Lagoon." Aunt Amelia looked directly at the Indialantic by the Sea Emporium's most recent shopkeeper and gave him a sly smile. Then she stepped off the stage to much applause, stopping when she reached none other than Samuel Clemens dressed as Huck Finn, barefoot and all. His gray ponytail was tucked beneath a ratty hat with fishing lures hanging from the brim. A fishing pole dangled with what Liz hoped was a rubber fish. Samuel Clemens was the name on his birth certificate, but everyone called him Ziggy.

Ziggy took Aunt Amelia's hand in his. If her great-aunt's face wasn't covered in white pancake makeup, she'd most definitely be blushing. Ziggy had rented a space in the emporium after last October's hurricane took the roof off his surf shop. He and Aunt Amelia went way back—sixty-five years back. They'd recently rekindled their friendship and a shared love of surfing. If Liz hadn't seen it for herself, she never would have believed her eighty-year-old great-aunt could ride a wave.

Ryan said something to her, but it didn't register. Liz could have sworn she saw someone she knew. Paula Resnick, her ex-boyfriend Travis Osterman's literary agent. Unless Paula had a twin, there was no mistaking her one-of-a-kind upturned nose and inner-tube lips. She said, "Hold that thought. I see someone I need to talk to." Then she raced off in pursuit of Lisbeth Salander from *The Girl with the Dragon Tattoo*.

Ryan called out, "You better be back before the countdown to midnight. I demand a kiss from your prim little mouth, Miss Eyre."

"But of course, Monsieur Valjean," she said, barreling across the dance floor. She tripped on the hem of her dress and fell headfirst into the paws of the Beast from Gabrielle-Suzanne Barbot de Villeneuve's fairy tale. Beauty looked on in alarm. Beauty had nothing to worry about; Liz already had her prince and wasn't in need of another. When she finally made it to the corner of the courtyard, she hurried through the doorway leading to the hotel's grand dining room.

There was no sign of Paula.

Chapter 3

The perimeter of the dining room had been set up with long buffet tables draped with white linen tablecloths displaying items for the silent charity auction.

Had it been Paula? Had Liz been hallucinating? She glanced toward the arched windows that faced the ocean and saw a figure pass by. Someone was on the terrace. At one time, during the Indialantic's glory days, the country's rich and famous had breakfasted on the terrace. Aunt Amelia had volumes of old photo albums to prove it. The terrace was the perfect place to sip ice tea under the striped awning while gazing out toward the sea. It was also where Chef Pierre had taught Liz how to play chess. He always joked that he wished he hadn't, because she always beat him. They still played on his good days, when Pierre's memory was shaper than Liz's.

She walked toward the arched French doors, then realized they were blocked by a row of tables. Whoever she'd seen must have left the hotel another way.

A man next to her, dressed as a wizard, was placing a silent-auction bid on renting out the *Queen of the Seas* for a private eco-tour, which included lunch for eight. The Indialantic's Captain Netherton was the ship's tour guide and pilot. Last month, Aunt Amelia came up with the idea of offering picnic lunches that could be purchased at the emporium's Deli-casies and brought onto the ship. "Good Luck," Liz said to the man, then glanced at her watch. Eleven fifteen. Only forty-five minutes until the fireworks. She hurried toward the door that opened to the hallway. She needed to see if the person on the terrace was Paula or a figment of her writer's imagination.

When she reached the lobby, she glanced around. No sign of the girl with the dragon tattoo. Impulsively, she went out the revolving door, turned right under the portico, and headed in the direction in which she'd seen the figure. The moon lit her way as she crept closer to the wild jasmine bushes in front of the terrace's iron railing. When a cloud covered the moon, the darkness was almost suffocating. Liz steadied herself, knowing she had to get back to Ryan before the stroke of midnight. To his strong arms.

She was being foolish. Things were good; she should just turn around. But something spurred her on. Like in a slasher movie, when one of the characters decides to go down the open cellar stairs after the power goes out. *Why would Travis's agent be on their small island anyway?* It was probably someone else, not a ghost from Liz's last few years in Manhattan. During that time, she'd been everyone's literary ingénue, not knowing she'd been caught in the barb-wired coattails of her ex-boyfriend's popularity until he sued her for defamation of character. When they'd first started dating, she'd signed a nondisclosure agreement. Travis claimed she broke that agreement when she'd dialed 911. The irony of it all. She'd won the case, but the pain of the trial and all the bad press stayed with her like the scar on her face.

It was amazing how quickly her thoughts could segue back to that terrible time in her life. One night, after consuming a boatload of alcohol, Travis had pushed her to the floor of his favorite bar when she tried to take away his glass after he'd had too many scotches. It was the same watering-hole his fans and fellow male authors hung out. She'd cut her cheek on a shard of glass from a broken bottle of Macallan scotch, Travis's signature anesthetic. It happened during one of his rages, after he saw a photo in the *Post* of him on his knees in the middle of the street during Little Italy's San Gennaro Festival, a crowd of gawkers looking on. Of course, he'd been drunk.

Travis had never laid a hand on her before, and she was sure he hadn't meant her injury. But that was the end of their relationship. Soon after, she'd returned home to the Indialantic.

Palm fronds rustled, which was unsettling because there wasn't a breeze. Feeling for the gate, she opened it, then stepped onto the terrace. The only light came from two electric lanterns on either side of the French doors. She looked in the window and saw that the dining room had emptied. Everyone was probably in the courtyard waiting for Aunt Amelia to announce it was time to go out to the great lawn. She turned to go. Then a voice from the shadows said, "Elizabeth."

But it wasn't Paula. The voice was male, and there was something familiar about its tone. The outline of a figure wearing a hat emerged from under a potted palm. The clouds parted, and the moon illuminated a thin man, on the short side, dressed in an Army uniform. And he was carrying a rifle.

"Travis," she said, "what the hell are you doing here?"

"Is that any way to greet the best thing that ever happened to your career?" he asked, moving toward her.

She couldn't believe his arrogance. "Your theatrics may have been good for my book sales, but it was a package deal when it came to my serenity. I'd give you every penny I ever made if that night could be erased and our whole relationship never happened."

He smiled. The gap between his two oversize front teeth, which at one time she'd thought adorable, now made him look like a deranged rabbit. "Come, come," he said in his usual patronizing tone. Something she once thought had to do with their twelve-year age difference, but now realized was just Travis being Travis.

He leaned the rifle, complete with bayonet, against the stucco wall, still within arm's reach.

She shivered.

"I think you're being a tad harsh, Elizabeth Holt," he said. "I'm new and improved. Haven't had a drink since that night. Do you like my costume for your little dance? I mean ball?" he said, adding a sneer.

He always was a snob. He stepped closer, and Liz stepped back. He was right. She didn't smell the usual scotch on his breath. But something about his eyes, even in the dim light, looked harder than she'd remembered. After their night of no return, her therapist had recommended that Liz go to a twelve-step meeting for people whose loved ones were affected by the disease of drugs and alcoholism. And even though right now she wanted to throttle him, she was hopeful he'd found sobriety through his own program.

She glanced at his olive-green uniform, affixed with shiny gold medals. "Haven't got a clue who you are. I really don't feel like playing games. I have to get back inside."

"To your new boyfriend? Sally told me all about him."

"Sally? Sally who?" she asked, balling her fists and digging her fingernails into the palms of her hands to stop herself from shaking.

"The local television news reporter. Buy her a few margaritas and you know every detail of her small life on this scrub of an island."

He had to be talking about Sally Beamon, who Liz had gone to high school with. Why would she be talking to Travis?

"So, this is the place you always wanted me to see. A tad on the quiet, boring side. Don't you think?"

"Travis, I have to get inside, and your name's not on the guest list. Please leave quietly, and don't make a scene." She was trembling, but her voice remained steady.

"You can't dismiss me so easily," he said, taking another step forward. "First, guess who I am?" He took off his hat, and she saw that his short, almost-white hair had been dyed carrot orange. "Then, we're going to have a little chat about what you can do to help my career. Like I did yours."

Liz felt her face heat. "I don't really care who you're dressed as. And I'll never help your career. I deserved my success and it had nothing to do with you. Leave, or I'll call security."

He ignored her. "Mickey, Mickey McAvoy."

Mickey McAvoy was the main protagonist from Travis's Pulitzer Prize–winning novel about a group of brothers during WWII. Of course, narcissist that he was, he *would* choose his own creation as his costume for the literary ball. "Swell. If you're not leaving, I will." Liz turned toward the gate.

Travis grabbed her right arm. She knew tomorrow she'd have a bruise from his grip. "Not so fast," he snarled, his eyeteeth reflecting moonlight. "I need you to go on a little publicity tour for *Blood and Glass*. Your 'no comments' and shunning the limelight because of your little scar has cost me in sales. My publisher is ready to drop me if they don't improve, and a movie deal hangs on the line because of your little shenanigans at the Pen and Pad that night. It's time to move on. You need to admit that almost everything in the book is true. I bared my soul in that novel."

She kept her voice low, but she couldn't push down the disgust she'd felt for the man in front of her. "My *shenanigans?*" she said in a low growl. "That isn't the reason I want nothing to do with your thinly veiled fictional account of our relationship, culminating in the night I received my *little scar*. I haven't read it. And I don't plan to. Yes, it's time to move on. Now move!" Her long-withheld anger bubbled up until she couldn't help but screech. "And your publisher should drop you, and I should sue *you* for slander! Or maybe I should tell them about what you stole from that poor vet at the VA hospital years ago. The one whose belongings mysteriously ended up in your apartment."

"Don't threaten me. Sgt. McPherson died while at the VA. I knew he had no family, so I kept his stuff. I was devastated when he passed away. He was my inspiration for *The McAvoy Brothers*."

"That's strange," Liz said, "because I saw an open letter on your desk from his daughter, asking if you had any idea where all her father's things were. I think I can even remember her name, and the Indianapolis postmark."

"I admire your moxie, but I think I'll have the last laugh," he said. "You either promote *Blood and Glass* or I'll tell everyone in the press that I wrote most of your own darling novel. And I'll sue you for a percentage of your royalties. I talked to Paula; she thinks we'd have a good case. She wanted to go ahead with litigation, but I thought I'd approach you like a gentleman..." He grabbed the rifle and stepped closer.

So, she *had* seen his agent. "I suppose that's Sgt. McPherson's rifle?" He smiled. "A M1 Garand." He pushed it toward her.

She pushed it back. "Are you insane? No one brings a gun to the Indialantic."

"It's not loaded, princess. Lends a dose of authenticity to my costume, though, don't you think?"

"You sound like a four-year-old," she said. Travis had been adopted and his only sibling, Taylor, hadn't. Travis always claimed his parents treated him differently than Taylor. Liz never saw it. Taylor took on the role of big sister and protector, even though Travis was five years older. "You?" Liz continued, in a shrill voice that sounded very unlike her own, "A gentleman? Get real." She waited until he placed the gun back against the trellised wall, crushing the scarlet flowers on her great-aunt's prized honeysuckle vines. "You didn't write one word of my novel."

"Every file of every draft you've written is on my hard drive. You told me yourself. Who's to say I didn't pen your little award winner?"

"Drop dead! I'm not scared of you. You're a liar. My manuscript was completed before I met you. I retyped it from a hard copy when my laptop was stolen. Remember, you borrowed it, went out drinking, and left it in the back of a taxi. Get a life and get the hell out of mine!" Liz felt like she was having an out-of-body experience. The words came out with such vehemence, it was like she'd been possessed by an amalgam of all downtrodden women who couldn't take it anymore. She stormed off the terrace, bumping into someone standing on the other side of the open gate.

The full moon shone down on a fairy with pink iridescent wings. Covering the woman's eyes, and her identity, was a glittery mask. Liz guessed she was dressed as either Tinker Bell or...she couldn't think of another fairy from literature except Titania from Shakespeare's *A Midsummer's Night Dream.*

She did remember some of the tales Aunt Amelia had told her as a child about the evil Cornish fairies called spriggans. They were grotesque, with crooked, skinny bodies and lived underground or in caves on the Cornish coast, cousins to the pixies and brownies. Only spriggans liked to perform darker deeds, like replacing human babies with changelings, or creating storms to kill travelers who trespassed on fairy lands. Liz wished she knew a real spriggan she could sic on Travis. Maybe Jean Valjean could hit Travis on the head with one of his candlesticks. Jane Eyre: How would Jane handle Travis? Probably the same way Liz had in the past. Go to her room and lock her door.

Well, no more! Liz brushed past the woman, tripping again on her long gown and elbowing the fairy in the chest before she righted herself. *How did nineteenth-century women deal with these blasted long skirts?*

"You don't have to be so pushy, Eliz-z-z-abeth," the fairy slurred. "You still have thirty minutes until midnight." Travis might not have been drinking, but this woman had. And it wasn't champagne.

She couldn't make out the woman's hair color because her head was covered with a crown of flora and fauna. Maybe she was a wood nymph. Whatever she was, Liz had no time for fairies or anything else. It was almost midnight. "Do I know you?" Liz asked over her shoulder as she walked away.

"All will be revealed after the stroke of twelve. Isn't that the way these masquerade balls work?"

"Whatever," Liz answered, still fuming about Travis invading her island. She wondered what the woman had overheard. What did it matter? All Liz could think about was getting as far away from Travis as she could and finding Ryan in time for her midnight kiss.

She followed the winding path leading to the front of the hotel. To her right, the ocean sparkled with gentle ripples of glistening moonlight. After a few feet and a few deep breaths, she relaxed, slowing her steps. When she was close to the entrance, she saw Travis's literary agent, Paula, exit the revolving door. She was dressed all in black, sporting a small gold hoop ring on her upturned nose. She came toward Liz, then walked past her without a glance. Travis's agent looked angry, her hands clenched at the bottom of her tattooed arms. Liz knew it had something to do with Travis. Or maybe something to do with her?

Paula Resnick was the kind of agent you'd want on your right side— never your wrong. She'd been in the business for over twenty years and would only take on authors who'd made it to the top ten of the *New York Times* Best Sellers. Liz's novel, *Let the Wind Roar*, had made it on the list. Back when Liz was living in Manhattan and dating Travis, Paula had approached her to join the agency. When Travis found out, he was livid. He'd always belittled Liz's literary accomplishments and didn't want to share Paula. He told Paula he would leave the agency if she brought Liz in, claiming Liz would be better off in an agency with fewer clients and could give her the individual attention she deserved. She'd had to admit he'd been right. Her agent turned out to be one of her best friends. Paula, on the other hand, couldn't have been colder to Liz, and she always wondered if perhaps Travis hadn't done more than threaten to leave the agency. Liz wouldn't put it past him to have sealed his future in the bedroom rather than the boardroom.

Liz pushed too hard against the revolving door and was spit into the lobby. She caught the hem of her dress and fell into the arms of the Beast from *Beauty and the Beast*. Beauty was nowhere to be seen.

"We'll have to stop meeting like this," the man said. Then he pounded his chest and roared.

When Liz righted herself, she laughed.

"I hope I didn't scare you?" he asked.

"Of course not. I know behind all that hair there's a prince hiding inside."

"I'm glad you can tell that I'm not dressed as the Cowardly Lion from *The Wizard of Oz*. Half of the people here think I am." He used his mouth to take off one of his paws, then reached into his blue velvet jacket pocket and retrieved a fat cigar. "My date is furious. Everyone keeps berating her for looking nothing like Dorothy Gale, especially without her red slippers and Toto. And who are you dressed as, Ms. Holt?"

"Jane Eyre."

"But of course," he said. The lobby's Lalique chandelier caught the glint of diamonds on his pinky ring. The ring was designed to look like a pair of gold dice, and the four and three spots on each die had small diamonds. He took out a cigar cutter and clipped off the end of the cigar. It went flying in the air, and Liz caught it. "Good catch, Miss Eyre. I should have recognized you by your mousy-brown, center-parted, bun wig and the brooch on your collar."

Liz didn't know if she was more amazed that there was a man who'd read *Jane Eyre* or that he knew her name.

"The only thing not in line with Miss Eyre is your cornflower-blue eyes and the scar on your cheek. I don't remember Jane having any scars—only Edward."

"The scar is real," she said, taking a step toward the arched doorway leading into the courtyard. "I should get going. I don't want to miss the countdown and fireworks over the lagoon."

"And I need to smoke my cigar. I hope there's a breeze. I'm dressed more for New Year's Eve in Times Square than an island in Florida."

"Don't you care about missing all the festivities? The fireworks will soon be displayed over the Indian River Lagoon at the rear of the hotel, not over the ocean."

"Always thought New Year's Eve was overrated. Never kept one of my resolutions. Plus, my date has disappeared. I won't have anyone to kiss. Unless you'd like to fill in?"

"Sorry. I have someone waiting inside. Where I should be."

"Mr. Rochester, I presume?"

"No. Jean Valjean."

"From *Les Misérables*. One of my favorite characters, and a little more inventive than one from a child's fairy tale, but I was roped into it by my date." He reached down and planted a kiss on her left cheek. "Happy New Year, Miss Eyre."

She pulled back and said, "Happy New Year, Beast. Hope you find Beauty."

He bowed and exited via the revolving door. Liz was almost positive she'd never met the man behind the beast before. Nothing about him seemed familiar, yet he knew her name.

Remembering that Travis was lurking somewhere on the Indialantic's grounds, she rushed out of the lobby and into the courtyard. She wouldn't tell Ryan about her and Travis's confrontation until after the fireworks. She refused to let him ruin their first New Year's. How had Travis even heard of the literary ball? No doubt from local newscaster Sally, always scrambling for the big story to get her a foothold into one of the major networks.

Sorry, Sally. No news story here.

Famous last words.

Chapter 4

"Betty, have you seen Ryan?"

"What's that, dear? The noise is deafening."

"Ryan. Have you seen him?"

Miss Marple dragged Liz over to an alcove in the corner of the courtyard, where they stepped behind a seven-foot potted palm. The male singer of the band was singing Dan Fogelberg's *Same Old Lang Syne*. Such a sad song to herald in the New Year. Aunt Amelia must have thought the same thing because Liz heard her interrupt the lead singer to announce that everyone should grab their champagne from the trays of the passing wait staff and follow her outside. Liz couldn't see her from behind the tree, but she heard the excitement in her voice.

"Why are we hiding?"

"It's less noisy here. And yes, Ryan was looking for you. Seemed in a sour mood when he couldn't find you. I tried to cover but had no idea where you were or what you were up to. Is there a game afoot?"

"Not a murder mystery to solve. But there is someone I'd love to murder."

Betty gave her a quizzical look. "And who would that be?"

"Travis Osterman!"

"He's here? Oh my."

"Oh my indeed. The one and only."

"Do you want me to kick him out?

"That won't be necessary. I think I was pretty clear I wouldn't put up with his games."

"Should I give your father a heads-up?"

She remembered how helpful her father had been during the defamation of character lawsuit and weighed getting him involved. There was still a chance Travis would leave Melbourne Beach peacefully. On second thought... "Yes, please warn Dad that he's skulking around. Not only Travis, but also his agent."

"The same barracuda he had an affair with? The one who reneged on letting you into her posh agency?"

"The same."

"Maybe I should go with you to find Ryan? I have a bad feeling."

"That's not like you—or Miss Marple. Hopefully, I set Travis straight. I was very forceful. I'll be fine. Remember, I took a few kickboxing lessons with Aunt Amelia. Puny Travis doesn't scare me. He should be the one afraid. No matter what he's up to, I won't let him destroy my serenity."

Betty gave her a gentle push. "Go, tiger. Find Ryan before you turn into Cinderella. Although, even dressed in rags, he wouldn't care a fig."

Liz smiled. "Any idea which direction he went in?"

"Sorry, I didn't see where he went. Did you try his cell?"

"No," Liz said, laughing, "duh." She took out her phone and called. It went to voice mail, and she left a message. Then she texted, *Where are you?*

"Boy, you must be frazzled if you didn't think to text Ryan."

Liz kissed Betty on the cheek. "'Traumatized' is a better word. I'm gonna find Jean Valjean. If you see him, tell him that I shared my location with him from my phone—he should just follow the blinking light."

"Follow the blinking light. Got it. Told you that feature on your phone would serve you well. And you weren't sure you wanted Ryan to know your every move."

Betty was the most tech-savvy eighty-three-year-old she knew. Hell, she was the most tech-savvy *person* she knew.

As Liz hurried out of the alcove, she saw snoopy Susannah Shay standing in front of her wearing her trademark frown. She said, "What's got you all riled up, Miss Eyre? Trouble in paradise?"

A few months ago, her great-aunt's thespian friend had come to stay in the hotel's Windward Shores Suite and never left. To cover her room and board, Aunt Amelia had given Susannah the title assistant hotel manager. When talking of her position, Susannah had a tendency to drop the "assistant" part of her title. Liz had no idea what she did around the Indialantic except write manifestos on the way the hotel *should* be run. Never implementing her directives or participating in any of the grunt work the huge hotel and emporium needed to run smoothly. Supposedly, Susannah was a distant cousin of Amy Vanderbilt, the American authority on etiquette and the author of 1952's etiquette bible, *Amy Vanderbilt*

Complete Book of Etiquette. Still in print today, as Susannah pointed out on numerous occasions.

"Were you listening to our conversation, Miss Shay?"

"I might have heard a snippet or two. If a lady wants to be discreet, it behooves her to move to a more private location. Did I hear your ex, Pulitzer Prize–winning Travis Osterman is here? I would so love an introduction."

Liz glanced at Susannah's Elizabethan costume. It looked familiar. And Liz realized why. It was the same one Aunt Amelia had worn in the Melbourne Beach Theatre Company's production of Shakespeare's *Macbeth.* The costume appeared to be altered to fit Susannah's thin frame. Her dark hair had been covered with a wig, no doubt also borrowed from Aunt Amelia.

"Let me guess who you are. The Queen of Hearts? You're the fifth one I've seen tonight." It was fun to rile up prim-and-proper Susannah.

"I am not the Queen of Hearts. A children's book? I have a little more imagination than that. No. I'm Lady Macbeth. As an author, I'm sure you've heard of her." Her ramrod-stiff spine got stiffer.

"Oh, now I see it. That was Auntie's costume. Correct?"

Susannah pursed her thin lips but didn't answer. For a moment, Liz felt bad she was picking on the elderly woman. She'd never liked the way Susannah had treated her great-aunt. But kindhearted Aunt Amelia had told Liz that Susannah had had a major sadness in her past and Liz should just ignore her haughty behavior.

"It looks good on you," Liz lied. She thought Susannah would have been a perfect Mrs. Danvers from *Rebecca.* "I don't believe Mr. Osterman is still here. In fact, I'm sure he's long gone. And it *behooves* me to go find Ryan."

"Aha, I was right. Trouble in paradise, confirmed. Your generation just can't seem to make a commitment."

Liz bit the inside of her cheek. There was no use in defending herself. She just wished of all people Susannah hadn't been the one to overhear her and Betty's conversation. Susannah was known to hire private investigators at a drop of a hat when she wanted dirt on someone. She had to admit Susannah's snooping had helped them find a killer last October, but that didn't mean she needed to butt into Liz's private life or past. She made it a point to have Aunt Amelia talk to Susannah before she lost her cool with the elderly woman.

A minute later, Liz got caught in the exodus filing out the courtyard doors for the countdown and fireworks. It was ten minutes until midnight. Ten minutes to find Ryan. Once she freed herself from the pack, she took off for the Indialantic's gazebo, where she and Ryan had shared many a romantic evening, hoping he'd be there.

But he wasn't.

She took out her phone and turned on the flashlight feature to make sure Travis wasn't lurking. How had he found out about the ball? A picture of petite newscaster Sally Beaman flashed in front of Liz. Sally's wide smile and large, trusting Bambi eyes made her easy to confide in. In high school, Liz had shared her worry that the boy she'd been dating was seeing a cheerleader on the side. Dumb Liz. Sally was also a cheerleader. And even though she acted like she'd take Liz's confidence to her grave, the next day Liz's boyfriend dumped her for not trusting him. Of course, soon after, he and cheerleading captain Amy Lisbon were inseparable. Now that she thought about it, the fairy she'd met after her confrontation with Travis was the same height as Sally.

Liz didn't have time to ponder the situation; she leaped down the gazebo steps and hurried to the path leading to the front of the Indialantic. Determined to find Ryan, all thoughts of her evil ex faded. She stopped next to the Indialantic's pool to check her phone. No text. No call. As she went to put the phone back in her pocket, she saw it was one minute until midnight. Defeated, she slumped down on a lounge chair to catch her breath. It was too late. She'd blown it. And she blamed Travis.

At the same time the first firework exploded over the Indian River Lagoon, she saw the silhouette of a bobcat. He turned his head in Liz's direction, then continued with his powerful stride toward the south side of the hotel's grounds. Fireworks rat-tat-tatted like the beating of her heart as she watched the cat melt into the darkness. *Some kind of omen?*

The view of the fireworks over the lagoon were blocked by the Indialantic, but she saw splashes of color through the opening in the bell tower. Disappointed at not finding Ryan, she got up from the lounge chair and walked toward the iron fence surrounding the pool. From the direction of the gazebo, there was the sound of someone running, almost galloping in her direction. The person stopped running when they saw her. Someone dressed in a French military suit with a huge pig head turned toward her. Its open mouth had large teeth that looked real. The eye closest to her was glassy in the moonlight, reminding her of a dead fish. In one white-gloved hand it held a cell phone. It slowed and waved in her direction, then took the path leading to the back of the hotel. The pig head was creepy. She shivered in the warm night as she watched it disappear from sight.

Disappointed she'd missed her midnight kiss, she decided to turn back the hands on her wristwatch to eleven fifty-five and find Ryan. She made her way toward the huge crowd gathered on the lawn in front of the Indialantic's dock. Between the bright explosions of light and the full moon, it seemed almost like daylight. Liz scanned the eclectic group of masqueraders for someone in army fatigues and a helmet, exhaling with relief when she didn't see Travis. She had a horrible vision of walking into her beach house and Travis sitting in the dark waiting for her. Holding his rifle.

Brushing away all negative thoughts, she moved toward the center of the crowd. Her father was standing next to a woman she assumed was his fiancée, dressed in costume. Agent Charlotte Pearson turned and waved her over. She was dressed as Scarlett O'Hara from Margaret Mitchell's *Gone with the Wind*, only instead of a bustled Civil War gown, emerald-green velvet draperies hung from a curtain rod that extended across her shoulders. The drapes were secured at her waist with a corded tassel.

When Liz reached them, she said, laughing, "Charlotte, what a fun costume. I didn't know you were a fan of old television shows." Liz was referring to the iconic skit on the *The Carol Burnett Show*, on which the comedienne played Scarlett in a mock version of a scene from the movie. No matter how many times they viewed the sketch, Aunt Amelia and Liz always got hysterical. She was thrilled that Charlotte, who used to be so serious and uptight, would choose such a fun way to celebrate the classic novel. This playful side of the detective seemed to bloom ever since her father came into the picture.

Charlotte laughed, and the ringlets on her auburn wig jiggled. "How can I not be a fan of old television shows with Aunt Amelia as a guide?"

Fenton joined in the laughter. "Nothing could be better than being with my two girls. Liz, can you come over to the lamppost by the dock? I have something important to show you." They excused themselves, and as soon as they were out of earshot, her father said, "Betty just told me Travis Osterman is here. Are you okay? Do you want me to get rid of him?"

"It's true, he's here," she answered. The knot in her stomach returned. "But I think I handled him. I'm quite proud of myself actually."

"Well, you stick nearby. I already have Charlotte on alert."

Ryan came up to them. "Alert about what?"

Fenton glanced at Liz, and she shook her head in the negative. Before anyone could explain, Kate ran up to them and said, "Come on, guys, you're missing the finale."

Ryan said, "One minute, Kate. I have some unfinished business." He pulled Liz to the side and whispered, "Where the hell have you been? I've been searching all over for you."

Before she could answer, he dipped her backward and gave her a kiss that surpassed any she'd experienced in the past. The fluttering of her heart told her this might be the real deal. And that scared her. "I've been looking for you," she said, once she was upright. "We must have gotten our wires crossed." It was a stretching of the truth, but the truth nonetheless. "I called and texted you. I even shared my location."

"Left my phone at home," he said. "The pockets in this monkey suit can't hold anything bigger than a quarter."

She looked up at him, seeing the exploding colors of the fireworks reflected in the irises of his deep brown eyes. Should she tell him about Travis? She was still in the doghouse for not disclosing the thinly veiled work of fiction Travis had written about their turbulent relationship, *Blood and Glass*, last fall. But this was New Year's. If she told Ryan that Travis was here, it would mar the rest of the evening and he'd probably go looking for him. She let it go.

Which turned out to be a big mistake.

Chapter 5

The next morning, as she was putting her coffee mug in the dishwasher, the phone rang.

"Elizabeth, this is Sally." When Liz didn't respond, she said, "Beaman, Sally Beaman. Where's Travis Osterman?"

Liz heard the panic in her voice, and someone in the background say, "Hand the phone over."

"Where is he?" a female voice said. "No time for games, Ms. Holt."

Liz recognized Travis's agent's gravelly voice. "How the hell should I know, Paula? I've gotta go." She ended the call. Hearing the newscaster's voice, then Paula's, told her that they were together, and solidified her hunch that Sally was the Tinker Bell she'd bumped into near the terrace last night. Liz felt relief. Maybe wishes did come true and Travis had left the island. She pictured him two thousand miles away in New York in his high-rise condo in the sky. She'd been forceful with him. *Hadn't she?* But she knew Travis too well. He'd never leave without getting what he wanted.

She pulled her phone off its charger and dropped it in her bag. Then she put Brontë in her basket, slipped the handle of the basket over her arm, and left the beach house. She paused on the deck for a moment and said good morning to the Atlantic. On most fair-weather mornings, Brontë and Liz would sit and admire the ocean vista with its bird and sea life.

Because of Travis, all Liz could see today was red.

Why would Sally and Paula assume she'd seen him this morning?

She'd woken at ten after staying up until three in the morning. The Literary Masquerade Ball had been a roaring success, which made Aunt Amelia happy because she envisioned many more events at the Indialantic to earn extra income for the running of the hotel and emporium. Last night Liz had been determined to salvage the evening, or should she say morning, with Ryan, and they'd done a good job of it. She felt guilty she hadn't mentioned her confrontation with Travis, promising herself she would tell Ryan tonight. She already had the whole explanation scripted in her head, reminding herself that Travis couldn't hurt her anymore. She owed him nothing.

For now, she was happy to be heading over to the Indialantic for New Year's Day brunch, a tradition she'd missed ten years in a row when she'd lived in Manhattan. Aunt Amelia made every holiday memorable. If there was a reason for a celebration, she'd find one. Every pet got its own birthday party, and if she didn't know the exact date the animal was born, her great-aunt would make one up. Last week, at Christmas, everyone got a stocking hung from the mantel of the mammoth fireplace in the grand library—including Barnacle Bob, Caro, Venus, and Killer. Ryan's pup, Blackbeard, and her kitten, Brontë, even had their own BABY'S 1ST CHRISTMAS stockings, hand-embroidered by one of the artisans from the Indialantic's emporium shop, Home Arts by the Sea.

On the short walk to the Indialantic, Liz conversed with Brontë about the pros and cons of calling Ryan ASAP and telling him about Travis. She took Brontë's silence as a sign that it would be better to tell him in person.

When they entered the lobby, she saw Barnacle Bob in his brass cage next to the 1920s art nouveau accordion-gate Otis elevator—a nonworking elevator, because Aunt Amelia still didn't have the funds to repair it and bring it up to code. It still made an impressive statement, along with the polished wood check-in counter and cubby mail-and-room-key sorter, where back in the day there might have been mail for Ginger Rogers or Fred Astaire. Supposedly, Mr. Astaire had done a short dance routine involving the revolving door and the bamboo coat stand that still stood near the door, displaying old bamboo canes and forgotten umbrellas.

As Liz got closer to the parrot, Brontë still nesting in the basket on her arm, Barnacle Bob squawked, "Meow. Meow." BB wasn't really a cat lover. Far from it, but he liked to parrot a few meows in the presence of the Indialantic's felines, fooling them into thinking he was one of them. He'd learned his lesson one day when Betty's cat, Caro, knocked over his cage and the door flew open. It took hours for Aunt Amelia to catch him. The next day, when she went to give him his breakfast of kiwi, she'd noticed all the feathers on top of his head were missing. Even though the macaw came off as a tough bird, with his foul-mouthed expletives, the vet said the whole episode had been so stressful, he doubted BB's feathers would ever grow back. It had been twelve years, and you could still see the pinholes on the top of his head.

"Howdy, Barnacle Bob. Happy New Year." Liz placed Brontë's basket behind the check-in counter so the kitten could explore the hotel, knowing she'd end up next to a stack of antique books in one of the wall-to-wall mahogany bookcases in the hotel's library. Brontë loved books, almost as much as Liz and Kate.

"Meow," Barnacle Bob answered, then changed his voice to a male TV announcer's. "Nine Lives, the nutritious food even finicky cats like Morris like." He referred to an old television commercial featuring a demanding talking cat, in which Aunt Amelia had played Morris's owner. The commercial only showed her from the neck down, but she was happy to have free 9-Lives cat food "up the kazoo" for the year the ad ran.

"Don't worry, BB," Liz crooned. "Brontë is a sweetie. She's never gone after a bird in her life. On the other hand, Caro is a different story."

Not believing her, the macaw's meowing followed her out of the lobby and down the hallway. She passed the enlightenment parlor, the screening room, and the library. At the end of the hall, she opened the door and entered the dining room. Her reaction to the aromas wafting from the sideboard were like a homecoming. It was easy to picture what ingredients would be included in the New Year's Day fare. All were based on Cornish and American traditions, to ensure prosperity in the coming year. Since her great-grandmother arrived almost a hundred years ago, the menu had included pork, where the expression "high on the hog," came from. The use of lentils represented wealth because their shape resembled Roman coins. Pierre always made a homemade pork sausage called cotechino, which he simmered in lentils, killing two traditions with one stone. Also included were two Southern traditional foods ensuring good fortune for the New Year: black-eyed peas and leafy greens. The leafy greens were obviously meant to symbolize *green*backs. Pierre had told her that using black-eyed peas in the menu dated back to the Civil War, after the Siege of Vicksburg. Because of Union blockades, the residents of Mississippi had to resort to eating peas usually reserved for their cattle. They survived the blockade, and from that point on, black-eyed peas or "cowpeas" were thought to bring good luck to all who ate them.

Under the dining room's chandelier, hung with sprigs of mistletoe, two tables had been pushed together in the center of the room. If someone wanted a kiss, they'd have to climb onto the table.

Seated with mimosas in front of them, the orange juice fresh from the Indialantic's trees, was Aunt Amelia, her father, Kate, Pierre, Betty, Captain

Netherton, Greta, and Ziggy. In other words, family. She realized she'd added Ziggy in the fold. He was Aunt Amelia's new companion of only a few months and made her great-aunt blush like a schoolgirl. Ryan was also considered part of the Indialantic's family, but because the emporium shops were closed, he was spending the day with his grandfather, Pops, who ran Deli-casies by the Sea.

"Over here. Grab some food. I saved you a spot." Aunt Amelia patted the seat of the chair next to her. Liz went and sat, reaching for the pitcher of orange juice. "Lizzy, guess who brought in the silver dollar?"

Leaving a silver coin on the doorstep for the first person visiting the house on New Year's Day was also a Cornish tradition. Liz didn't have to guess who'd found it. Judging by the huge grin on Bastian Caruthers's face, she knew it was him. Bastian and Susannah sat at their own table near the French doors that opened to the inner courtyard. Susannah, aka Miss Etiquette, didn't like to mix with the help, even if she was one.

"I was happy to bring good fortune into your household for the coming year," Bastian said, raising his champagne flute in the air. "To the wonderful Amelia Eden Holt and her hospitality. You look the same as you did forty years ago on the set of *Dark Shadows*." Bastian was in his late seventies, with a full head of slicked-back, noticeably dyed ebony hair. In the center of his forehead was a widow's peak, similar to Eddie Munster's in the '60s television sitcom *The Munsters*, on which Aunt Amelia had once played an Avon lady Grandpa had set his cupid's arrow on. She'd shared that Al Lewis, who played Grandpa, was a year younger than actress Yvonne De Carlo, who played his daughter, Lily. "The opposite of what usually happens in Hollywood, with most actresses of a 'certain age,'" her great-aunt had remarked, adding quotation marks in the air.

"You haven't changed a bit, Bastian," Aunt Amelia called out. "I'm fifty pounds heavier than the last time you saw me and as wrinkled as an elephant's hide. How long has it been?" Even though she didn't think it was possible, Liz saw her great-aunt's cheeks redden under her bright-pink blush. Aunt Amelia was known for her flair for the dramatic. Her flame-red hair coifed on top of her head in soup-can curls, trademark baby blue eye shadow, and thick black liner that extended over her sea-green eyes just added to her larger-than-life persona.

"Forty years, give or take," he replied. Last evening, at the ball, Bastian was dressed as the Prince of Darkness, Bram Stoker's Dracula. This morning, he wore a black turtleneck, slacks, and a suit coat, keeping the vampire vibe going. Liz had learned from her great-aunt that Bastian had been on the *Dark Shadows* writing staff for only a short time before going on to write a copycat spin-off called *Fog and Mist*. Instead of a vampire, like *Dark Shadows'* Barnabas, *Fog and Mist* featured a werewolf. Both *Dark Shadows* and *Fog and Mist* were filmed live, which was the reason *Fog and Mist* failed. The seasoned actor who played the werewolf couldn't ad-lib and keep rollin', as actor Jonathan Frid could as Barnabas. Four werewolves later, the show was canceled; however, *Dark Shadows* continued for six more seasons. According to Aunt Amelia, Bastian had a long career as a television writer, which included as one of the writers on *Night Gallery*. Now in retirement, he was staying with a grandchild in Melbourne Beach while deciding where to live out his golden years—the East or West Coast.

"It's been forty-one years to be exact, Bastian dear," Susannah said, not wanting to be left out of the conversation.

Susannah was frowning. No doubt upset Bastian hadn't mentioned her in his toast. He'd recently joined the community theater, of which Aunt Amelia and Susannah were players. Bastian had been given the role of Aunt Amelia's character's husband in Melbourne Beach Theatre's production of *Mousetrap*. Susannah had the part of Mrs. Boyle, the stern and unpleasant guest at Monkswell Manor. The last play Aunt Amelia and Susannah were in, Susannah had had the coveted lead role. Now it was Amelia's turn. The new owner of the theater, Ziggy, was also a bone of contention with Susannah, causing a fair share of grumbling from her thin-lipped mouth: nepotism being the nicest of her accusations. Not to mention, her dissatisfaction with her friend and employer having the role Agatha Christie had originally cast as a young twentysomething, not an old eightysomething.

"Well, I rest my case, Amelia," Bastian said. "You're still a stunner."

Ziggy, who was sitting next to Aunt Amelia, covered her hand with his. Their eyes met, and Liz saw reassurance from her great-aunt that Ziggy had nothing to worry about with Bastian Caruthers.

Liz excused herself from the drama and went to the sideboard. She started piling the New Year's fare on her plate, knowing she'd be back for seconds. Suddenly, the door to the dining room slammed open. Liz turned and saw Paula Resnick, Travis's agent.

Paula strode to the center of the dining room and put her hands on her hips. She had mahogany shoulder-length hair highlighted in shades of red. Her face was tan; a spray tan, Liz was sure. Paula had her own personal esthetician who made house calls. The faint shadow of yesterday's temporary tattoos was visible on her arms.

"What the hell have you done with Travis Osterman, Elizabeth? The last I heard, you and he had a heated discussion with more than a few threats from you. He hasn't been seen since! We've notified your rinky-dink sheriff's department, but they won't do a thing until he's been gone twenty-four hours."

"I have no idea where Travis is. And what threats are you talking about?" Liz placed her plate on a nearby empty table.

"Sally Beaman contacted me. She said she saw you last night and you were fighting with Travis. He's scheduled to do a book signing at the Windsor Polo Club in thirty minutes."

Fenton Holt got up from the table and moved toward Paula.

Go, Daddy, Liz thought, and her breathing slowed.

Usually the most mild-mannered of anyone she knew, her father said, "You're interrupting our family gathering. My daughter has informed you she has no idea where Mr. Osterman is. Perhaps you'd better search on your own until the twenty-four hours are up; then I'm sure the Brevard County Sherriff's Department will be more than accommodating." Before semiretirement, her father had been Brevard County's lead defense attorney.

Kate, Liz's bestie, called out, "Have you checked the bars? Or his most recent female acquisition's bed?" Kate was a little on the impulsive side—always had been. Usually, Liz would tell her to tone it down a notch. But not this time.

Liz charged over to Paula and her father. "I have no idea where he went. If you're truly concerned," she glanced at Paula's smooth, Botoxed-and-filled face, then searched her eyes for a view into her soul, as Aunt Amelia had taught her. Liz saw more anger than worry. "I'll come after brunch to wherever Travis is staying and see if we can figure out where he is." Liz just wanted Paula to leave, before she upset Aunt Amelia.

"The least you can do," Paula retorted. "You owe him your career."

"And he owes me more than a career." She felt the area under her scar pulse with heat. A purely visceral reaction. The pain felt real nonetheless. After winning a Pen/Faulkner Award, Liz's novel immediately hit the top of the *New York Times* list. That was when their relationship changed. Travis had always called her his Eliza Doolittle, and she'd been the fool to let him. Yes, associating with a Pulitzer Prize–winner hadn't hurt her career. But even after the lawsuit Travis filed against her, which she won, and all the blacklisting in the Manhattan publishing world after he'd called in a few favors, her book sales were brisk. She hoped it had to do with the quality of her writing, not the publicity. Bad or otherwise.

"Here." Paula reached into her turquoise Birkin handbag with little gold locks and retrieved a business card and pen. Paula collected Hermès handbags like Aunt Amelia collected grocery coupons. After jotting down an address on the back of the card, Paula held it toward her, then purposely let it slip to the floor so Liz had to bend to pick it up.

Liz stood. In what she hoped was a voice of authority, she said, "Okay, Paula. Time to scoot." But her composure melted when she glanced at the address on the back of the card. "He's staying this close to the Indialantic!"

"See you in an hour," Paula said. "We'll be waiting."

We'll, Liz thought, as she watched Paula, dressed in one of her Balmain designer power suits, exit the dining room.

Fenton wrapped his arm around Liz's shoulders.

Everything was going to be okay.

Wasn't it?

Chapter 6

Instead of taking Betty's ancient blue bomber Cadillac Deville, Liz and Betty cruised down the sidewalk that ran parallel to scenic A1A in one of the Indialantic's golf carts. The beachfront estate Travis was staying at was close enough to walk to. Liz preferred the security of the golf cart in case they had to make a quick getaway.

"They need seat belts in these things," Betty said, hanging on for dear life as Liz avoided a gopher tortoise snailing its way into the underbrush of dense palmettos lining the sidewalk. When the cart righted itself, Betty placed her hand on Liz's arm, giving it a gentle squeeze of reassurance.

Liz loved Betty's hands. They were a writer's hands, a crafter's hands. And even though eighty-three, Betty presented herself as decades younger. Today, her long gray hair was pulled back in a loose chignon. She met Liz's gaze with pale gray eyes blooming with youth, especially if a mystery needed to be solved.

Liz had to admit that since she'd returned home, they'd had their share of mystery, not to mention murder. Betty had a confidence in herself that never wavered. She'd come to the Indialantic when Liz was eight, three years after she and her father came to live with Aunt Amelia following the death of her mother. In those early years of loss, Aunt Amelia and Betty helped her and her father deal with the pain. Aunt Amelia, fun and flamboyant, Betty, a born teacher and nurturer. It was because of Betty that Liz had become a writer. In the '60s and '70s, Betty worked for the Stratemeyer Syndicate as a ghostwriter for five Nancy Drew mysteries under the pseudonym of Carolyn Keene. Even under duress, she never revealed exactly which books she'd written. Betty had also written her own series, The Island Girl Mysteries, starring Kit and her plucky sidekick dolphin,

Misty. Even though she'd written them in the '60s, Liz had enjoyed them in her teens, along with the vintage yellow hard-backed Nancy Drews—a mystery is a mystery, no matter in which year they were written.

"Are you sure you want to do this?" Betty asked.

"Yes, I'm sure. I need to face Travis one more time to make it clear I want nothing to do with him. Thanks for coming with me."

"Of course. The captain wanted to come along and bring Killer," Betty said.

Liz and Aunt Amelia had a game they played where they assigned '60s TV-character names to their lookalike residents, guests, and shopkeepers at the Indialantic. It was mutually agreed that Captain Netherton, with his Van Dyke beard and mustache, tall, lean frame, and erect posture, was the spitting image of the actor Edward Mulhare, who played Captain Daniel Gregg in the television show *The Ghost and Mrs. Muir*. She realized next month was Valentine's Day, and it seemed love was in the air at the Indialantic. There were budding relationships between Betty and Captain Netherton, Greta and Chef Pierre, Aunt Amelia and Ziggy, and, of course, she and Ryan. Even her best friend, Kate, had a new beau.

"Killer would lick Travis to death," Liz said as she idled the cart to let a long line of cars pass so they could cross the highway. "And afterward, Travis would probably insist on getting a rabies shot." Captain Netherton's Great Dane always found himself in precarious situations because in his mind he was the size of Brontë but, in reality, was taller than Liz's five-foot-eight if he stood on his hind legs. One time, Killer followed Carolyn Keene under the stadium seats in Aunt Amelia's screening room and got stuck. They'd had to call her father to unbolt the seat from the floor to free the crazy mutt.

"Why don't you fill me in a little on last night?" Betty said. "You didn't come to blows, did you?"

"No. I never touched him."

"It wasn't him I was worried about."

When Liz had woken this morning, there'd been a bruise from where Travis grabbed her arm. "I'm not saying I didn't *want* to slap him, especially after he tried to blackmail me."

"Blackmail?"

"He said he would tell everyone he was the one who wrote *Let the Wind Roar* because it was on his hard drive. Sally Beaman, our very own newscaster, was only a few feet away being all fairylike, three sheets to the wind. Which might be a good thing because she won't remember all the shouting."

"And what, pray tell, did you shout?"

"I really don't remember. All I know is he pushed every button he could, and I reacted. I'm such a loser."

"You're no such thing."

"How's the new series coming?"

"Smooth segue. We'll revisit the Travis problem later. I would suggest if he answers the door, you let me do the talking." She reached in her goliath tote bag and took out an envelope, opened it, and extracted the contents. "I'll pretend I'm a process server and I'm about to hit him with a lawsuit. He'll turn tail so fast, he won't ever bother you again."

Liz laughed. "You and your bag of tricks. Seriously, tell me about your London Chimney Sweep Mysteries." When visiting England last October, Betty, an esteemed member of the Sherlock Holmes Society, had procured a three-book deal with a top London publisher. Her new mystery series was about a sixteen-year-old female chimney sweep who dressed as a boy to assist Sherlock with some of his smaller cases to earn money to support her widowed mother and three sisters. It was a man's world, even a boy's world back in nineteenth-century England. If Liz knew Betty, her protagonist's small cases would morph into something much grander.

"I love the time period. No DNA to deal with, just good detecting. I'm having a fun time with it," Betty said, pointing to the sky at a half-dozen parachutists floating down to land on Paradise Beach. A pretty common sight; a sky-diving school was nearby in Sebastian on the other side of the lagoon.

"Will the reader ever get to meet Sherlock?"

"Oh, no. He and Watson are strictly in the background. They communicate with my protagonist through invisible ink letters left in a bin in an apothecary shop that's really a front for Sherlock's brother's British intelligence work. At first, I thought the series would have readers more in the Nancy Drew age group, but my publisher, after seeing the pages I'd turned in, wants the readership to be older, more young adult."

"How exciting. Can't wait to read it."

"We'll both have to wait until after our teaching gigs at the Abbey have ended. And don't forget, we have to take another pottery lesson from Minna at Home Arts."

"I don't know about that. Even Aunt Amelia, who's been displaying my artwork since I was five, was at a loss to identify the lopsided pot I threw. We decided it was an incense burner, and she put it in the Indialantic's Enlightenment Parlor." Liz had given Betty a gift certificate at Christmas for pottery lessons at the emporium shop Home Arts by the Sea, and Betty had given Liz the same. "It looked a lot easier in the movie *Ghost*."

"And romantic," Betty said, laughing. "You just need your Patrick Swayze, I mean Ryan, behind you to help form the clay."

"You're incorrigible, and you're starting to sound like Aunt Amelia," Liz said, putting the golf cart in gear.

On the beachside of A1A, they stopped in front of an ornate iron gate. In the far distance, there was a sprawling oceanfront house with a glimpse of the Atlantic peeking through keyhole openings in a white brick wall. On a pillar next to the gate was an intercom. She leaned out and pushed the button. When she released her finger, a voice said, "Come in, Ms. Holt," and the gates swung open.

Liz drove through and parked at the edge of a sweeping circular drive. Turning to Betty, she said, "The voice on the intercom sounded familiar. But it wasn't Travis's."

"The porridge thickens, as my protagonist Julia, aka Julius, would say,"

"Love it," Liz said before stepping from the cart.

Betty grinned, grabbed her tote bag, which held her iPad, her version of a trusty sidekick, and hopped out of the golf cart. They met at the bottom of the marble steps leading up to one of the most amazing beach houses or beach mansions Liz had ever seen. It glistened white in the midday sun. Like many of the oceanfront estates on the island, its architecture was in the Mediterranean Revival style, with a center entrance and two flanking arched pavilions. Travis had money, but she would bet this place was way above his means, especially if what he said was true, that *Blood and Glass* wasn't selling. His literary agent Paula repped many top authors and had way more money than Travis. But Paula wasn't big on sharing her wealth, even with golden-boy Travis. She was a taker, not a giver.

"Let's get this over with," Liz said, leading the way to the portico. When they reached the two arched doors, they automatically opened inward.

A man stood in front of them dressed in a white linen shirt, beige linen pants, and brown loafers—no socks. He had an amazing tan that accentuated his pearly whites. Something about his thick-lashed hazel eyes... Then she saw his pinky ring.

"Beast!" Liz called out. Now she knew why his voice on the intercom sounded familiar.

"Don't call him that. You're the beast," Paula said as she shot venom from behind Beast's wide back. "I know all about you—you've always had it out for Travis. He told me he wrote most of your precious Pen/Faulkner winner. You better come clean with where he is." Then she stepped in front of Beast. His mouth was open, ready to introduce himself but not having a chance.

Paula had changed her outfit from when they'd seen her earlier at the Indialantic. She wore a caftan made of a gauzy cotton, printed with palm leaves outlined in metallic gold. Around her wrinkly neck, the only thing that gave away her age, was an oversize tribal-style necklace with gold claw-shaped beads interspersed between large turquoise stones. She held a tissue to her nose. When she removed it, the tip of her nose was beet red. If Paula had been crying, Travis hadn't shown up.

Even Liz was beginning to think something might have happened to him.

Chapter 7

Beast channeled his king-of-the-jungle chutzpah and said in a deep voice, "Ladies, ladies. Let's go out to the lanai and discuss things." He led them through the high-ceiled foyer, down a wide-tiled hallway to a large great room decorated with tasteful modern art and cream-colored chaises and loveseats. Glass tables trimmed in gold were accented with ocean accessories: gold-dipped conch shells, large pieces of endangered red coral, and wire trays holding exotic seashells. On one wall, Liz spied a huge mixed-media piece signed by the Indialantic Emporium's resident artist, Minna Presley. Liz elbowed Betty, then nodded her head in the direction of the canvas. Betty smiled but was unusually quiet, taking in her surroundings. No doubt analyzing and storing away what she was viewing in case they needed it later.

At the rear of the great room were open sliding glass doors. They filed out onto the lanai. Liz and Betty took a seat on a cushioned-bamboo wicker sofa. Beast, whose real name they still didn't know, went behind the bar.

The lanai was spacious, almost the size of Liz's former SoHo loft in Manhattan. It even had an outdoor kitchen and brick fireplace. Paula anchored herself onto the sisal carpet and faced Liz and Betty. She placed her hands on her hips like an inquisitor. "Okay. Spill," she demanded through puffy lips, practically foaming at the mouth. "What did you do with him? I'm sure you wanted revenge for what he did to you." She sniffled, then retrieved a tissue from her pocket and held it to her nose.

"Paula, I think that's quite enough," Beast announced, exasperation in his voice. "Why don't you offer our guests a cool drink?" Paula looked at him with anger in her muddy-brown eyes but decided to do as she was told. As he came from behind the bar, he told her, "I've already started some Arnold Palmers; you can finish them up." Paula took the pitcher from his hand and he came and sat on a chair across from Liz and Betty. "I apologize for all the theatrics. We're concerned about Mr. Osterman, as you can well guess."

Liz couldn't hold back any longer. "I'm sorry, but who are you?" He laughed, the sound emerging from low in his gut. His laughter was contagious. Liz and Betty joined in, even though they didn't know what was so funny. "I'm Stevenson Charles," he replied, taking a sip of his drink, then focusing on Liz's face.

"As in my publisher, Charles and Charles?" Liz asked, astonished.

"One and the same. Great-granddaddy Stevenson the first started the operation. Now there's just me and my father."

It was hardly just him and his father at Charles & Charles. They were a multinational publishing corporation with hundreds of *New York Times* best-selling authors under their umbrella. "So why are you concerned about Travis Osterman?" Liz asked. "His publisher is Minton and Castle."

"Not anymore it isn't," he said. "We bought Mr. Osterman's contract in a bidding war last spring. Now we seem to have a rogue author."

"Would it be too much to ask why Travis, you, and Paula are here in Melbourne Beach?"

"That's something I would rather discuss with you over dinner," he said, glancing at Betty. "Alone. The matter is quite delicate."

"Can we pleaz-z-z move on to where Mr. Osterman might be?" a female voice asked, walking onto the lanai from the interior of the house. It was newscaster and last night's Tinker Bell, Sally Beaman. Following behind her was a pale-faced woman around Liz's age with strawberry-blond hair and too-blue/almost-violet eyes. Colored contacts? From the shape and unusual color of her eyes, Liz recognized Beauty, Beast's better half from the masquerade ball.

"Elizabeth, I overheard you arguing with him last night," Sally said, "even threatening him." She had cookie-cutter Stepford-wife good looks—a bland version of Charlotte, her father's fiancée. Her shoulder-length platinum-blond hair was plastered with hairspray so that when she turned her head, her helmet hair remained stationary.

Liz stood. "I seem to remember that when I left him on the terrace, you were standing nearby. So why don't you ask yourself the same question, Sally. Where did Travis go after you saw him?"

"We chatted for a few minutes, then he went to view the fireworks..." She paused for effect. "And look for you."

"Well, he never found me. It was a mistake to come here."

The young woman standing next to Sally tugged on her sleeve, then whispered something into her ear. Sally said, "Oh for gosh sakes, Hallie. Just introduce yourself."

The woman walked toward Liz, holding out her hand. "Hello, Ms. Holt. I'm a huge fan. I've been following your career and I adored your novel *Let the Wind Roar.*"

Liz was taken aback. "Thank you," she said, shaking her hand. Liz gave Stevenson a questioning look.

"Hallie is our new intern, assigned to Travis," Stevenson explained.

Good luck with that one, Liz thought as she sat back down.

Paula put a tray on the glass coffee table in front of Liz and Betty. "Okay. Drink up. And let's get down to the nitty-gritty. Where is Travis?"

"You were dressed as the Girl with the Dragon Tattoo last evening," Liz said. "And I seem to remember you passing me after coming out of the lobby, minutes before midnight, heading in the direction of the terrace. Maybe you were the last one to talk to Travis?"

"I admit to dressing as Lisbeth Salander, but Travis went his own way last night after the limo dropped us off. And I didn't go anywhere near the terrace. I came back here to Stevenson's. Had one of my migraines."

"This is your house?" Liz asked, looking over at Stevenson.

"One of our board members has it as a timeshare," he said.

Sally sat next to Stevenson. She leaned forward in Liz's direction and said, "You know I'm a seasoned television reporter, Elizabeth."

"Yes, I know. We've known each other since high school, Sal, and please call me Liz."

"As I was saying, I have a stellar reputation for looking at all angles of a story, and in this case, it seems your involvement with Travis must be related to his disappearance."

"How exactly did you meet up with Travis? As far as I know, Sally, you've lived in Melbourne Beach your whole life."

"When you wouldn't give me an interview last October about your ex-boyfriend's upcoming book, I contacted his agent. Travis himself took the time to call me back."

"From what I've heard, *Blood and Glass* is fiction, Sally. What am I missing here?"

"I'm only saying, we all saw Travis last night," she said. "He didn't come home, and he hasn't contacted any of us. And you seem to be the only one who's got something against him."

Betty came to Liz's defense. "Let's take a step back. When was the last time Mr. Osterman was seen?"

Before anyone could answer, Hallie asked, "Who are you? Liz's granny?"

"I should be so lucky. I'm Betty Lawson, and I think it's time to put the recriminations aside and get down to brass tacks. I'll ask again. Who saw Travis last?"

Stevenson slapped his knee. "Well, I'll be darned. Betty Lawson as in the author of the future London Chimney Sweep Mysteries! What an honor to meet you. You're one lucky lady. It's rare for the estate of Sir Conan Doyle to approve the use of Sherlock in a series. They must have been impressed. You should have had your agent come to our little house to publish."

"Little house. Not quite," Betty said. "I went with a London publisher."

Liz interrupted, "Excuse me. Can someone direct me to the powder room?"

Paula pointed to the door Sally and Hallie had come out of. "First door on your right. Don't be long."

Paula must have read Liz's mind, but that didn't mean she would abandon her plan to check out the rest of the house. Specifically, Travis's room. Maybe she'd find some clue to where he'd gone that the others had missed. And if she got caught, she would just tell them she was trying to help figure out where Travis had gone.

The door Paula mentioned led directly to a tiled hallway. She passed the bathroom and stopped in front of a closed door to the right. She opened it and looked inside. The room was huge. One of Paula's Hermès Birkins sat on a credenza. She closed the door. The next room was a sitting room with a pullout sofa in the open position. This, she guessed, belonged to Travis's intern. There was a printer on the desk and an open laptop. She left the room and continued down the hallway. She heard Betty and Stevenson talking about books. Good. Betty probably had caught onto what she was up to.

The next door opened to Travis's room. There was no doubting it. His Louis Vuitton suitcase was on a luggage stand with his gold-stamped monogram on top: TPO—Travis Peter Osterman. She hurried toward it and unzipped it. It was empty. She went to the dresser drawers and opened them one at a time. Nothing. Everything was perfectly organized by color and type of clothing. Travis was nothing if he wasn't neat. Everything had its place in Travis's world. Shoes had to be taken off at the door, no red wine in the living room on the white rug, and books had to be shelved, even if you were in the middle of reading.

In the drawer of the nightstand next to the king-size bed, she found his return ticket to LaGuardia, a set of keys with a gold Cartier key tag, and a debit-card receipt from Deli-casies by the Sea from three days ago.

Travis must still be on the island. Maybe he'd found an adoring fan and stayed the night with her? She quickly closed the drawer and moved to a connecting door. She turned the handle. Locked. She went back out to the hall and tried the other door to the connecting room. Locked.

Glancing down the hallway, Liz saw Travis's intern coming toward her. She took a step back from the door, turned, and waited until Hallie was a few feet away before saying, "I think I got lost. This place is huge."

"It is. Paula sent me to fetch you."

"Of course she did," Liz said under her breath.

If Hallie heard, she didn't let on. "I can't wait to read your next book. Can you give me an idea of what it will be about?"

"It takes place in Cornwall…"

Paula came stomping toward them. "Hallie, what's taking so long? I asked you to get her, not gush all over her. This isn't a social occasion. We must find Travis. He's scheduled for a book signing in the morning, then we have to get to the airport for a six o'clock flight."

Liz had no choice but to follow Paula out to the lanai, where they joined Sally, Betty, and Stevenson.

Stevenson stood. "Ms. Lawson said you must be getting back. I'm sure Mr. Osterman will show up sooner or later."

"He better," Paula said, looking at Liz.

A phone rang from inside the house. "Maybe that's him!" Paula said, running off.

It wasn't him.

But it was *about* him.

Chapter 8

The rain was torrential. What had started out as a perfect New Year's Day dissolved into an evening of thunder and lightning that would charge Mary Shelley's Frankenstein enough to outrun the Energizer Bunny. Paula had heard from the Sheriff's Department that Travis's cell phone had been found in the dumpster outside the Indialantic's Emporium. It had been found by Brittany Poole, owner of the women's clothing boutique Sirens by the Sea. What pretentious Brittany had been doing dumpster-diving was beyond Liz's comprehension. Kate, on the other hand, the owner of Books & Browsery by the Sea, never met a dumpster she didn't like.

"Thanks for the tea, Auntie," Liz said, sitting at the kitchen's long farm table.

"Can you pass the sugar, please?" Betty asked, sitting across from Liz. Liz handed it to her.

"Yes, thanks, Amelia. It hits the spot," Betty added. "You're the best tea maker in Melbourne Beach. Even in London. When I had high tea at the Shelbourne, it didn't compare to your secret blends." She placed her nose above her cup and inhaled the distinctive aroma.

Liz's great-aunt was an awful cook, but she made up for it with her tea-making skills.

Greta stood at the double sink. After she rinsed her teacup and placed it on the drying rack, she turned and said, "I think I'm on to you, Amelia Eden Holt. I've whittled it down to spearmint, lemon verbena, rose petals, licorice root, cinnamon, and, of course, orange peel from our very own trees. The only thing I might have wrong is the cinnamon...it could be allspice."

Aunt Amelia sat at the head of the table, her "dogs" resting on a chair. "You're close, Greta. You left out yerba santa and hyssop. And it *is* cinnamon. Pierre helped me prepare it. I'm calling it my New Year's Bliss blend."

Liz filled Aunt Amelia in on what they'd just learned about the phone. "Thanks for keeping me updated. Have you talked to Ryan about everything?"

"Waiting for him to come back from being with Pops."

"Well, next time Mr. Osterman threatens you, I'll bring Ziggy and a posse of his biker friends over to frighten the coward. No one ever has to know they're the most nonviolent group I've ever met."

"Aw... my champion," Liz said, blowing her a kiss.

"Admittedly, finding his phone in the Emporium's dumpster is a bit perplexing," Aunt Amelia said, stuffing one of Pierre's mini cornbread jalapeño muffins in her mouth, then washing it down with a gulp of tea.

"What phone?" Ryan asked, walking into the kitchen.

Uh-oh. "You're back," Liz choked out. Today, he had the pirate look going. Liz was very partial to pirates.

"Yes, I'm back. Why do you all look guilty about something?"

Betty picked up her napkin and held it to her mouth. Liz knew her "tell" was an urge to smile in sad or serious situations. Aunt Amelia just gave Liz a you-know-better-than-this-missy gaze about the fact she hadn't told Ryan about Travis.

Liz shot up and grabbed Ryan's arm. "Come into the butler's pantry. There's something I need to tell you." She had to half-drag him forward. Once inside, she closed the doors.

"What's going on, Liz?" he asked.

"What's going on, Liz?" Barnacle Bob repeated. "Travis was here last night! Travis was here last night!" Barnacle Bob liked to mine people's conversations like he was digging for gold. Aunt Amelia had gotten him from a parrot rescue shelter, and Liz had an inkling of why he'd been abandoned. There wasn't a curse -word he didn't know, and coupling that with his uncanny ability to go for the jugular by repeating a few choice words, it was clear why the parrot was usually quarantined to the butler's pantry. Aunt Amelia never saw it. Or maybe she did, but chose to look for the best in him, just like she did with everyone else.

"Eavesdropper," Liz hissed into the macaw's ear.

"Say what!" Ryan shouted. "Your ex was here at the literary ball and I find out now, from him."

He pointed at the bald-headed parrot, who ruffled his feathers, then said in an innocent voice, "Polly wants a cracker."

I'll give you a cracker. "Yes. I meant to tell you this morning, but you had plans with Pops, so I was waiting until you got back. And here you are!" she said a little too cheerily.

"Let's hear it." A lock of glossy, deep-brown hair covered his deeply furrowed brow. His voice took on a patronizing tone, but instead of confronting him, she tucked her tail between her legs and said, "And there's more."

"More?" Lightning flashed behind him through the window over Pierre's desk. The same place the chef had written the day's menu for over thirty years. Thunder followed, matching the anger in Ryan's almost-black accusing eyes.

"Travis is missing, and they just found his phone in the Emporium's dumpster." Her tone was squeaky at best, like a TV cartoon mouse's. She had an urge to run out into the storm with the goal of being hit by a lightning-felled palm tree. It would be better than becoming a recipient of Ryan's ire, especially with the way he was looking at her.

He must have noticed the panic on her face, because instead of chastising her for not telling him sooner, he gently pulled her toward him and whispered into her ear, "We'll handle this together."

Her shoulders relaxed, and she realized there was something to be said about having a boyfriend who put his needs and ego aside to comfort her.

She collapsed onto Pierre's desk chair. She explained everything from the night before, starting with when she'd first seen Travis's agent, then found Travis on the terrace dressed in a WWII costume, holding a rifle—all the way to the news about Brittany and the phone.

After thinking things through, something that must come naturally to a former arson investigator on the FDNY and her dad's current PI, he said, "I think we should search the grounds. If you're not up to it, I understand." He grabbed her hands, then pulled her up from the chair.

"My father said Charlotte has decided to vacate the twenty-four-hour rule and is sending over a few cars."

"Okay. We'll wait until they arrive. Let's go powwow with Betty and Aunt Amelia. We need a plan."

Ryan held open the pantry door and they walked into the kitchen at the same time someone threw open the outside door. Pierre shuffled in, wearing a black-hooded rain slicker. Water sluiced onto the terra-cotta tile. In one hand he held a wire basket filled with mushrooms. In the other, a World War II Garand rifle—complete with bayonet.

The same rifle Liz had seen last night.

Travis's rifle.

Chapter 9

Agent Charlotte Pearson and her team of CSIs were inside the cordoned-off area where Travis Osterman's body had been found. The Brevard County Sheriff's Department hadn't been the ones who'd secured the site. It was the Barrier Island Historical Society, in conjunction with the Florida State Native American Anthropology and Genealogy Department. Last October, a Native American dugout canoe was found on the Indialantic's property near the Indian River Lagoon. A few weeks ago, hidden beneath the canoe, they'd found the over three-hundred-year remains of an Ais Native American tribal chief. It was one of the reasons the Indialantic had been deemed an official historical site. The chief had recently been removed for further study. Now, it looked like Travis's killer had swapped the chief's final resting place for Travis's. Not that his body had been hidden when Pierre stumbled upon it. The torrential rain had caused the thin layer of top soil to wash away, revealing Travis's corpse and the rifle.

Liz, her father, Betty, and Ryan stood on the perimeter, looking in. Travis was still dressed in costume from last night. He wore a smile on his face. *Or was it a sneer?* And his eyes were open. Liz turned away when she saw a bullet hole in the middle of his chest. If not for the palm trees, she would have thought he was playing a role in a WWII movie, shot in the trenches by an enemy soldier.

The rain had stopped, but there were still cavalcades of thunder echoing off the Atlantic. "How is this possible?" Liz whispered to Ryan. "Wouldn't we have heard gunshots? And I'm pretty sure Travis wasn't stupid enough to bring a loaded gun to the literary ball."

"I have a theory," Ryan said. "He must have been shot during the fireworks. The noise would cover the sound of a gunshot. We'll know for sure when the coroner rules on time of death."

Aunt Amelia had stayed behind with Pierre. Earlier, Ryan had known enough to bag the rifle Pierre had brought in. Apparently, Pierre had been foraging for mushrooms in the middle of the thunderstorm. Not the wisest place to be; Florida had more lightning strikes than any other state in the country. Just another reason they had to keep a closer eye on the absentminded chef. Guilt tugged at her heart. Pierre had always been so independent. She didn't blame him for sticking to his routine. But now, having him find Travis's body might have been a little more than even he could handle. Luckily, Pierre had thought the body and the rifle had been there for years, not less than twenty-four hours. Aunt Amelia had done what she did best: She sent Pierre to bed with a cup of her soothing herbal tea to promote brain function—sage, holy basil, rosemary, oregano, spearmint, and gotu kola.

Liz turned to tell Betty about Ryan's theory about the fireworks masking the sound of gunshots, but Betty had moved away and was examining the ground near a park bench with a view of Aunt Amelia's cutting garden. She watched Betty pull something from her pocket and stick it in the ground. She tugged on Ryan's T-shirt and pointed. "I think Nancy Drew may have found something."

As they approached, Betty said, "We better leave this area alone until the forensics team can secure it." She'd left a piece of Wrigley's Spearmint gum on the ground as a marker. "There's a button on the ground," Betty answered their inquisitive gazes, "a brass army button. I'm sure the body didn't fall directly into the grave after being shot. I'd bet he was killed here, then dragged. The rain would have erased the drag marks, but the button proves he sat on the bench."

Liz glanced at the bench, imagining Travis's ghostly shape holding the rifle. Aunt Amelia already thought the bench was haunted. But haunted in a good way, with healing, loving spirits. A large brass plaque on the back of the bench listed all the Indialantic's pets that had passed over the rainbow bridge since her great-aunt was a child. Aunt Amelia had told her, "Every flower I've planted is in memory of my beloveds, and look at what a colorful, fragrant tribute I've created." As a child, Liz thought the daisy-shaped, golden-yellow Florida state flower, Coreopsis, was the Pookie flower until she saw a photo of teenage Aunt Amelia holding an arctic-blue-eyed Himalayan fuzzball. The inscription under the photo read, "Pookie and me."

At the thought of all things great and small being deceased, the full impact of Travis's death—or murder—hit Liz. She'd been angry with him, but never wished him dead. What was the motive for his death? A disgruntled lover? Something to do with *Blood and Glass*?

At the beginning of their relationship, Travis had seduced her with his words. Carefully chosen words that pushed all her romantic buttons and made her feel she'd brought out the poet in him. He'd told her she was his muse. As time went on, especially after a night of drinking, he used his words as weapons. Now, someone had used a real weapon on him.

But who?

There wasn't time to analyze the situation as she turned her attention to a shouting match between Charlotte and a man in a rumpled blue suit. They both wore disposable booties so as not to tamper with trace evidence. Slightly ludicrous, seeing the area around the grave was a river of mud.

"Give it up, Agent Pearson," the rumple-suited man said to Charlotte. "I just heard from a newscaster that your fiancé's daughter threatened the deceased just last night. It's a definite conflict of interest. And brass agrees."

Charlotte looked over at Liz, Ryan, and Betty, then to her fiancé, Fenton, standing a few feet in front of her. Embarrassment flushed her perfect-featured face. She slumped her shoulders, ducked under the crime scene tape secured between two huge palms, and walked in the direction of the Indialantic's parking lot. Charlotte rarely gave up so easily. Why now? She was a tough homicide detective who never cut Liz a break when she had "stuck her nose in police business." Now that Charlotte and her father were engaged, it made for quite a sticky wicket.

Liz called over, "You better go after her, Dad. It's not her fault, but I know whose it is. Sally Beaman's."

Fenton glanced at Liz, then toward Charlotte's retreating figure, and came over to them. "Okay. But I want you to be careful. Don't say anything to the press and meet me in my office in an hour. I want to hear everything that happened between you and Mr. Osterman last night. And bring Ryan." He gestured toward Betty and Ryan, who were talking in whispers a few feet away.

"Are you speaking to me as my attorney or my father?"

"Both," he said, wrinkling the brow of his handsome face.

"Then I'd better give you this." She dug in her jeans pocket and took out a dollar. "Your retainer."

An obvious stickler for the law, he took it. "Behave," he ordered, scurrying after his fiancée.

Liz saluted his back. Which only reminded her of Travis's uniformed body. His dead body.

Betty tapped her on the shoulder. "Earth to Liz. We'd better get going, I think the sky is going to let loose again."

"Oh no, what's happened now?"

"I was referring to the weather. Why did Agent Pearson leave in such a hurry? Wanted to tell her about the button."

"She's not on the case. That guy is," Liz said, pointing. "Conflict of interest because of me."

"Never seen him before. Have you?" Betty took her elbow as they walked toward Ryan, who was still examining the area where Betty found the button. "Maybe we should have Ryan tell the new guy about the button. I live at the Indialantic and you're a suspect."

"I am? Darn. I am." Tears stung the corners of her eyes.

"Hopefully not," Betty said. "But I think we should have Ryan break the ice. Judging by the new guy's tank-shaped body, no neck, and Marine buzz cut, he looks like he might relate better to a former FDNY arson investigator rather than a little old lady or the deceased's ex-girlfriend."

"Betty Lawson, are you typecasting? You must remember this isn't the days of Sherlock Holmes. A woman can be a woman. They don't need a macho male to talk to an authority figure. Look at Charlotte. A tough and capable woman."

"Just sayin', it can't hurt. Plus, I might have pocketed something else I found under the bench, and I'm not giving it up. Yet."

"Oh boy. I should've known. You better go give my dad a dollar too. We might both be in the stewpot before long."

"I have a high tolerance for heat. And so do you." Betty squeezed her shoulder in reassurance.

"I don't know if that's true where Travis is concerned. Shh, the new guy is coming over here."

"Look innocent."

"I am innocent." That wouldn't be the first or the last time she'd utter those words.

After stiff introductions and a few innuendos alluding to the fact that they would be seeing a lot more of Agent Crowley, Betty and Liz stepped onto the path leading to the back of the hotel. If Sally Beaman was waiting in the front, Liz planned to avoid her. Ryan stayed behind to talk to Charlotte's replacement about the button. Liz heard the detective say in a gruff voice, "Drop the agent. Just call me Crowley." Maybe Betty was right, and he was one of those stereotypical drill sergeant types featured on hard-boiled detective shows.

There was a cooling drizzle, and Liz enjoyed the feel of it on her face. It seemed, since being scarred, she'd been hiding under hats or wearing protective sun lotion—afraid of the elements you encountered when living on a barrier island. The gentle rain was cathartic, in stark contrast to what was going on around her. When they reached the turnoff toward the rear of the Indialantic, Liz stopped next to a cement birdbath. On its rim was a cupid type angel sitting on a lily pad. Kate had rescued it from an estate that was being demolished. Kate rescued used objects for her shop the way Aunt Amelia did pets and people.

"Did he have any family?" Betty asked as they continued on.

"Oh my God. Taylor! Travis's sister. I have to contact her before it's too late."

Betty pointed ahead. "It might already be too late." Even though the early evening sky was dark, the front of the Indialantic was lit up like Marlins Park. News vans had invaded the entire circular drive in front of the hotel's main entrance. Liz froze and took a step backward. "These aren't local news reporters. This is more like a media frenzy. I refuse to run and hide like I did with Travis's lawsuit. Let's go face the cameras. Someone killed Travis and I want to find out who. Haven't you always told me from reading your true-crime books that murderers usually stick around to gloat. Maybe we'll spot him or her in the crowd. Posing as a bystander."

"That's true, but that rule usually refers to serial killers or something you'd see on an episode of *Criminal Minds*. But I like your thinkin', kid." She looped her arm through Liz's, and they marched toward the front of the hotel. "We might as well check out the lookie-loos. As Sherlock said, and I quote, 'What is out of the common is usually a guide rather than a hindrance.'"

"So, look for the uncommon in the crowd of gawkers?" Liz asked.

"Yes. But remember, Sherlock is fictional."

"But you're not, Betty. And with all your research on Sir Arthur Conan Doyle, I'm sure you have an edge."

"Doyle might not have been in law enforcement before he started penning his Holmes tales, but he was a physician before the advent of IT forensic evidence in crime detecting. Doyle's deductive mind, inherited by his protagonist Sherlock, is why I love writing mysteries the old-school way. Not based on black-and-white printouts analyzing someone's spit."

"Ugh. Why did you have to bring that up? Who knows what trace evidence of mine might show up on Travis?"

When they reached the crowd, Liz saw Captain Netherton standing erect with US Coast Guard posture. He was waving his walking cane to ward off the piranhas advancing toward him and Aunt Amelia. Little did the captain know, her great-aunt could handle herself, especially in front of an audience. But like the captain, Liz had an urge to protect her.

She pushed her way through the wake of vultures, one of which shoved his microphone against her mouth, causing her lip to bleed. Liz knew the official name for a group of flying vultures was a "kettle"; vultures hanging around trees or on the ground were called a "committee"; but when talking about a slew of vultures feeding on carrion, the correct term was a "wake". What was in front of her was definitely a wake and she was their corpus delicti.

When Liz reached the portico, she planted herself next to the captain.

"Is it true, Ms. Holt, that your ex-boyfriend was murdered at your family-run hotel?"

The lights were blinding. She couldn't see who'd asked the question but knew for sure, it wasn't Sally Beaman because the reporter was male. Unlike the last time she'd been attacked by the media, she was ready to shout it from the Indialantic's bell tower that she was innocent. Then she remembered her attorney father's voice: *whatever you say, they will twist and rearrange to sell their story.* It didn't matter anyway; just as she opened her mouth—her bleeding mouth—Agent Crowley pushed her aside. Before facing the cameras, he turned to her and said, "Nice bruise. Were you in a scuffle?"

She followed his gaze to her right arm. An eggplant-colored bruise had formed on her upper arm. The same arm Travis had grabbed last night as she was turning to leave. She wasn't surprised at the detective's next words. "See you at the station. Bright and early, Ms. Holt."

She stepped back and was enfolded in Aunt Amelia's embrace. Finally choking out, "I'm good, Auntie. You can let go."

Aunt Amelia released her, and the captain squeezed her elbow. "You okay, kiddo?"

Liz smiled and nodded, then they turned their attention to Agent Crowley's responses to the press. He handled himself well. Not disclosing anything. Yet you had a sense when he did learn something related to the case, he would share it for the common good. What she hadn't expected was the fact that Captain Netherton knew him. When Crowley was finished, the captain approached him and gave him a hearty pat on the back. Crowley returned a manly version of a hug.

If the captain liked Crowley, he couldn't be all bad. Could he?

Certain there was no more flesh to be had, the maddening crowd dispersed. Aunt Amelia, Captain Netherton, and Liz entered the Indialantic's lobby through the revolving door, and Liz looked back, hoping to see Betty. Stealth sleuth that she was, Liz knew Betty was scoping out the crowd for Travis's killer. Maybe when Liz woke up the next morning, the headlines would read Suspect Arrested in Pulitzer Prize–Winning Author's Murder.

But that wouldn't be the case...

Chapter 10

"Taylor, what are you doing here? I mean..."

Monday morning, Travis's sister stood outside the doorway to Liz's beach house, looking worse than something the cat dragged in. She appeared waiflike and vulnerable as she turned her large, watery green eyes on Liz. Her long, flame-red, stick-straight hair blew in the ocean breeze, windshield wiping her delicate-featured face left, then right. Giving Liz just enough of a glimpse to know she'd been devastated by her brother's death.

When she saw Liz, a smile transformed her face, then quickly disappeared. "Oh, Liz, isn't it terrible? I can't believe he's dead."

"Come inside. Do you have any luggage?"

"No. Aunt Amelia paid the cab driver and had my overnight bag sent up to the Oceana Suite by a Mrs. Shay. After giving me a huge hug about the loss of my brother and a cup of tea, which I swear worked like magic, your great-aunt insisted I stay at your hotel. I know you told me how wonderful she is, but something about her made me feel like I was coming home. Not here to plan a funeral," she added, sniffling. "She's leaving soon for the Melbourne Beach Theatre and invited me along. I wanted to say hi to you first. When I told her I once took acting lessons at the Strasberg school in Manhattan, she insisted I come with her to critique her performance in *The Mousetrap*. Do you believe it?"

Liz did believe it. Aunt Amelia was the most kindhearted person on the planet. And Taylor, who'd taken so much grief from Travis over the years, deserved to be enfolded in Aunt Amelia's ample, loving arms. "I'm sorry I didn't call you myself. I wanted to wait until the morning and here you are. How did you hear about your brother?"

"Well," she said, hesitating, "it was Paula Resnick, his agent, who made the call. She also told me some things about you. I didn't believe them for one second. I can't believe he's gone." She dissolved into a bout of crying.

Even at Travis's verbal abuse, she'd never heard Taylor say anything negative about anyone. Liz was happy Taylor hadn't believed whatever Paula had told her on the phone. And why would Paula call Taylor in the first place? As far as she knew, Paula and Taylor had never met. Travis had been embarrassed by his younger sister. She wasn't the cosmopolitan type who'd fit into his circle, dressing in vintage clothing, more comfortable in the East Village than the new "in" neighborhood of the moment where he hung out.

"Have a seat." She led her to the sofa, where she collapsed into the cushions like a deflated balloon. Liz sat next to her. "I was just going down to the police station to give my formal statement. Then, this afternoon, I have to go teach a class at a nearby writing workshop."

"Are they sure he was murdered?"

"I'm sorry, Taylor. Yes, they're sure."

"Why would anyone want to kill him? Everyone loved him."

Liz paused for a moment before speaking. She wanted to say, *there was one person who didn't love him*, but instead she said, "I don't know, Taylor. We'll have to wait and see. I'm sure the Sheriff's Department will want to talk to you. Did you know Travis was coming to Melbourne Beach?"

"No." She started crying again.

Liz jumped up and took a few steps to the kitchen, which was part of the great room, grabbed a roll of paper towels off the counter, and brought it to the sofa. She tore off one section at a time as Taylor cried into them. A soggy pile grew on the glass coffee table.

After composing herself, Taylor said, "We had our differences, but I always took care of Travis. Two months ago, after our parents died, I moved into the house in Connecticut."

Her and Travis's childhood home was a rattling old nineteenth-century Colonial on five acres in Greenwich, Connecticut.

"I think the reason he'd recently cut ties with me had something to do with either Sammi the golden retriever I rescued or the video."

"Why would he care if you got a dog? He lived in the city."

"I told him I was too lonely in the house and needed a companion. He claimed a *slobbering dog* would bring down the value of the house when he went to sell it."

"*He* went to sell it? Wasn't it left to both of you?"

"Well, actually," she picked at the cuticle of her right thumb, then looked up, "Mother and Father left everything to me. Even Silver Lightning."

Silver Lightning was the million-dollar racehorse owned by the Ostermans. The horse had won the Preakness twice and was now used as a stud for producing more champions.

That sounded like Travis, denying his sister any pleasure. He'd claimed he was allergic to dogs and cats alike and hadn't even allowed Taylor to have one in her apartment, in case he dropped by. Which he never did. Once, Liz had brought up how much she missed Aunt Amelia's zoo at the Indialantic and mused about getting a kitten. Travis had had a fit. She doubted he had pet allergies. It probably had more to do with him being a fanatic when it came to cleanliness. Not that Liz had time for a pet anyway at the time—too many events and book signings, his and hers. She wished she'd slowed down to smell the fur, like she did every night before kissing Brontë good night on the top of her tiny head.

One night, near the end of her relationship with Travis, Liz had invited Taylor over for dinner at Travis's penthouse. Taylor told her brother she was thinking of finding a pet that wouldn't affect his allergies. He'd slurred, "Maybe I'll allow you to get a guinea pig. Then when the smelly thing kicks the bucket, Liz could whip up some cuy, roasted guinea pig, for dinner. It's a delicacy in Peru."

The meal hadn't gone as planned. Travis got drunk on crème de violette champagne cocktails and Taylor had been embarrassed by his verbal diatribe about how his parents always favored her.

Liz had spent hours that evening preparing dinner, making all Travis's favorites, hoping to create an exceptional meal that would bring brother and sister closer together. She'd been Pierre's sous chef since she'd moved to the Indialantic as a child. Pierre had been classically trained in Paris, and in turn, Liz had been classically trained by Pierre. Sometimes Liz worried she wasn't the great writer everyone who'd read *Let the Wind Roar* thought she was, but she'd always been confident in her cooking skills. Travis hadn't been impressed that night, or any other that she'd cooked for him. He enjoyed dialing up a gourmet delivery service and ordering the best cuisine from the top-rated restaurant du jour in the Zagat's guide. Plus, he was a freak when it came to germs, as evidenced by the sparse, antiseptic décor in his penthouse. Not a comfy spot in the whole place to curl up with a cozy quilt and a good book.

In the past, when all these negative thoughts about Travis surfaced, her therapist had instructed her to write a page of all his positives. They had existed. But for now, she couldn't remember one. Was it wrong to despise a dead man? Where was her compassion? She made a mental note to dig out her old journals from when she and Travis first met to reread them. She'd thought it was love at first sight.

"I know when I was with him, he wasn't close to your parents. I assume they didn't patch things up?"

"I don't think they had an argument. Travis basically lost touch with them once he won the Pulitzer. I know there was some incident about a year ago. Someone came to the house and told my parents all these bad things about Travis. But no one ever discussed it with me. In fact, they refused to talk about it."

"Did you see the person?" Liz couldn't help but think the visit might be related to Travis's murder.

"Yes. I answered the door. It was an older woman. In her fifties or sixties."

"Do you know what bad things she said?"

"No. My parents took her into the study. Do you think the woman might have something to do with Travis's murder?"

"I have no idea," Liz answered. "But you might want to tell the Sheriff's Department about it. I was so sorry to hear about your parents' automobile accident. I wanted to come to the funeral, but, well, you know... I hope you got my donation and flowers?"

"Yes. They were beautiful."

"You said Travis was upset about either Sammi or the video. What video?" Liz felt guilty grilling Taylor while she was in such a delicate state. Just not guilty enough to stop.

"Oh, it's stupid really. I don't know why I brought it up."

"What happened?" Liz asked gently.

"It was the day of my parents' funeral. I left Travis in the living room talking to people who'd come back to the house from the cemetery."

Liz knew the "house" was more like a rambling mansion.

"You know how great Travis was in front of a crowd. Most of the people there were his friends or business associates." The tears started again. "I went into my father's study and picked out a home video with my parents in it. I just wanted to see their faces one more time..."

"Hold that thought." Liz got up and hurried to the bathroom. She grabbed a box of tissues from the counter and the small wastebasket under the sink, then went back to Taylor and sat down. She held out the box of tissues.

"I should buy stock in the tissue companies. I can't seem to turn off the waterworks." She grabbed a tissue, held it to her nose, and blew.

"What a beautiful ring. Aquamarine?" Liz asked. The size of the stone overtook the ring finger on Taylor's right hand. The stone was pear-shaped and appeared flawless.

"Yes."

"Your birthstone?"

"No, it was my mother's birthstone. Daddy gave it to her on their twenty-fifth wedding anniversary." She grabbed another tissue and honked into it.

"You were telling me about the day of your parents' funeral."

"Yes. I'd chosen a video to watch that they'd taken the day they brought me home from the hospital as a newborn. Travis was five at the time."

"Your parents adopted him when he was two, right?"

"Right. Anyway, I didn't realize it, but the day of their funeral, he and his buddies had come into the room to see some of my father's hunting trophies. When Travis saw himself in the video, he made a joke like *"Who would've thought that skinny little kid would turn out to be so famous."* As the video progressed, everyone watched as Travis came over to the bassinet with me inside. My parents were in the foreground, talking about how blessed they were, but in the background we all saw Travis rip the pacifier out of my mouth with a mean look on his face. Then he dangled it in front of me, then pulled it back again when I opened my mouth. Before my parents turned to see what the crying was about, he hid the pacifier on the windowsill behind the curtains."

Liz patted her hand. "I think any child psychologist would say that's normal behavior when a new sibling comes into the home,"

"Tell that to Travis. He was livid that his friends had witnessed it. He stormed over, ejected the DVD, and threw it at me. From that moment on, he barely talked to me. You know how he's always been so sensitive about being adopted. My parents didn't think they could have any biological children. I was a surprise."

Liz did know about Travis's obsessive feeling that his parents loved Taylor more than him. Liz had only met his parents a few times. Once, she was at one of Travis's book signings and saw him treat them like strangers off the street who wanted his autograph.

Taylor continued, "It's been two months since the funeral. Did Travis come to Florida to see you? Did the two of you rekindle your relationship?"

That one took Liz off guard "Egad! No." She covered her mouth.

Taylor looked at her with understanding.

"I think it had something to do with me and his last book," Liz said. "But let's just wait until we learn more."

"It's too awful to consider someone killing him. Could the rifle have gone off by accident?"

Before Liz could answer, Brontë, who'd been snoozing on a section of classic novels in the bookcase flanking the window seat, came to see what the crying was about. She rubbed against Taylor's black Lycra leggings, leaving behind a smooth frosting of gray-and-white cat hair.

Distracted, Taylor cooed, "Isn't she adorable. So-o-o tiny. Is she a newborn?"

"No, actually, she's ten months old." Liz picked up Brontë and handed her to Taylor.

"How precious." Taylor scratched behind her ears.

"She loves it even more when you rub the area on her back closest to her tail. You'll soon have a friend for life."

Brontë's rattling purr confirmed Liz's warning.

Taylor looked over at her. "I see your scar is looking much better. You know, I tried to see you when you were in the hospital, but Travis's lawyer's put a stop to it because of the lawsuit."

"Don't worry. I understand. I got all of your letters and they really meant a lot to me."

When Liz had returned from Manhattan to the Indialantic, she'd told her great-aunt all about Taylor, especially Travis's poor treatment of his sister. During the trial, his lawyer had even called Taylor as a witness, trying to make Liz out to be a monster. Travis claimed Liz purposely antagonized him that night, and when she'd called 911, her goal was to make Travis look bad in the press and destroy his reputation. "Taylor, I'd better get going. Do you want to come with me to the station?"

"Aunt Amelia—she told me to call her that—said I should lay low as long as I can. She's going to call someone named Ryan to take me when I'm ready. She also promised a tea-making lesson after we go to the Melbourne Beach Theatre. And even gave me a copy of her play." She rooted in her canvas bag and extracted a well-worn copy of *The Mousetrap* and held it in the air. "She says I remind her of a young her."

Liz did see a slight resemblance between Aunt Amelia and Taylor and was pleased her great-aunt had taken Taylor under her wing. She knew what was going on. Aunt Amelia wanted to distract Taylor from the death of her brother. So far, it seemed to be working. She also knew, by having Ryan escort Taylor to the police station, he might overhear information Liz wasn't privy to that might prove her innocence.

Taylor and Liz left together in the old Cadillac convertible Betty left parked at the beach house for Liz's use. Betty hadn't driven in a year, seeing everything she needed was at arm's length between the Hotel and Emporium shops, not to mention a couple of oceanfront restaurants within walking distance. There was also the little matter of Betty's driver's license having expired. Liz was on the lookout for her own car, but in the meantime, she'd recently invested in having the car's convertible top fixed. Now she could cruise and gawk at the ocean scenery. Even though she'd grown up on the barrier island, its wildlife and sea life never got old.

Betty insisted Liz should drive the blue bomber until the engine rusted through the chassis and ended up on the road. By the squeaking and grinding noises as they pulled under the canopy at the Hotel's main entrance, that might happen sooner rather than later.

Taylor got out and waved farewell before disappearing inside the revolving door. *Thank you, Auntie.*

As she pulled away, Liz glanced at the area in front of the Hotel's main entrance. It looked like a parade of elephants had trampled through, crushing Aunt Amelia's prized flower beds and beheading a dozen hibiscus in Liz's favorite color—coral. There were even cigarette butts floating in the fountain that had just been repaired after last October's hurricane. The media might have pulled down their tents and gone away, but their presence was still evident. On her way out the circular drive, she gunned it past a lone News 12 van lurking on the shoulder of A1A, then turned north toward the Sheriff's Department. Inhaling deep gulps of tangy sea air, she steadied herself for the upcoming interrogation. Knowing that was what it would be. She and her father had talked last night. He'd told her that even though there'd been only one bullet in Travis's chest, forensics had found another one lodged in the trunk of an oak tree behind the bench where Betty had found the button. Liz recalled that Betty had found something else under the bench. Something she'd refused to share with Liz.

"So, it could have been a struggle? An accidental shooting?" she'd asked her father last night.

"It was no accident, because he was buried in the ground," he'd said. Now, she was wondering how much detail she should give the detective about her confrontation with Travis on New Year's Eve. Did she have to say anything or just let him ask the questions? She started rehearsing her side of the events, then grew anxious. There was nothing to rehearse. She was innocent. Lost in thoughts of the murder, she absentmindedly took her hand off the steering wheel to rub the sore area of her upper arm where Travis had grabbed her. She wasn't paying attention and nearly back-ended an SUV that had stopped for a trio of blue herons parading across A1A. She wished she'd worn long sleeves. But it was too late; Crowley had already noticed her bruise. Another nail in her coffin, she thought. While she waited for the herons to cross, she tapped the steering wheel to the beat of the *Jaws* theme and glanced toward the Atlantic. There wasn't a cloud in the sky and the temperature hovered somewhere between seventy and seventy-five. It was a picture-perfect Florida Monday. If only she could get another picture out of her head: the one of Travis's corpse in the mud with his dead eyes gazing upward.

Last night on the news, there'd been photos of the nor'easter that was walloping the East Coast with snow. Taylor had been lucky to get a morning flight out of New York. If Paula had called Taylor, did that mean she was Travis's heir? For some reason, she didn't think that was the case. Plus, Travis knew how to blow money. Never caring when his credit card bill came, usually handing it over to Liz, who would send it on to Paula. He'd told Liz she needed to help him increase the sales of *Blood and Glass*. Did that mean he'd been broke?

Liz was confident she had a stellar team on her side: her attorney father, his homicide detective fiancée, her private investigator boyfriend, and Betty, the best cyber sleuth around. Liz might be at the top of everyone's suspect list. But who would be at the top of hers? It was early, but she postulated that whoever killed Travis must be someone who knew him. As he himself stated, he'd never been to the island before. Could it be Paula, his manipulative agent? Stevenson Charles, head of Travis's new publishing company? Should she add reporter Sally Beaman to the list? Why not. She was sure it was Sally who'd thrown her to the paparazzi. Although for the life of her, she couldn't imagine Sally murdering Travis. It was probably just as likely that Sally was trying to get the scoop about Liz and Travis's relationship. Sally was all about getting the story.

Travis had been an international celebrity author. *The McAvoy Brothers* had won him the Pulitzer, and the literati thought he could do no wrong. So, what had changed with *Blood and Glass*? Liz hadn't read it, but under the circumstances, maybe she should. She would discuss it with Ryan before she did. Not that she was scared he'd forbid her. They didn't have that kind of dynamic, where one bossed the other around or made unreasonable demands. She just didn't want to be in the doghouse again for not reasoning things out with him before she acted.

When she reached the town hall, she parked in the small lot. Crimes like murder were rare on the island. On second thought, since Liz had returned from Manhattan, there had been three murders in less than a year. All on or near the Indialantic by the Sea Hotel and Emporium. Maybe she really was a murder magnet, as one of the reporters had shouted at her yesterday.

As she got out of the car, she had another thought. Taylor. What if Taylor killed Travis? It would be easy to find out if she'd flown out before the New Year's Eve ball. And what about Hallie, the new intern? She'd been at the Indialantic the night Travis was murdered. Being Travis's gofer entailed more than the usual intern's job. Hallie resembled Liz, with her strawberry-blond hair and blue eyes. Was that why Travis had chosen her to be his intern?

Pushing her troubling thoughts aside, she headed up the steps to the police station, holding open the door for someone coming out. Susannah Shay, the hotel's new assistant manager. What was she doing here? Tattletailing? Liz wouldn't put it past her.

Chapter 11

The desk sergeant directed Liz to the interview room. As she walked down the short hallway, she was happy to see Charlotte's name plaque was still outside her office door, reassuring Liz that her father's fiancée hadn't been taken off all her cases. Only the one involving her.

An elderly male figure exited from the last door on the right and scuffled toward her.

"Grand-Pierre! What are you doing here?" Liz rushed toward him and took him in an embrace.

"Lizzy, ma chérie, you're crushing my backbone."

She removed her arms and stepped back. "Are you okay? Are you alone? Why are you here?"

"Calm yourself, ma petite." He reached out to push aside a curl on her forehead that had escaped her ponytail, and she saw his fingertips were lightly stained. He'd been fingerprinted!

"I hope you weren't bamboozled by Crowley. He had no right to talk to you without you having someone with you. And you definitely shouldn't have volunteered to be fingerprinted!"

He gave her a knowing gaze. "Don't worry, Lizzy bear. I was the sticky web in our little chat. The detective, the fly, so to speak." Then, he grinned.

Liz smiled back. Pierre had learned all about interrogation dos and don'ts from his alter ego, Hercule Poirot.

After an officer passed them by, Pierre whispered, "I wanted to see if I could be of any use in the investigation of the soldier found at the Indialantic. I am sure there's family looking for him. I was assured by Agent Crowley that the man's family has been notified."

"Pierre! Pierre! There you are!" Greta came running from behind them. "I'm sorry, Liz. He was busy in the pantry planning the morning's menu. Next thing I knew, he was gone. Captain Netherton told me where you were. You naughty boy," she scolded. Then she laughed when she saw his gaze was clear. "Come, the brioche is ready to be made. You know I'll make a mess of it."

"It's wonderful to have such beautiful women worrying over me. To the brioche!" he said, then marched forward.

"I would come with you, but I have an appointment." Liz nodded her head in the direction of the room Pierre had just exited.

Greta winked and took Pierre's arm.

As Liz watched them disappear around the corner, she took a deep breath. Pierre had been the one to find Travis. He'd also brought the rifle with him into the Indialantic's kitchen. His fingerprints would be all over that rifle. There was no way Pierre had killed Travis. Anyone who knew Pierre knew that. The only problem was, Crowley didn't know him. Crowley didn't know anyone from the Indialantic. Except Captain Netherton.

On the way to the interview room, she glanced longingly at the water cooler. Not for a drink. She had an overwhelming urge to stick her head under the spigot and douse herself with icy water to wake herself from this nightmare. How was it possible Travis was dead? Murdered. Instead, she kept walking, put her hand on the doorknob, took a deep breath, and entered the room.

Before Agent Crowley could open his mouth, she said, "How dare you fingerprint and interview Pierre Montague without someone with him for support?" When it came to protecting the man she thought of as a grandfather, she found the courage to stand her ground. "Pierre is eighty-one, and he's had a few medical issues recently. Anything he told you should be assessed knowing those facts. It's obvious his fingerprints would be on the rifle, seeing he found it and brought it into the hotel."

"Have a seat, Ms. Holt." He nodded toward the aluminum chair across from him. He was seated in a padded desk chair. His light brown hair buzzed close to his scalp, military style. He had deep squint lines by his gray eyes, like he'd spent a lot of time in the sun. Unfortunately, there weren't many laugh lines around his mouth.

"Have a seat," he repeated. "Time is of the essence. The first twenty-four hours are important after a murder. Unless you're here to confess?"

She pulled out the chair, purposely dragging it back so the metal legs scraped against the linoleum with a jarring, nails-on-a-chalkboard sound, then placed her handbag on the table and sat. Feeling she'd made her point with the chair scraping, she looked ahead and braced herself for his next words. Something along the lines of, *Elizabeth Holt, I'm placing you under arrest for the murder of Travis Osterman.* "No, I'm not here to confess," she said with a slight tremor in her voice. "Are you saying the coroner is positive it wasn't an accidental death? That the gun didn't go off by mistake? Maybe a bobcat surprised Mr. Osterman and the rifle backfired? I know a bullet hit the oak tree behind the bench where the button from his uniform was found."

"Ms. Holt. Slow down. There is no question it was murder. And I'm not allowed to share anything from the medical examiner having to do with the case. And how do you know about the second bullet?"

"I plead the Fifth."

She saw a slight upturn to his lips.

"Do you always call your ex-lovers by their last name?" he asked, then opened a file in front of him and withdrew two pieces of paper. "I have a sworn statement that you were overheard arguing and threatening the deceased."

"Who told you that?"

He looked down at the papers in front of him. "I'm not obliged to tell you my sources. If you want to go get a lawyer, feel free."

"I don't need a lawyer, because I didn't kill him."

"So, you do admit to threatening Mr. Osterman's life?"

A sweat broke out on Liz's upper lip. "No. It was the heat of the moment. I don't remember exactly what I said. But trust me, I never wanted him dead. And I didn't kill him." Wait until she got hold of newscaster Sally Beaman. Even though she'd dressed as a beautiful fairy for the ball, she was more of a spriggan. And she obviously hadn't been as drunk as Liz thought.

Liz changed tactics. "What do you want to know?" she said, pasting on a smile.

"I want to know when you first learned Travis Osterman was in Melbourne Beach and what you were arguing about."

Liz filled him in. Giving him only the basics about her and Travis's relationship. Let him dig into their checkered past in Manhattan. From living with her lawyer father, she knew how to say the right things without incriminating herself. She didn't need her father now. But when the time came, she knew he'd be by her side.

After she'd finished, he said, "I also want to know where you were between the hours of eleven forty p.m. and one in the morning on New Year's Day."

"You've pinpointed time of death to such a small window? Must hand it to you, Crowley. Your team are miracle workers. I know a little about these things and I can't see how you can be so specific."

"We know the window for time of death because we have a witness who saw him at eleven forty." His hand was poised over his notepad. "Can you please articulate where you were during those times? And be specific."

He gave her a sly smile, just as Aunt Amelia burst into the room. She sashayed up to Crowley, the scent of her perfume following in her wake. Today's diaphanous caftan took on a life of its own as she stopped short and said, "Agent Crowley, Captain Netherton told me you and he are old maritime buddies. I'm so happy you've met my beloved great-niece. As proprietor of the Indialantic by the Sea Hotel and Emporium, I am more than happy to enlighten you on the Literary Masquerade Ball and share any information on catching this fiend."

He grabbed a pair of reading glasses from the table, then flipped through the pile of papers until he found the one he wanted. Then he looked up. "I believe you were scheduled for later this afternoon, Mrs. Holt."

"Oh, mercy me, it slipped my mind. And it's *Miss* Holt, but Amelia is fine."

"If you want to wait in the vestibule, Amelia, there are some *People* and *Entertainment Weekly* magazines out there. Your reputation precedes you. I loved your performance as Maggie in *Cat on a Hot Tin Roof* last year."

"Gee, Agent Crowley, you'll make a girl blush. But I didn't play the part of Maggie. I played Big Mama."

"Outstanding performance, then. I could've sworn you were the lead. You can call me Crowley; drop the Agent."

With flushed cheeks, Aunt Amelia dug in her bag of tricks and retrieved two pink tickets. "Here are two tickets for front row seats opening night of *The Mousetrap.* Don't tell anyone I gave them to you—they're very hard to come by." She batted her false eyelashes so hard, one looked ready for flight.

"Well, thank you, Amelia. I look forward to attending." A grin spread from one side of his mouth to the other as he reached for the tickets.

She handed them to him and asked, "Detective, has anyone ever told you that you're the spitting image of Lucas McCain?"

Crowley said, "Who?"

"Chuck Connors. You know, *The Rifleman?*"

Liz knew that in an episode of the '60s television show, Aunt Amelia had played competition for the Rifleman's love interest, Lou Mallory. They'd just watched the show together on a streaming network. Now, she didn't know if any title with the word "rifle" in it was appropriate, seeing Travis had been shot with one.

"Lordy, I'm such an old fool. Of course you wouldn't know who the rifleman was. What are you? In your early thirties? Thirty-five at the most, I'd bet."

Crowley looked to be in his fifties and nothing like the actor who played the rifleman. Whoa, Aunt Amelia was laying it on thick. Too thick. Any more flattery and she'd find herself behind bars for solicitation. Liz relaxed for a moment, happy for the breather. Then she saw her great-aunt's left hand was shaking. Aunt Amelia was worried about her. If she was worried, Liz should be *really* worried. Had she heard something new?

"Why don't you let my Lizzy go get us some refreshments, then you and I can have a little chat?" She sidled up to him and put a bejeweled hand on his shoulder. Her stack of twenty bracelets, which Liz called her "bojangles" chimed when they hit her wrist. When she and Kate were adolescents playing dress up, her great-aunt would give them full access to her theatrical trunk and jewelry box, which included dozens of bojangles.

"Auntie, I'm fine. Why don't you wait outside and read some magazines, as Agent Crowley suggested? I think I saw a *People* magazine with a retrospective on the celebrity stars from the old *Hollywood Squares* game show." A teensy white lie.

"Oh my gosh! My favorite '70s game show, with the glorious Paul Lynde, Joan Rivers, George Gobel, Rose Marie, Karen Valentine, Charo, Harvey Korman, and the inimitable Vincent Price." Her great-aunt hesitated for a millisecond, then air-kissed them good-bye, almost leaving skid marks as she barreled out the door.

She can't be that worried if she was so easily distracted, Liz thought. Aunt Amelia always called Liz an old soul; maybe that was because they'd watched so many *old* television shows together in the Indialantic's screening room.

Sometimes, Liz wondered if she hadn't led such a perfect sitcom life before moving to Manhattan, she might have seen Travis for who he truly was. Life in the world of '60s and '70s television was a lot different from reality. And she had the scar to prove it.

"Thank you for the tickets, Miss Holt," Crowley called to Aunt Amelia's retreating back.

Aunt Amelia's voice echoed in from the hallway, "Make sure you visit backstage after the performance."

Crowley got up and closed the door. He went to his chair and sat, the smile from Aunt Amelia's visit had faded as soon as she'd left the room. He sent Liz a penetrating stare that made her squirm. "The grounds of your friendly hotel are now a crime scene. I need to get a handle on all this before things turn cold. And I'm afraid now that your future stepmother is off the case, you're stuck with me. No special treatment from here on out."

Stepmother? Now, that was something Liz hadn't thought about. Charlotte was in her early forties, though she appeared only thirtysomething. "There was no need to take her off the case. She's a professional. And it doesn't matter, because not I, nor anyone else at the Indialantic, killed Travis Osterman. I suppose you want to take my fingerprints also. Or did the rain wash away trace evidence on the rifle?"

"Good try, Ms. Holt. We don't need your prints; they're already on file."

"How is that possible? I've never been charged with a crime before."

"You seem to be forgetting last April. After the death of someone at your hotel, you were fingerprinted. How many murders does this make that you're directly involved with? Three, if my calculations are correct."

She'd forgotten about being fingerprinted. "The Sheriff's Department took my prints to eliminate mine from the killer's. I had an alibi."

"Speaking of alibis...where were you during the times I asked you earlier?"

"Do I need a lawyer?"

"Not now, you don't. But when forensics comes back, you might."

"Around eleven forty, I was in the Indialantic's courtyard where the literary ball was going on. Betty Lawson can vouch for that, and most likely so can Susannah Shay."

"Okay. Keep going."

"I left before midnight to find someone."

"And who would that someone be?"

"Ryan Stone."

"And did you find him?"

"Yes."

"At what time?"

"It was after midnight, about twelve fifteen, if I had to guess. Then I was with him until after your window closed for time of death." She stuck out her chin with a *so there.*

He arched his eyebrow. "Are you and this Mr. Stone lovers?"

"We're in a relationship. But that's none of your business." *Cool it, Liz,* she thought. She'd watched her father in the courtroom on numerous occasions, and not once did he lose his composure, no matter what the prosecution presented. Telling her, *It's not about my ego; it's about giving my client the best defense.*

Crowley took his time writing notes in a black notebook. After he closed the notebook, he said, "So, there was opportunity for you to kill

Mr. Osterman. Let's say eleven forty-five until twelve fifteen. Thank you, Ms. Holt."

"Wait! I forgot something. Before I returned to join the crowd watching the fireworks, a person dressed as a pig came running from the direction of where Travis was found."

"A pig?"

"Yes. He or she was wearing a huge pig head the size of a giant piñata, something you might wear at the Mardi Gras parade in New Orleans. It was quite disturbing."

"Did you talk to the pig?" he asked with a sly smile.

"No. He or she just waved and went toward the lagoon."

"So, you don't know if this pig creature was a man or a woman?"

Liz searched her memory but couldn't tell which sex the pig was. "No. It could have been either. I assume you have a guest list from the party planners."

"Ms. Holt, let us do our job and you concentrate on providing a *concrete* alibi. You can leave now. And send in your aunt."

"Great-aunt. You can't dismiss me so easily…I, uh…" She needed to find out who was dressed as a pig, even if she had to call everyone invited. Then she remembered that as far as she knew, Paula, Stevenson, Travis, and Hallie hadn't been invited. Or had they? Liz needed to call Travis's publicist, hoping, now that Travis had switched to Charles & Charles, they shared the same one, Molly Freeman. Molly had always been a friend to Liz, even during the bad press and throughout the trial. If what Ryan said was true, the sound of gunshots had been masked by the fireworks exploding over the lagoon. Then she only needed an alibi for the short time before she found Ryan.

Her right knee quivered as she stood up. She looked toward Crowley and heard her father's voice saying, *Don't engage, remain calm, and only answer in short sentences—leave out the emotion.* "Thank you, Agent Crowley. Please let me know if there's anything else I can do for you. I'll go fetch Auntie now."

She saw the surprise on his face at her sudden sweetness. "Please do," he said, matching her smile.

A few minutes later, Liz escorted Aunt Amelia down the hallway to the interview room. As they walked, Liz reiterated that everything was fine. No one from the Indialantic was under suspicion—a real whopper. However, she knew her great-aunt would do anything to protect those she loved, including lying. It would be so simple to ask Aunt Amelia or her father for an alibi for the postage stamp of time her whereabouts were unknown. Well, maybe not her father, because he'd been with Charlotte/ Scarlett O'Hara, chief homicide detective of the Brevard County Sheriff's Department. And perhaps not Aunt Amelia, because she was front and center the entire night. Kate. Kate would have her back like she'd had since they were five years old. *Darn.* Kate had been with Ryan, watching the fireworks. No, she wouldn't even entertain the idea of a false alibi. Liz had learned after the lawsuit with Travis that truth always was the safest route to redemption. Innocent till proven guilty. She glanced down at the bruise on her arm from Travis. Yesterday, it had been a deep purple; now there were golden yellow marks where his fingers had grabbed her flesh. She knew it was wrong to be angry at a dead man. But she was. Someone else had been angry—deadly angry. But who?

She opened the door and ushered Aunt Amelia into the empty room. Crowley had taken his files, but his closed notebook remained on the table.

"Okay, Auntie. Don't worry about anything. Just tell the truth and keep it simple. Pretend you're Della Street from *Perry Mason*. Calm, cool, and supercollected."

"Great reference, darling. But are you thinking what I'm thinking?" She gestured to the closed notebook with the two pink theater tickets sticking out. Aunt Amelia reached into her handbag and retrieved her phone. "I'm just going to take a gander." With her phone in hand, she slunk over to the other side of the table.

"Oh no, Auntie. Bad idea."

"I'm only going to see what he wrote down about you." She put her hand under the top layer of her caftan and opened the notebook.

Liz couldn't help but be impressed; she wouldn't have thought of using chiffon as an impromptu glove so as not to leave fingerprints. "Hurry," Liz whispered, curious about what the detective had written about her, and at the same time petrified her aunt would get caught. She leaned out the open door and glanced down the hallway, checking for Crowley.

"Oh pshaw," Aunt Amelia said, then commenced with her picture taking. "I have the perfect cover. I'll say I thought I gave him the wrong theater tickets and was checking the date. You leave, Lizzy. I won't have you prosecuted for my shenanigans."

"You'll be the one who'll be prosecuted."

"I have a good lawyer. Now go, lovey. I'm ordering you. We're wasting precious time."

"I'll wait for you outside."

"No need. I came with Ziggy on his bike." She made a shooing motion with the hand not under her caftan. "He's waiting next door at Burt's."

Ziggy's bike was a Harley motorcycle and Burt's was a dive bar where local bikers and nonbikers like to hang out. Burt's had the best Mahi grilled fish sandwich on the island and live entertainment seven days a week.

Confident in her great-aunt's skills as an actress, Liz obeyed. She left the room, shut the door, and went down the hallway. She wished her father wasn't at the courthouse delivering his closing arguments defending a local fisherman who'd been denied disability because he'd missed two insurance payments while laid up in the hospital.

Liz slunk out of the interview room, making sure the coast was clear. As she approached Charlotte's office, she heard raised voices. She crept up to the door, which was slightly ajar, and leaned in to hear Crowley's distinctive Midwestern accent. Charlotte was reading Crowley the riot act or, more succinctly, the Liz act. Defending Liz with the same vehemence she used when grilling a murder suspect. "You can't take this new evidence to the press. It would jeopardize the entire investigation. Liz isn't a murderer. Hell, she helped us twice catch a killer. Things get blown out of proportion on a small island town. And remember, one of the witnesses and suspects is a TV newscaster."

"Isn't Ms. Holt a native? The prodigal daughter."

"She is, but she's also had some bad press from when she lived in New York. All unfounded."

"And that bad press revolved around her relationship with Travis Osterman. Our dead guy." Crowley obviously knew about what had gone down with the defamation of character lawsuit. Which meant he also knew the case had been dropped.

"All I'm sayin' is, wait until ballistics comes back to match the rifle to the bullets. Fingerprints on the gun don't necessarily mean she's guilty, especially where you found them. Nowhere near the trigger."

"She could have wiped them off."

Liz almost slipped to the floor in a dead faint. She remembered pushing away the rifle, disgusted that Travis had used a weapon as part of his New Year's Eve costume. She scurried away from the door and went barreling out of the police station. When she was standing in the parking lot, she left a voice mail on Ryan's phone, trying to keep the panic out of her voice.

He called back immediately. "Where are you?"

After she told him, he said she should meet him at Deli-casies. "And not to worry."

Not to worry, she repeated in her head as she left the parking lot. It seemed in the past few days, she and worry were joined at the hip.

Chapter 12

Feeling out of sorts, Liz pulled into the Indialantic's Emporium parking lot. She parked in one of the farthest spots, happy to see the lot was full of cars and the Emporium seemed to be flourishing. The shops in the Emporium had been Aunt Amelia's idea to help keep things afloat. After a fire in 1945 caused the entire midsection of the original hotel to burn down, Liz's great-grandfather left the northern section untouched, only rebuilding the main part of the hotel. It wasn't until recently that the north section of the old hotel had been renovated into a shopping emporium. Short, four-foot-tall partitions separated one shop from the other, making the Emporium come off like an open-air market. Similar to something you might find in London's Covent Garden.

She got out of the car and glanced toward the river. The Indialantic by the Sea Hotel and Emporium was sandwiched between the Atlantic Ocean to the east and the Indian River Lagoon to the west. It was Monday, so the hotel's sightseeing and eco-tour boat, *Queen of the Seas*, had left its slip on the river with Captain Netherton at the helm. She was reminded of the captain's Coast Guard connection with Agent Crowley and made a note on her phone to talk to him, if Betty hadn't already. She didn't lock the car, because who would want to steal it, and hurried to the Emporium's main doors. She only had an hour before she and Betty needed to leave for Vero Beach to teach their first class for the writers' retreat, but she wanted—no, needed—to see Ryan and Kate for moral support. Kate always cheered Liz up. She could count on one hand the times Kate had cried in the twenty-three years she'd known her. She was also looking forward to seeing Ryan at his grandfather's gourmet deli for a macchiato and a hug.

As she approached the main doors, they opened, and Home Arts by the Sea's Francie came out, her arms loaded with bolts of fabric that looked like they came out of a 1960s time capsule. Liz trotted over to catch the door. Home Arts sold handmade items and art, along with offering lessons in quilting, knitting, crocheting, pottery, mixed-media art, and painting.

"Thanks, Liz. I'm on my way to a needlecraft expo in Orlando. I'll be demonstrating how to make clothing from a few of my new patterns."

"Here, hand me a couple of bolts," Liz said. "I'll walk you to your car." Francie was not only co-owner of Home Arts by the Sea but also produced women's sewing patterns based on vintage midcentury styles that she copied to fit today's women.

Francie popped the trunk.

After Liz put the fabric in the trunk of Francie's Prius, she said, "Have a great time. You'll do great. Someday you'll have to teach me how to sew on a button."

"Hey, I taught you how knit a scarf, so don't sell yourself short."

Liz smiled. "Guess what? Aunt Amelia is going to use the scarf as part of her costume for *The Mousetrap* because the play takes place during a blizzard."

"See, and you were worried you would never need a winter scarf in Florida." France got inside her car and put down the window. "I'm sorry about all the trouble having to do with your... uh, ex. When I came in this morning, a cop from the Sheriff's Department was questioning Brittany about finding his phone in the dumpster. I hadn't watched the news, so it was a shock to find out about the murder." She looked toward the packed parking lot. "Seems it's good for business."

"Did you happen to overhear any of Brittany's answers?"

"No, but I did hear her mention your name. I don't know how her finding the phone had anything to do with you."

"It doesn't. But you know Brittany. We aren't exactly besties—more like worsties."

"I'd stay away, as much as you can. Good thing she sticks to her clothing shop and doesn't have a crafting or artistic bone in her body, so I've never had to deal with her," Francie said.

"Oh, she's crafty, all right. Just not that kind. Do you know why she was dumpster diving?"

"Said she was throwing out the trash and heard a phone ringing, so she climbed inside to fish it out."

"That makes sense. I guess." Liz felt slightly better about the phone because she knew it would prove Liz and Travis hadn't been in contact with each other. She hadn't had one phone conversation with Travis since moving back to the island.

"Liz, if you want me to skip going to Orlando, I have no problem with that."

"That's ridiculous, Francie. Even though I'm everyone's number-one suspect in Travis's death, I'm sticking to my schedule of teaching a writing course at St. Benedict's Abbey this week."

"That's the spirit! I'll be back on Thursday. Minna is holding down the fort. In the meantime, text me if you need me. I owe you one. I'll never forget how you helped me last April."

"I'll be fine. You have fun. By the time you come back, I'm sure everything will be solved."

Francie pulled away. As Liz waved good-bye, she thought, *from my lips to God's ears*, then went inside the Emporium.

Minutes later, Liz tracked down Kate and Ryan in Deli-casies. They were seated at the coffee bar, being catered to by Ashley, the Melbourne Beach High School student who worked as part-time barista. Behind the bar, made from old, recycled barnwood, was a floor-to-ceiling blackboard. A wood ladder leaned against the blackboard for spry, seventysomething Pops to climb on to list his food and drinks specials in chalk with his perfect, fluid handwriting. Pierre had similar handwriting when he wrote out the daily menu at the hotel. A lost art, Liz mused. She couldn't remember the last time she'd used script to write anything except her signature on a check, and even that was rare because everyone took debit cards.

Liz felt like she was back in time in the old, general-store-type setting. Wood crates displayed jams, bottled sauces, pasta, and the like. There was a fresh produce section Pops recently added. Ryan and his grandfather had drawn up plans for a farmers market to be held twice a month in the Emporium's parking lot for the months of February to May, inviting local farmers and vendors. Aunt Amelia had been enthusiastically on board with the idea. Having lived on the island most of her life, except for the years she lived in California as a television actress, Aunt Amelia was one of the community's biggest supporters.

"Have a seat," Ryan said, getting up and giving her a quick kiss.

"Ryan was just filling me in on things. I had no idea all this was going on." Kate's sleek ponytail swung from side to side as she jumped up to give Liz a bone-crushing hug. "You know I don't own a television. Only watch old TV shows with you and Aunt Amelia. I can't believe Travis Osterman is dead. Why didn't you call me?"

"Weren't you on the other side of the state at an old plantation estate sale?"

"Yes. But I got back last night. I tried to call you, but it went right to voice mail."

"I turned it off. Didn't want any more calls from Sally."

"Sally Beaman? That's funny, I got a voice mail from her too. Wonder what she wanted."

"It's clear what she wanted. Me and my story, from one old school chum to another."

"I should've known. I just told Ryan you should come stay with me for a while. Get away from the spotlight. You can have my bed; I'll sleep on the porch."

Kate lived in a tiny cottage on the beach. Barely enough room to turn around in. But she did have a huge screened-in porch with a bed swing; perfect for sleeping and reading. Or talking to her books. One of Kate's idiosyncrasies was conversing with characters in novels. She did it partly in jest, but mostly out of habit from when they were children exploring the Indialantic's massive library.

"Thanks for the offer. But so far, I'm okay. I think the media believes I live at the Indialantic, not the beach house. I feel sorry for Auntie; this publicity isn't good for the hotel."

"But it's good for the Emporium," Ryan said, handing her a macchiato.

Liz looked behind her. Pops was at the checkout counter ringing up items, a huge line snaked between the two refrigerated cases that held gourmet cheese, olives, and Pop's signature cold salads. On the blackboard was listed today's salad as Curry Shrimp Salad, with golden raisins and pineapple.

Ashley took off her apron, came from behind the counter, and stood next to Ryan. "Boss, do you mind working the coffee bar? I'm going to rescue Pops from the hordes of customers who want to dispose of their cash."

"Sounds good, Ashley. Tell Granddad to go rest."

Liz watched Ashley shooing Pops away from the cash register and take over. "What a godsend," Liz said.

"She sure is. Next fall we're going to lose her to USF. She'll be majoring in photography. I think her camera is permanently attached to her hand." He looked at Liz. "How would you like to take over Ashley's job as barista when she leaves? We could work together."

"I'd rather work with you on one of Dad's cases. I think we make a pretty good team. Maybe I'll apply for a PI license."

"Go for it," Kate said, enthusiastic about doing anything outside the box. When the choice came, she'd always take the road less traveled.

"What about your writing?"

"I should be finished with *An American in Cornwall* next week. If my editor thinks it's a flop, I might hang up my papyrus and move on to detecting. Or if I'm arrested, I'll do a tell-all like Travis did to keep the Indialantic afloat."

"Oh stop, negative Nancy. You're not going to be arrested. Ryan will catch the real killer. Won't you, Ryan?" Kate looked at Ryan.

Liz saw he was avoiding Kate's gaze.

"What is it, Ryan Stone? What do you know that I don't?" She would rather face the music than miss the concert.

"Let's go in the back room and I'll tell you." A piece of dark hair fell across his brow. His smile had turned to a scowl. He was mad about something. She just hoped it didn't have anything to do with her.

"I need to price some precious junk I got at the estate sale," Kate said, getting up from her stool. "Liz, come find me when you're done."

"If I can, in that mess." Kate's shop was packed with vintage and antique items, along with thousands of volumes of used books. Kate never ran into a book she didn't love. Well, maybe one: Travis's *Blood and Glass*. As Kate passed, she elbowed Liz, letting her know she'd better fill her in on what Ryan said.

A few minutes later, Liz stumbled into Books & Browsery, finding Kate on top of a bookcase feather dusting a vintage globe. She looked down at Liz's face, then hurriedly climbed onto the step-ladder and came to her side. "What is it? What did Ryan say?"

"He said he found out there's a chance that very soon I might be arrested for Travis's murder. When he took Taylor to the station, he overheard Charlotte telling my father to get bail money ready."

"That's ludicrous!" Kate stomped her sneakered feet. "I'm going down there right now. There's no way I'm letting them arrest you. And I know your father won't allow it either!"

"Slow down, sweet protector. I can understand why I would be their top suspect. I didn't do it."

"Of course you didn't." She took both Liz's hands and looked into her eyes. "Think of this as an adventure. We'll band together and find this person, or animal. Here, have some of my green drink." She forced the cup to Liz's mouth and made her suck on the straw.

"Bleh! What is this? My throat's on fire."

"Cayenne and jalapeño are good for you. There's just a smidge."

"More than a smidge," Liz said, coughing, "It is quite tasty once my taste buds recover from the hot pepper. I know cayenne is good for memory loss. I have no problem with my memory. Remind me to order this from Deli-casies minus the jalapeño."

"Ha. You just said, 'remind me.' It's not from Deli-casies; it's from Café Latte Da, and the green comes from an avocado. They even pulverize the pit. It will help boost your immune system."

"Pulverized pit?"

Kate took the cup from Liz's hands. "There's tons of medicinal value, and in your case, you need all you can get."

"Will it keep me out of jail? Hand it back."

Kate handed it to her and Liz took another sip.

"You won't spend a minute in jail. I don't think you'll be arrested anyway. Based on what Ryan told me, they don't have enough evidence."

"I just told him the police have my prints on the rifle used to kill Travis."

Surprise showed in Kate's chocolate-brown eyes, but true friend that she was, she didn't say anything.

"I pushed the gun away when Travis and I argued, and that's how my fingerprints got on the rifle."

"Boy, that was fast work by the cops."

"They had my prints on file."

"You've never been arrested. Unless you were holding out on me about your crazy Manhattan lifestyle the ten years you lived there?"

"Of course not. My prints were on file from April, after the murder at the Indialantic." Liz glanced up at the clock resting on an old fireplace mantel. "Is that the time? I must run, I have to get to St. Benedict's for the writers' retreat workshop. Although I should cancel."

"Go. It will do you good. Get your mind off things."

Liz didn't hear the last words Kate said; she was halfway out of the shop.

When she got in the car, she took out her phone to check her voice mail. Sure enough, her father had left one.

It was short and to the point. "Elizabeth, I just want to give you a heads-up that Agent Crowley has a search warrant for the beach house. You don't need to be there. Charlotte and I will oversee things. Stick to your schedule. We've got your back. Love you tons."

Her lawyer father and his homicide detective fiancée had her back. Even with that assurance, Liz felt a sudden light-headedness and had to grab the steering wheel to keep the interior of the car from spinning around her.

Chapter 13

Liz pulled up to the main entrance of the Hotel. Punctual as usual, Betty waited under the awning. She wore cool tan linen pants and a white cotton sleeveless shirt with her collar turned up. Liz hoped she looked as beautiful when she was eighty-three. That's if she made it to eighty-three and didn't die in prison after being framed for Travis's murder. Remembering what her therapist always said, *You can't change the past or the future, only today*, she pasted on a smile and said to Betty as she got in the car, "Ms. Lawson, you're looking fresh as a daisy, as Auntie always says about everyone."

"Yes," she said, adding a laugh. "Even if they're as wilted as a dandelion." Betty threw her satchel onto the back seat. Her satchel held her trusty iPad. Betty prided herself on always being connected to cyberspace. "So, tell me," she said, her gray eyes sparkling as she got in.

"Tell you what?" Liz asked, putting the car in gear. She checked for traffic before turning right on A1A and setting out for St Benedict's Abbey.

Betty turned toward Liz. "How'd your interview go? I've been looking into Crowley's background. He seems to be a good cop. As you said earlier, I shouldn't typecast people."

On the short drive to Vero Beach, Liz filled her in on her morning at the sheriff's station, the news about her fingerprints on the rifle, her imminent arrest, and the fact that right now, the police might be rifling through her belongings. "Other than that, it's been a great day."

"As for the fingerprints on the rifle," Betty said, "you have a good explanation because he shoved it toward you and you pushed it back. If Sally Beaman witnessed your exchange with Travis, she'll be able to collaborate hearing you tell him to get the rifle away, then see you leave minutes later. Regarding Crowley's time-of-death window, my guess would be that Sally was the eleven-forty witness he told you about, the last one to see Travis alive."

"Oh, I almost forgot! Wait until you hear what Auntie did at the police station." After disclosing Aunt Amelia's daring undercover escapade of photographing Crowley's notes, Liz said, "I swear, Betty. She was brilliant. Even used the fabric of her caftan so she wouldn't leave fingerprints."

"Didn't know she had it in her," Betty said, laughing. "She's an exceptionally good actress, but sometimes the situation calls for a more understated part."

Liz smiled, feeling lighter now that Betty was with her. "Aunt Amelia? Understated?"

"You're right; it will never happen."

"If I'm not dining on bread and water in a locked cell, Auntie's meeting me at Squidly's for an early dinner. Why don't you join us? Ryan's going to try to make it. It'll be like old times. The three detectiveteers. Or four, if you count Aunt Amelia."

"I'm game. Let's just hope the lessons I gave Amelia about her cell phone paid off. She's a pro at pulling up YouTube videos of midcentury TV shows and commercials. Especially those she had a part in. But using the camera is another story."

"She also started doing some basic texting. You're a good teacher, Ms. Lawson. Just hope I'm as good at teaching this writing class. Except for the few times I filled in being a teaching assistant for a professor at Columbia, I've never been in front of a classroom."

"You're an award-winning author and you're instructing the class on the importance of setting in a novel. A no-brainer for you. I've been reading your manuscript and I felt like I was in Cornwall from page one. Your sense of place comes through loud and clear, and it's time to share your knowledge with other writers."

"Time to pay it forward, like you've done with me. Look at the help you've given me and are still giving me."

Betty reached over and squeezed Liz's knee. "How about all the book signings you've done? I know at Beachside Books they were lined up out the door when you came back to the island last spring."

"That's because they wanted to see the girl behind the tabloid stories. Oh my. The tabloids. Have you read the papers? Maybe I shouldn't keep to my schedule. How embarrassing. What if in the middle of class, I'm hauled off to jail?"

"Thought that scar made you tougher."

"This scar," she said, pointing to her right cheek, "might also be the reason people might think I wanted revenge on Travis and killed him."

She stopped in front of the stone gates of St. Benedict's Abbey and rested her head on the steering wheel. "I don't know if I can go through the hoops of another media circus. I was just starting to relax and feel myself again. Why did he have to come here?"

"Look at me," Betty said. "We'll find out who killed him. You have a lot of people in your corner this time. You're not alone like you were in Manhattan. You're home. We have to take it one day at a time. And today, you're teaching a workshop on the Importance of Setting in a Novel. Focus on that. Now, put this blue monster in drive and get on with it. No pity parties. What would Nancy Drew tell you to do? I know what," she said, "because I wrote the book—or should a say, a few books. Nancy would say *follow the clues.*"

"Speaking of clues: What did you find under the bench near where Travis was found? And why haven't you shared your discovery with me or Ryan? The three detectiveteers—all for one and one for all. How soon they forget," she said, adding a grin.

Betty squirmed in her seat, pulled down the visor mirror, and applied coral lipstick.

"Betty Lawson! I thought we were partners in crime. What did you find?"

"I just need some time to make sure it's related to your ex's murder. If it is, I promise to tell you."

"Now that you know he was most likely killed near Aunt Amelia's garden bench, it stands to reason whatever you found was either his or the killer's."

"Give me a day."

"You're being very evasive. I'll get it out of you—mark my words."

"I'm sure you will…when the time's right."

They pulled through the open iron gates. Liz parked next to a stone carriage house covered in white hyacinth vines. Stepping from the car, she drank in the scent of earth and sea.

Betty got out and walked over to her. "Where could you imagine a more glorious spot to get the writing juices flowing? I can imagine a monk in robes moving silently beyond that trellised arbor, cutting flowers and placing them in a basket on his arm, painted buntings singing from their nest in the belfry, and the scent of baking bread coming from that outdoor brick oven."

"Well done, Betty. You've just demonstrated the importance of setting by using all five senses."

"I didn't include touch," she said, strolling over to a bench under a white lattice arbor. On the bench, she traced a small brass plaque with her fingertips.

Liz followed her, reading the inscription: *How Lovely Is the Silence of Growing Things*. She put her arm around Betty's shoulders. "Thanks, friend, for *setting* me on the right path. One covered in pebbles and seashells."

A few minutes later, Liz stepped into the space where she was to lead her class. The walls were white stucco with curved doorways and stone floors that shone like they'd been recently scrubbed. The entire eastern wall had arched, floor-to-ceiling windows looking out to a splendid garden and, beyond, to the sea. Liz remembered taking art lessons at St. Benedict's as a youth, and the feeling of her brush against the canvas as she gazed out the monastery's windows. Not that her final product was anything gallery worthy—there was a reason she was a writer instead of an artist. But she could still remember the way the garden-and-ocean vista made a visceral connection between her brush and the canvas. When she'd gotten home, she'd tried to hide the painting under her bed but was tsk-tsked by Aunt Amelia, who had it framed and hung on her sitting room wall. Where it still resided today.

She went to the podium and put down her notes, feeling a lump in her throat as she gazed toward the twelve desks facing her. Brushing away her anxiety, she concentrated on placing a handout summarizing the course on top of each desk. One by one, they filed in. Liz greeted them with a smile and a handshake. Eleven of the twelve desks were taken. She tapped her foot, glancing at the clock, not exactly the Zen posture her surroundings inspired. After ten minutes, she announced, "Let's get started. Might as well do a quick warm-up exercise. Pen and paper ready, please. Now, close your eyes for a moment and…"

The door to the room opened and in walked Hallie, Travis's gofer intern and Beast's Beauty. She said, "Sorry I'm late, teach. What did I miss?"

Surprised, Liz looked down at the class list, and there it was: Hallie Corman. "We were just starting. Please have a seat."

The first hour and a half went by quickly. When it was time for a fifteen-minute break, Liz followed Hallie out to the reflecting pool near the front garden, calling out, "Hallie, can we chat for a second?"

Hallie turned. Her frown quickly changed to a smile. "Of course, teach."

Liz joined her on a marble bench near the pool. For a moment, they were silent, watching giant koi aimlessly swim back and forth, acting like they had somewhere important to go, only to turn around and continue their endless loop.

"Are you enjoying the class?" Liz asked.

"Yes. Never thought about setting as such an important part of a story. Mr. Osterman always said character is what drives good fiction. I thought working with him would help me with my novel, but that hasn't been the case."

"If I can give you some unsolicited advice, I would say, write your first draft on your own without outside influence. Then, for the second draft, it's always good to give it to a friend who enjoys similar fiction, or join a writing group where you can read excerpts aloud for constructive criticism. But never change anything if you know in your gut it's what you wanted to say. Just tweak it so it's clearer."

"Thanks, Ms. Holt. That's good advice."

"Please, call me Liz. Mr. Osterman has, I mean *had* a point about character being the driving force behind a well-written novel. But setting's important too. It draws the reader into your world so that they feel they're right with you."

"True. That's why I originally wanted to work with Mr. Osterman. My novel takes place during WWII, the same setting as his first novel. The Pulitzer Prize one. Mine's about a British nurse who falls in love with a wounded American soldier."

"It sounds interesting. Was Mr. Osterman working on anything new? His sequel to *The McAvoy Brothers*?"

"How'd you know? *The McAvoy Legacy.* Up until this morning, I had no idea how much he'd written because he always locked himself in his office when he was working. Wouldn't let me near him. I'd only be called in to clean up after he was done writing for the day. Ms. Resnick was the only person who had access when he was 'in the zone.'"

"His death is quite tragic," Liz said.

"You mean his murder." She gave Liz a look that was almost gleeful. "It is tragic. But I didn't know him that well. I'm doing a lot better than Ms. Resnick. I've never seen her so upset. She seems just as mad with him for dying as she was before he died. This morning, after the police left, I was packing Mr. Osterman's toiletries in the suite bathroom and I overheard Ms. Resnick shouting, but no one else was in the room. She had no clue I was there."

"What was she saying?"

Hallie hesitated, then looked around, making sure no one could hear. "She was talking to his empty desk chair and stomping her feet. *You rotten thief, scoundrel, and cad, you deserve what you got. Lies. Lies and more lies. It was all lies.*"

Liz took a moment to process Hallie's words. Travis's agent could have been talking about their personal relationship or something to do with his writing. She stored the information in her mind for when she got arrested and needed the police to look at other people with a motive to kill Travis. Paula Resnick moved to the top of Liz's list. "Do you have any idea what she was talking about?"

"No, but when I came out after she left, a few pages from his sequel, *The McAvoy Legacy*, were scattered on the floor."

When Liz was in the picture, Paula always bowed down to her meal ticket, even though Travis verbally abused her on more than one occasion. "You said you were in the suite bathroom. Was there an adjoining door from the next room?"

"Yes."

"Whose room?"

"Ms. Resnick's. How'd you guess? Why? Do you think they were having an affair?"

Liz didn't answer. "Had you been working long with Tra...Mr. Osterman?"

Hallie twirled her strawberry-blond hair around her finger, looked at it, and after a few beats, said, "Only a few months. I really didn't get to know him that well. Not like you did, I'm sure." She put her hand to her mouth, like she regretted her words. "He kept me busy, that's for sure."

So, she too had seen Travis for the arrogant egomaniac he was.

The sun shone in Hallie's eyes, confirming that she wore blue, almost teal-colored contact lenses. The vanity demonstrated by changing her eye color didn't mesh with her simple way of dressing. Today, she wore a sundress in a faded tan batik print and simple brown sandals. Liz was struck once again at how Hallie's looks were similar to her own. Travis must have thought he was in heaven when Liz Number 2 walked into his life.

"You look surprised. Do you think Ms. Resnick killed him? Usually, when they argued, your name was mentioned."

"In what context?" Liz was taken aback.

"Something about you not endorsing Mr. Osterman's latest book. I think it was Ms. Resnick's idea to come down here, so he could talk you into it in person."

Liz wanted to say, *he did a bad job of it*, but instead asked, "Did you see him New Year's Eve?"

"We all went together in a limo. But once we were dropped off, I didn't see him. The first thing I knew about his disappearance was New Year's morning. I came to the room he was using as an office at the usual time."

"What time was that?"

"Ten. We usually met then to go over the day's schedule and I gave him a report on any recent reviews or important emails."

When Liz and Travis had been together, he'd barely cracked open a bloodshot eye till noon. "I take it he wasn't too happy with the reviews on *Blood and Glass*?" Even saying the title of the book upset her.

"That's an understatement. I'll be honest: From what little I saw of the few pages of the manuscript, *The McAvoy Legacy*, he had a long way to go if he wanted another bestseller. I don't know if this is right, but one minute the main character would say, *I* went to the butcher, and in the next sentence he would say, *he* went to the butcher. It was very confusing. Don't you agree?"

"As a rule, you stick to one point of view, either first person or third. Yes, it sounds very confusing. And not like Mr. Osterman at all." Liz had written *Let the Wind Roar* in third person, using "she" instead of "I." Travis had used first person, using "I" instead of "he" in *The McAvoy Brothers*. Many a night, they would argue over which was best.

Hallie stood. Liz followed suit, torn between getting back to the classroom and questioning Hallie for more information.

As they walked toward the entrance. Hallie said, "*Blood and Glass* wasn't his best work. Nothing like *The McAvoy Brothers*. But I'm sure as a writer, you know the pressure of living up to another best seller. I can imagine it must have been overwhelming in Mr. Osterman's case, especially after winning a Pulitzer. What's your opinion of *Blood and Glass*?"

Liz glanced at her watch before saying, "I never read it."

Surprise showed in Hallie's eyes, but she didn't question her further.

"We'd better hurry."

"You won't be giving homework, will you?" Hallie swallowed, and pink flushed her cheeks.

"No homework. Just some short, in-class assignments. I want to inspire, not overwhelm."

Liz placed her hand on the girl's shoulder for reassurance. "Don't worry. Nothing is graded and there aren't any wrong answers." There was a naiveté about Hallie, who she thought was in her early twenties, perhaps younger. She just hoped Travis hadn't taken advantage of her youth.

As they walked inside the cathedral-ceilinged vestibule, Liz asked, "All things considered, did you enjoy the Literary Masquerade Ball?"

"Oh, it was fabulous. I wanted the evening to go on and on. Stevenson— Mr. Charles—was such a wonderful escort. We danced the night away."

"Were you together at midnight for the fireworks over the lagoon?" Liz asked slyly, thinking she knew the answer.

"Yes. It was magnificent."

Liz stopped short. She'd seen Stevenson in the hotel's lobby, minus Hallie, at about twenty to twelve. He'd also said he didn't care about New Year's, and that his date had disappeared. Was Hallie telling the truth? If she wasn't, what could be her motive for lying?

Stevenson had called this morning and left a message on her voice mail, saying he still wanted to meet Liz for dinner. She'd planned to call to tell him she couldn't make it. Now that Hallie had said she was with Stevenson during the time Travis was murdered, she reconsidered. Curiosity and self-preservation won out. She'd call him back after she returned from the monastery.

Looking toward the ocean, Hallie said, "It looks like Mr. Osterman's sequel to *The McAvoy Brothers* will never make it to print. What a shame." Instead of sadness in Hallie's unnatural blue eyes, there was excitement. "That's why I want to get my story out, before something happens to me."

A strange comment, Liz thought, before she asked, "Where do you go from here? Stevenson said you were interning. Will they assign you a new author?"

"Oh no. I just got word that my mother has taken a turn for the worse. I'm needed at home. But no one from the timeshare can leave right now, per Detective Crowley."

"They call detectives 'agents' at the sheriff's department," Liz interjected.

"Anyway, when Agent Crowley says we're allowed to leave, I'm going home to help Mom and write my novel. I must admit I'll miss Manhattan, but I always felt like a fish out of water. Now that I have some connections, I'll be able to get my foot in the door for publication. I have a few credits from a social work degree, so I could always fall back on that after..." Tears pooled. Liz finished her sentence in her head: *After... my mother dies.*

Chapter 14

The sky over the ocean was layered in pink as they sat on Squidly's deck. The ramshackle structure stood perilously close to the shore. Ready for the next squall to take it out to sea.

Ryan had secured an out-of-the-way corner table for four next to clear plastic awnings lowered to protect them from the wind and sea spray. "I took Mr. Oster..." Ryan looked over at Liz, "Osterman's sister to the station and then to the morgue, where she had to identify him. She was pretty upset."

"Understandable." Liz was happy they hadn't asked her to make the identification. The vision of him lying in the former Native American chief's grave would haunt her for years. Ryan had gone well beyond the role of her boyfriend by helping Taylor. She reached under the table and squeezed his hand.

Betty leaned in. "Did she tell you anything that might clear Liz as a suspect?"

Ryan reached for a conch fritter and dipped it in Squidly's signature Cajun remoulade sauce. After swallowing and moaning in ecstasy, he said, "She was pretty open about her relationship with her brother. Just like you told me, Liz, even though she was younger, she took on the role of caretaker. I could tell she had a lot of guilt because her brother was adopted and she wasn't."

"You should have seen the way he treated her," Liz said, wiping her mouth with a napkin before reaching for a tuna tartare nacho drizzled with avocado aioli.

Betty, who didn't trust anyone, asked, "Does she have an alibi for New Year's Eve? Did she mention what flight she was on this morning?

I checked LaGuardia and Kennedy's schedule, and most flights were canceled because of a snowstorm yesterday. However, New Year's Eve, all flights left on time."

"She could have flown out of Newark."

"Checked also."

"I'm sure Crowley will get around to verifying everyone's alibi," Ryan said.

"Including mine," Liz said, feeling her heart hiccup. "As Crowley pointed out, there's definitely a short span of time I can't account for. I wonder if..." Before she could finish her sentence, Hurricane Amelia blew into the restaurant, laughing and shaking hands at each table she passed. Liz noticed the blank look on a few faces. They had no clue who her great-aunt was but still smiled and shook her hand. Giving her the same deference they would a former president or reality TV star.

Ryan got up and pulled out a chair. "Thank you, Ryan," Aunt Amelia said as she sat. "It's quite blustery out there. Thank goodness we had perfect weather for the Literary Ball."

"Yes. It was a perfect night for murder," Liz murmured

"Elizabeth Amelia Holt! Stop the pity party. No one's going to accuse you of anything. After we look at Agent Crowley's notes, we'll be able to get an inside track on what he has and prove your innocence."

"I already know what he has. Motive, opportunity, and my prints on the murder weapon," Liz moaned.

"Pshaw," Aunt Amelia said unconvincingly, the pink on her rouged cheeks deepening. "Betty, here's my phone." She handed the phone across the table.

Betty wiped her hands on a napkin and took the phone. They all leaned in, waiting for the aha moment. She swiped her finger across the screen to view the photos. Then she giggled. She had a dry sense of humor and rarely laughed out loud, just adding a smile or two when she thought something was funny. But nary a giggle had come out of her mouth the entire twenty years Liz had known her. Wordlessly, Betty handed Liz the phone.

On the screen was Aunt Amelia's blurred face covered in transparent orange and fuchsia paisley. "Oh my," Liz said, passing the phone to Ryan. Aunt Amelia had pressed the icon that reversed the photo. She'd taken a series of selfies instead of capturing the page of Crowley's notes.

Ryan's dark eyes focused on the screen. "It's just as well. We don't need anyone spending time in jail for meddling in an investigation. I know you wanted to help, Aunt Amelia, but I think to get the spotlight off Liz, we should focus on other people who had a motive for murder."

He handed the phone back and Aunt Amelia stowed it in her bag. "I'm so sorry, Lizzy dear. It seems I should leave my sleuthing to the professionals; private eye Ryan and homicide detective Charlotte."

Betty reached into her satchel and brought out her iPad. "Let's make a list of everyone we think had an opportunity to kill Mr. Osterman. When we're done, I'll message everyone the list."

"You can do that?" Aunt Amelia asked. "I feel like such an old fool when it comes to technology."

"You're not an old fool!" they all said in unison.

"Okay, let's start with Paula, his agent," Betty said. "Liz told me that she said she went home early with a headache. No alibi there."

"I saw her leaving the Indialantic after my confrontation with Travis," Liz reiterated.

"Good." Betty typed in Paula's name.

"But what would her motive be?" Aunt Amelia asked.

"Let's stick to alibi first. Then we can go forward and dig around for motive." Betty looked up from the screen and said, "Next."

There was silence for a minute, then Ryan said, "Taylor Osterman."

"Oh no," Aunt Amelia said. "That sweet thing? Why, she flew in this morning. I think the agent is a better bet. I remember once when I had a two-day shoot on *Mannix*, the plot had to do with a dead author. All fingers pointed to his cutthroat agent until the big reveal."

"Let me take a shot," Betty said. "A jealous author?"

"No, the head of the publishing company. But good thinking."

Liz snapped her fingers. "The Beast should be next on the list. I saw him at the front of the hotel right before midnight."

"Who's the beast?" Aunt Amelia asked, her gold hoop earrings banging against her cheeks in excitement.

There was a reason Liz, Betty, and Ryan had left her great-aunt out of the last two murder investigations at the Indialantic. Patience wasn't one of her virtues, and sometimes her acting was over the top—luckily not on stage, just in reality. Liz said, "He's the CEO of my publishing company and, apparently, also Travis's. At the Literary Ball he was dressed as the Beast from *Beauty and the Beast*. Stevenson Charles is his name."

Aunt Amelia took a sip of her mai tai, then slapped the table. "I remember now. That square-jawed, handsome Detective Mannix—played by Mike Connors—found out the publishing company was a front for money laundering. The murdered author had found a ledger saying his royalties on the books were listed as ten times more than he was paid. He confronted the head of the company and later found himself bludgeoned in a back alley."

"I doubt that's the case here," Liz said. "Although it's pretty strange that the head of a publishing empire would come to our little island for a local charity event."

"Now that you mention it," Aunt Amelia said, "I remember seeing the Beast. I thought he was the Cowardly Lion from the Oz books. But then I saw Beauty. For a minute, I thought she was you, Liz. Same color hair and blue eyes."

"Hallie, Travis's intern." Liz pointed to Betty. "You can add her to the list. She showed up for my class at the monastery. Said she was with Stevenson during the fireworks, but I saw him before midnight. He'd told me she'd disappeared and he planned to smoke a cigar while looking out at the ocean, not the river. Didn't seem a big fan of New Year's Eve. He wants to meet me to discuss something in private. I think I'll take him up on it, now he's a suspect."

Ryan looked her way but didn't voice an objection.

Betty added Hallie's name, then said, "Sally Beaman."

"The newscaster, right?" Ryan turned to Liz. "She was the one you said dressed as a fairy and overheard you arguing with... Osterman."

It was understandable why Ryan was having a hard time calling Travis by his first name. "Yes," Liz said. "It would be interesting to find out if she had an alibi for the time after I talked to Travis. Auntie, I also think your buddy and assistant manager of the hotel, snoopy Susannah Shay might have told the police about a conversation Betty and I had about Travis. It was right before midnight. This morning, I saw her coming out of the sheriff's station as I was going in. She wouldn't meet my eyes."

"Susannah wouldn't do that," Aunt Amelia said, taking a gulp of her cocktail, the paper umbrella close to poking out an eye.

"I have an idea, Auntie. Let's try to get Susannah to use her powers for good, instead of evil."

"A wonderful idea, Lizzy. She'll feel purposeful. We all know she has enough connections to ferret out the tiniest speck of dirt in the recesses of anyone's closet."

"Is that it, then?" Betty asked.

"Unless it was some kind of accident and he tripped and fell on his gun?" Aunt Amelia asked, already knowing the answer. "Wish I hadn't made such a boo-boo with photographing Agent Crowley's notes."

"An honest mistake, Auntie," Liz said.

"Maybe my nephew can convince his fiancée to share what she knows."

"Let's not forget the person dressed as a pig who I saw running from the direction of where Travis's body was found." Liz passed the platter of crab cakes to Betty. "I'd be curious to find out if the pig had any relationship to Travis."

"Curiosity..." Betty said.

"I know, killed the cat."

"I was about to say, *Curiosity keeps leading us down new paths.* It's a quote from Walt Disney: *We keep moving forward, opening new doors, and doing new things, because we're curious and curiosity keeps leading us down new paths.*"

"Hmmm. A pig," Aunt Amelia mused. "I don't remember anyone dressed as a pig. Was it one of the pigs from 'The Three Little Pigs'?"

"Maybe Wilbur from E. B. White's *Charlotte's Web*," Betty countered.

"This person was dressed in a seventeenth- or eighteenth-century military uniform, I would guess French or English, and had a huge papier-mâché pig head."

"I've got it!" Aunt Amelia jumped up and her chair fell to the floor. "Ashley!"

Ryan got up and picked up her chair. After she was seated, he said, "Yes. A wonderful idea."

He returned to his seat, and Liz and Betty looked at each other, clueless.

"Ashley, Deli-casie's teenage barista, killed Travis dressed as a pig? I doubt that," Liz said.

Aunt Amelia, laughed. "Of course not! That powder puff of a girl wouldn't kill a spider if it was crawling on her arm."

"Ashley was hired as the house photographer the night of the Literary Masquerade Ball," Ryan said. "She took hundreds of photos to use for her college portfolio, including ones taken outdoors during the fireworks. It'll be a good way to find out who was where when the murder happened."

"Go, Auntie!" Liz shouted, then they fist-bumped. "We'll be able to track everyone, including Travis."

"And your pig," Ryan added.

"Did I redeem myself?" Aunt Amelia asked.

"You certainly did," Liz answered for the table. "Another thing that might help, Auntie, is to get the list from the party planner of everyone invited to the ball."

"I'll do it first thing in the morning. You can count on me."

Liz gave her great-aunt a kiss on her soft cheek. "Thanks for everything, Auntie."

"You don't have to thank me, Lizzy."

Then Liz explained to Aunt Amelia about the conversation she'd overheard at the police station between Charlotte and Crowley. "Ryan, why don't you tell them about the bail and search warrant?"

After he did, they all were silent for a few minutes. Earlier, when Liz had returned home from St. Benedict's, the police had come and gone. She was surprised her home hadn't been in shambles, like in TV detective dramas. She was sure it had something do with her father and Charlotte overseeing the operation. The only thing amiss was that Brontë wasn't in her usual lounging spot on the second row of books next to the window seat. Liz had seen why. The books had been replaced neatly, but they'd been returned out of order, not leaving a flat surface on top for the kitten to lie on. Her father had left a note that they hadn't taken anything. Which sounded like a good thing.

Liz doubted Charlotte would be sharing any inside information with her. Even though her prints might be on the rifle, she believed her father's fiancée believed in her innocence. Now they just had to prove it.

When their main dishes arrived, Betty put away her iPad and they talked about better things: the successful Literary Ball and Liz and Betty's first day at St. Benedict's Abbey. Liz mentioned she'd been surprised that Hallie was one of the writers in her workshop. Now that she thought about it, how far ahead of time had Hallie signed up? She should have asked. Something was off. Liz hadn't seen the list of names of those attending the workshop, but she had received a number. That number was twelve, the exact number of participants, including Hallie. She'd received that number in an email a week ago. That meant Travis and his crew must have been planning the trip to Melbourne Beach for a while.

Liz thought of a way to get more inside info. After excusing herself from the table, she stepped outside. Following the side deck, she stopped on a small balcony that hung over the lagoon and took out her phone. Giggles and smooching noises were coming from behind the wooden partition next to her. Then a couple stepped under the lamppost. Susannah Shay was arm in arm with a man dressed in black. Liz said, "Bastian? Susannah? What a surprise to see you here. Was all that noise coming from you two?"

Susannah smoothed out imaginary wrinkles on her navy shirtdress. Liz had never seen her blush before—it made her appear almost human. She also seemed, for the first time Liz had known her, at a loss for words.

"Elizabeth, how wonderful to see you." Bastian came toward her and gave her a New York–style air-kiss. "Are you with your charming auntie? Ms. Shay and I were practicing a scene for *The Mousetrap*. It seems you've caught us in the act, so to speak. The second act."

"Yes, I'm here with Aunt Amelia. She's inside. Why don't you go say hello? I'm sure she'd love to see you."

"I surely will," he said and headed for one of the doors leading inside.

Susannah went to follow him. Liz said, "Susannah, do you mind if I have a word?"

She looked torn at whether to follow Bastian or stay. She stuck her nose in the air and took a step toward the interior of the restaurant. Liz put her hand on her wrist and pulled her to a stop. "I'll make it quick."

"Well, go on, Elizabeth. You're being rude."

"I'm being rude? Are you kidding me? I saw you at the police station. Why were you there? As if I didn't know."

"I was doing my civic duty and reporting on what I saw on the night one of our great American authors was murdered. I pride myself on remembering details other's might not."

"You snitched about a conversation you overheard between Betty and me and thought it was important to throw me under the bus without first getting my side of things. Did it ever occur to you what might happen when your friend, and employer finds out you did that to her great-niece?"

"If I did talk to the Sheriff's Department, it's confidential. Now take your hand off me, this instant. I said nothing that would hurt Amelia. She and I might not get along sometimes, but I would take a bullet for her."

Liz wanted to believe her. "Well, next time, maybe you should talk to her beforehand."

"I don't need advice about proper protocol on how to handle myself. My cousin wrote the book."

"Is making out in a public place proper protocol?" Liz couldn't resist.

"I never!" she said, taking a step toward the restaurant.

Liz hadn't even realized she was still holding on to her wrist. Feeling embarrassed by her aggressiveness, she released her hand. Susannah walked away with perfect posture, her head held high. Aunt Amelia had confided in Liz that she'd recently found out from one of the former cast members on *Dark Shadows* that Bastian had a girlfriend back in LA. Her great-aunt didn't want to tell her friend that she'd set her sights on a two-timing man because she knew Susannah would end it immediately. Liz guessed Susannah already knew about the other woman. If there was one thing she knew about Susannah Shay, she was a pro at learning everything there was about someone's background. Last October, Susannah had hired a private investigator to look into someone at the Indialantic, which had helped catch a murderer.

A pelican startled Liz by landing inches away on the railing. She placed a call to Stevenson Charles. When she got his voice mail, she said, "Stevenson, this is Elizabeth Holt. I got your message and I'd love to meet you." *If I'm not in prison*, she thought. "We could go out on the *Queen of the Seas* for a tour of the river." She left her phone number, even though she knew he already had it, then hung up and went back inside Squidly's.

As she approached their table, Ryan gave her a quizzical look for being gone so long. She leaned in and whispered, "Everything's okay."

But was it really?

Chapter 15

Tuesday morning, a sheriff's car stood sentry at the entrance to the Hotel. Other than that, everything seemed back to normal. Even Barnacle Bob's hissy-fit wasn't out of character after she'd brought him his kiwi and forgotten to leave the skin on. Her ears were still ringing from the four-letter words coming out of his beak.

She sat with her father on the Indialantic's front cobblestoned terrace. The same spot where she'd had her confrontation with Travis. A sea swallow danced in front of them over the rough ocean. A storm was brewing.

"Daughter, I have a confession. I feel partially to blame for Travis Osterman seeking you out and threatening you."

Liz turned and looked at her father. "That's ridiculous. How could you be to blame? You've been my biggest rock from when I first called you from my hospital room in Manhattan. I don't know where I'd be if you hadn't rescued me, Dad."

He clenched his clean-shaven jaw, and she saw his green eyes, the same color as Aunt Amelia's, were watery. Liz wasn't used to her father showing so much emotion. Seeing him like this showed her how grave her situation really was.

"I feel I've made an error," he said, rubbing the space between his eyebrows, as if he had a migraine coming on. "I gave you some advice months ago not to read *Blood and Glass*, and not to communicate with Mr. Osterman or his mouthpieces."

"I wouldn't have read it even if you'd said I should. He had no right to intimidate and blackmail me. I'm sorry he's dead. But it's definitely not your fault."

"Well, I got a printed copy of the book yesterday from Beachside Books. And I read as much as I could stomach."

"And?" she asked, her gaze following an osprey heading for the Pelican Island Wildlife Refuge "Is it as bad as they say?"

"It's hard for me to believe it was written by the same person who wrote *The McAvoy Brothers.* I don't know much about syntax, but it's quite a mess. You told me he switched publishing houses. I can't believe it went through a seasoned editor's hands at Charles and Charles."

"I'm not sure if Travis signed onto Charles and Charles before or after *Blood and Glass.* I do know he was writing a sequel, *The McAvoy Legacy,* with them."

"There's something interesting in the book that might have a bearing on Mr. Osterman's death. In the story, the lead character, the author..."

"Thinly disguised as Travis," Liz interjected..

"...was getting threatening emails and letters. When you were together, do you remember anything similar?"

"All I remember is all the fan mail. That *is* strange. If *Blood and Glass* is a depiction of our relationship, then the hate mail he mentions might be real too. Do you have any idea if the police have his laptop?"

"No. Sorry. I don't."

"Travis's intern is taking my class at St. Benedict's. I'll make sure to ask her. She's staying at the same oceanfront beach house with Travis's agent and Stevenson Charles. Told me it was routine to go over Travis's mail with him every day."

They were silent for a moment.

Greta came out the French doors and placed a tray on the marble and wrought-iron bistro table. "Lemon scones straight out of the oven, mango chutney, and freshly squeezed orange juice. Your favorites, Liz. Can I bring anything else?"

Before they could answer, Taylor and Aunt Amelia joined them on the terrace. Aunt Amelia wore a winter coat, scarf, ear muffs, and boots. "We're off to town. It's the first dress rehearsal, as you might have deduced from my garb. Would one of you mind checking on Barnacle Bob? He's been pouting about something, and I can't for the life of me figure out what."

Liz knew why. "I didn't prepare his kiwi to His Majesty's liking."

The housekeeper laughed. "He does have exacting standards."

"Well, that explains things," Aunt Amelia said. "I'd already fed him his kiwi. It also explains why he was repeating the old Alka-Seltzer jingle, *I can't believe I ate the whole thing,* then went on with some disgusting belching noises that I'm sure he learned from his previous owner, not me."

"One thing about Barnacle Bob," Fenton said, "he never forgets anything he's heard, even if it was over thirty years ago."

"Your parrot is over thirty years old? How old can they live to?" Taylor asked.

"A macaw's lifespan is usually fifty. I got him from a shelter thirty years ago and he already had the vocabulary of drunken sailor," Aunt Amelia said with a giggle. Her fondness for the macaw shone bright in her emerald eyes.

Taylor laughed. "I had a cat once that lived until it was twenty-two. Travis used to lock—"

Susannah's grating voice called out from the open terrace doors, interrupting their conversation. "Amelia. We can't be tardy. Bastian's waiting in the car. Meet us in the front."

Aunt Amelia came next to Liz and whispered in her ear, "Susannah promised to help me with the other matter."

"What other matter?" Liz asked.

Her great-aunt pinched her shoulder.

"Ouch! What'd you do that for?"

Aunt Amelia didn't apologize, just winked.

Uh-oh. She was up to some covert mission to save the day by enlisting Susannah's help in catching the murderer. Liz just hoped Susannah wasn't dead set on serving Liz up on a sterling-silver chafing dish to Agent Crowley.

Aunt Amelia kissed Liz on the cheek, then blew a kiss to her nephew.

"Bye, Liz," Taylor said cheerfully. She looked at Fenton. "Nice to see you again, Mr. Holt. And thanks for your advice. I'm so happy Ryan told me to go see you. It's one last thing off my mind."

Liz had no clue what they were talking about. If it wasn't under the heading of attorney/client privilege, she would find out. At least she could ask Ryan why he'd sent Travis's sister to see her father.

"Have fun," she called after them. Liz hadn't had a minute to talk to Taylor alone. She had been attached to her great-aunt's hip like the Wham-O Shoop Shoop hula hoop from the '60s television commercial Aunt Amelia had appeared in. She'd told Liz last night that Taylor planned to have a quiet memorial after Travis's body was released from the coroner, not the big event his agent, Paula, was pushing for. She had a feeling Paula would go ahead and do her own memorial, and possibly print whatever he'd finished on *The McAvoy Legacy* posthumously. Maybe even the movie version of *The McAvoy Brothers* would make it to the big screen, depending on who he left his estate to. She assumed Taylor was Travis's only heir. But with their rocky relationship, it was uncertain who would benefit from his death. Perhaps no one. Especially if he'd died a pauper.

Taylor and Aunt Amelia left via the iron gate, taking the path to the front of the Hotel. Liz couldn't just sit around; she had to do something to save herself. She jumped up and said, "Dad, I've gotta run."

Greta stood next to Fenton, shaking her head and looking down at Liz's plate, where she'd placed a scone. "Can't you stay and have your scone? Pierre would be very disappointed if you didn't try at least a bite."

Liz went to the table, grabbed the scone, slathered it with chutney, and wrapped it in a napkin. She chugged the OJ, then stepped toward the door leading into the dining room.

"Dinner's at seven," Greta called after her. "Pierre and I are making your favorite meal."

Her last meal before the electric chair? Florida had capital punishment. "Thanks, Greta."

It was time to stop making light of her situation and become more proactive. She had an idea. She took out her phone and called Ryan.

An hour later, Betty, Liz, and Ryan sat on one side of the rectory table in the Indialantic's library. Ashley, Deli-casies part-time barista, was seated across from them. Heavy rain splashed against the bow window blurring the view of the gazebo. Liz thought back to New Year's Eve, when she'd gone looking for Ryan. The gazebo was a hundred yards from where Travis's body had been found, and just a few feet away from the garden bench where Betty had found the button from Travis's uniform. She shivered at the thought that Travis's body could have been so close to where she'd stood. But no. The timing was off. She was there before the fireworks. He was most likely still alive. There would be no mistaking the sound of gunshots on that still night.

A ten-foot Christmas tree stood in front of the bow window looking out at the parklike tropical grounds. Usually, Amelia, Fenton, and Liz took down the Christmas decorations on the second of January. That wasn't going to be the case this year. Due to Travis's death, they'd decided to postpone it. Liz was relieved, because she always felt a little melancholy packing away the generations of passed-down ornaments and decorations until the following year. There was only so much sadness she could take. She looked over at the ornately carved mantel still hung with stockings and imagined the ghosts of Christmases past whooshing down the chimney of the massive fireplace.

Above the mantel hung a portrait of Liz's great-grandmother Maeve. Maeve had Aunt Amelia's and her father's green eyes, but her hair color was the same as Liz's, strawberry blond. Around her neck was a strand of emeralds that had been handed down to Aunt Amelia. Seeing as her great-aunt had never married or had children, one day the necklace would belong to Liz.

Liz tugged on Ryan's sleeve and gave him a quick peck on the cheek. "What's that for?"

"Nothing." She felt her cheeks heat, realizing that where Ryan was concerned, she was becoming vulnerable. It had been a while since she'd worn her heart on her sleeve without someone taking target practice on it.

"Ashley, thanks so much for doing this," Betty said.

The girl grinned and looked toward Ryan. "Anything to help out the boss. Thanks to him and Amelia, I got the gig of photographer at the Literary Ball. It was a blast." She made eye contact with Liz. "Sorry about the other thing."

Yes, the other thing, Liz thought.

"Liz, a few minutes ago, I sent all the photos taken that night to the email address you gave me," Ashley said. "I'll stay until you open them, then I'll be on my way."

Liz opened the email program on her laptop and said, "Got it!"

"Good," Ashley said, standing up. "I sold a few of the photos to the *Melbourne Beachsider* and the *Vero Beach Beacon*; they're the first four in the file. Officially, I'm now considered a paid photographer. I better hurry back to Deli-casies. Sometimes Pops has a hard time taming Maleficent."

Pops had assigned Deli-casies' new top-of-the-line Bunn espresso maker the name Maleficent because it spit clouds of steam like they were coming from the mouth of a dragon. Business had become so good, he'd had to replace his old machine with a "newfangled" one.

Thinking about the espresso maker reminded Liz of the receipt from Deli-casies she'd found in Travis's room. She'd already asked Pops and Ryan if they'd seen Travis in their shop on the date of the receipt and they'd both said no. That left Ashley. "Ashley, can you come over here for a moment? I want to show you something and ask you a question."

"Sure." She came next to Liz and looked at the laptop screen, where Liz had found a recent photo of Travis. "Do you remember him coming into Deli-casies on Dec. 30?"

"Yes. Only he had bright orange hair." The caption under the photo read *Travis Osterman*. "That's the dead author, right? He came in for a triple espresso. He wanted to talk to me, but I had a long line of customers."

"Did he come in alone?" Betty asked.

"Yes. But Brittany came in a few minutes later. She was all over him. At the time, I didn't know why. They sat together at one of the bistro tables."

Liz glanced at Ryan. Brittany, shopkeeper of Sirens by the Sea, had a crush on Ryan. He'd be able to talk to Brittany about her meeting with Travis and get a lot more out of her than Liz ever could. Brittany had also been the one to find Travis's cell phone in the dumpster on New Year's Day.

Liz crossed out the page with Travis's face staring back at her and returned to the photos from the ball.

"If these first photos are any indication of your talent," Ryan said to Ashley, "you're going to have a successful career in front of you." He pointed to the screen showing Aunt Amelia talking to Mayor Hitchens, who was dressed as Snape from *Harry Potter and the Sorcerer's Stone.*

Liz barely recognized the normally bald mayor with his shoulder-length black wig.

"Thanks, Ryan." Ashley went around to the other side of the table and grabbed her backpack off the chair. As she headed to the door, she stopped and admired all the leather volumes stacked ten feet high in the mahogany bookcases that lined the room.

"No, *thank you,*" Ryan said, giving her one of his rare smiles. Not that he was a sourpuss; he just had those bad-boy dark looks that many a female drooled over. Including Liz.

After Ashley left, Ryan tapped the screen, and the next photo appeared. In front of them was a shot of the Indialantic's interior courtyard packed with guests. The lens centered on the champagne spewing from the ice sculpture of Ernest Hemingway. There wasn't one guest with a frown on their face, except for someone wearing a full-headed pig mask, holding a copy of George Orwell's *Animal Farm.*

Napoleon the tyrannical pig had haunted many of Liz's dreams after she'd first read the novel at age thirteen. Liz tapped her finger on the photo of the pig figure. "There's the pig I saw running from the direction of where Travis was murdered! Still can't tell if it's a man or a woman. Anyone else have a clue?"

"It's too hard to tell," Betty answered, leaning in to look at the screen.

"I wonder where you'd get a costume like that around here," Ryan said.

Liz picked up her pen and said, "How disturbing is that huge head? I'm going to write down the photo number, and when Aunt Amelia gets the guest list, we'll try to find out who it is by process of elimination."

They looked back at the screen. Ryan said, "Look in front of Mr. Piggy— is that someone dressed in a WWII army uniform?" He opened his hand and placed his fingertips on the screen, spreading them to enlarge the photo.

Sure enough, they saw Travis's back as he was heading out the open French doors leading to the rear of the hotel.

"Look," Liz said, excitement in her voice. "Napoleon the pig's right foot is forward, like it intends to follow Travis out of the courtyard."

"That might be a bit of wishful thinking," Ryan said. "You can't tell if the two are related."

"Regardless, I'm submitting this to Ashley now. We need to learn what time the photos were taken ASAP. And you need to go see your friend Brittany so she can tell you about her little tête-á-tête with Travis at Deli-casies."

"Okay, Bossy Pants!" he said, grinning.

"It's about time you realized I wear the pants in this relationship."

"I wouldn't go that far. How about a challenge between the three of us? The winner will be the person who finds the killer. The losers must go up to Susannah and give her a big kiss. On the lips."

"On the lips!" Betty said in mock horror. "She'll turn to dust, or melt or something."

"Like the witch in *The Wizard of Oz*," Liz said, laughing. "We don't want to upset the woman, especially if Aunt Amelia's going to recruit her to help us."

"True," Ryan said.

"She's not as prim and proper as she comes off." Liz told them how she'd discovered Bastian and Susannah kissing at Squidly's.

Ryan turned to Liz. "I don't think she's that bad. She's always been nice to me."

"Of course she has. I'm surprised she didn't come to you on New Year's Eve after she overheard Betty and me talking about Travis and tell you about it."

"Now that you mention it, she did seek me out. It was at the same time you found me and Kate watching the fireworks. I have a new proposition. How about the two losers have to go surfing with Ziggy and Aunt Amelia?"

Liz extended her hand and they shook. "You're on, city boy." Ryan still liked to dress four out of seven days a week like a New Yorker in black jeans and a black T-shirt. Liz tried but failed to get him to dress more Florida preppy, but he refused to wear any kind of clothing with a logo on it—no alligators, polo players, or penguins.

Betty handed her a pad of paper. "Here. Before we move forward, we'd better jot down what literary characters everyone on our suspect list was dressed as."

"Good idea," Liz said, getting out a pen. "I'll list them in the order I saw them: literary agent Paula Resnick was dressed as Lisbeth Salander from *The Girl with the Dragon Tattoo.* Stevenson Charles, my—I mean, *Travis's and my* publisher—was dressed as Beast. Hallie, Travis's intern, was Beauty." She waited, then went on. "Newscaster Sally Beaman was a fairy and, of course, Travis wore a WWII army sergeant's uniform, masquerading as Mickey McAvoy, the protagonist in *The McAvoy Brothers.*"

"That's a short list. You should add Napoleon the pig," Betty said. "You can send the photo file to my iPad and we can circle back to the start of the night and independently look over the photos at our leisure."

"Sounds good," Ryan said, moving his chair closer to Liz. "Don't forget, we have to put his sister, Taylor, on the list. Unless one of you can prove she wasn't here the night he was murdered?"

"I agree," Betty said. "Liz, we'd better wrap things up before we go to St. Benedict's."

"I almost forgot. Maybe I can get more information out of Hallie?" Then Liz told them everything she'd learned from her the day before. Leaving out the part where Travis and Paula always argued about Liz.

The previous evening, before going to sleep, Liz had looked through the one-page writing assignments she'd given the class. They all were stellar, with one exception. Hallie's. Liz felt bad Hallie planned to go home to take care of her dying mother and write a novel with the hopes of getting published. Maybe it was a fluke, and Hallie was just having an off day. If not, Liz could try to help her. With only four more days of the workshop, it seemed a daunting task.

Liz shut down her laptop. As she was putting it in its case, Aunt Amelia ran into the library. She was breathing heavily and had snowflakes in her hair. "Guess what! Susannah is already on the case. Her family in Boston is acquainted with the Charles family, as in Charles and Charles Publishing and, more succinctly, Stevenson Charles." She collapsed onto the leather sofa, snow falling around her. She laughed and said, "Looks like I need some Head and Shoulders. Wonderful company; they sent me a year's worth of dandruff shampoo after I did one of their commercials. A camera followed me around a train station, then onto a train, where people kept pointing out the white flakes on my navy suit. The best was when a boy pointed to the back of my head and said, *Look, Mommy. That lady has dandruff.* The end shot had me standing in the shower with my head lathered up. The shot took six hours. For the final take, the water turned ice cold and I ended up a frozen prune."

Everyone laughed.

"You were great in that commercial," Liz said. "I remember you wore a blond wig and bubblegum-pink lipstick."

When Liz had first gone out in public after the night she was scarred, children would point at her face and ask what had happened. It'd never bothered her compared to when the media hounds tried to snap photos of her after the bandages came off.

"What a great memory you have, Lizzy," Aunt Amelia said, interrupting Liz's dark thoughts. "I remember you and Kate playing with that wig and my go-go boots."

"You'll have to show me the commercial, Aunt Amelia," Ryan said.

"Oh, what an old fool you must think I am, Ryan. Going on about my glory days."

"You're not an old fool," they said in unison.

"Unfortunately, even though I got the stuff for free, I didn't have dandruff. Gave a couple of cases to one of my exes. He didn't seem too pleased, but the next time I ran into him—no more dandruff. And the girl he was with was touting an engagement ring. Thank you very much!"

They all laughed.

"Auntie, there's something important you have to remember: Don't discuss anything relating to Travis's murder with Taylor."

"Why, Lizzy? Because she's a suspect? That's ludicrous. I'm a good judge of character and she isn't a killer—I'd bet my life on it. Her grieving for her brother is real."

"You need to listen to Liz, Amelia." Betty got up and sat next to her on the tufted brown leather couch. "You know better than anyone, that someone with the right motive could be a killer. It happens every day. It even happened here. You see the best in people, and nothing's wrong with that. Just keep quiet about anything we say. It shouldn't interfere with your relationship with Taylor. And there's a very good chance you're right. We just need to keep our cards breasted for the time being."

Aunt Amelia patted Betty's hand. "Good advice. I promise not to divulge anything we learn. I'm going to leave looking into her whereabouts on the night Mr. Osterman was murdered to you and the police."

"Thanks, Auntie," Liz called out.

"But, I still say she's innocent."

Liz hoped she was.

Chapter 16

Liz sat on the window seat with her laptop open and Brontë snuggled at her feet. The weather was still volatile; the pounding rain had let up, but the sky looked ready to unload its wrath like it'd done during her three hours at the monastery. Earlier, she'd had to change her plans for her in-class writing assignment. She'd originally wanted to bring everyone outdoors to write a piece about a sun-filled day on a tropical island. Instead, the new assignment she'd given them was to look into their own past and describe a room that played an important part in their life—good or bad—remembering to use all five senses when describing it. She looked forward to perusing the class papers before going to bed. Especially Hallie's.

She closed her laptop. "Brontë, I can't look at another photo from the night of the ball without some sustenance." She'd only found a few of the photos worth jotting down. In one of the ones she'd tagged, it showed Hallie, Stevenson, and Paula entering the courtyard at the beginning of the evening. Travis hadn't been with them. Another showed Sally lurking behind her and Ryan while they were talking near the band. Liz hadn't noticed Sally at the time, but of course, everyone wore a costume. Plus, all she'd had eyes for was the dashing Jean Valjean. It was hard to believe that hours later, someone would be murdered. And even harder to believe, that someone was Travis Osterman. How had he known she would find him on the terrace?

If he'd lived to blackmail her into promoting *Blood and Glass,* what was his agenda after that? There had to be something more he needed from her. Something more they *all* needed, or Travis could have come alone. She laughed at herself. Travis was never alone; he'd always had a posse trailing behind him.

Brontë snoozed next to her, her rhythmic purring better than a meditation mantra as Liz glanced out at the ocean. A turbulent ocean, which meant a turbulent Indian River Lagoon. She prayed her time on *Queen of the Seas* with Stevenson wouldn't be canceled due to the weather.

As she wondered if she should call the captain, her phone rang. It was Molly, her publicist at Charles & Charles. They chatted for a while about her next book, then Molly mentioned Travis. "I was so sorry to hear about Mr. Osterman. Have they found out anything about his murder?"

"No. The police are still investigating. Molly, I called because I wanted to ask you who Travis's publicist is. Or was."

"Well, that's easy," she said with a laugh. "Me."

"That's a surprise."

"For me too. I didn't think after everything... the two of you'd gone through, you would share the same publicist, let alone publishing house. But Stevenson insisted. I only took over a couple of weeks ago."

"Molly, were Travis, Stevenson, or Paula Resnick invited to a Literary Masquerade Ball in Melbourne Beach on New Year's Eve?"

"A what?" she asked.

"A charity ball."

"Why, no. There was nothing scheduled for him. No one does tours during the holidays unless the novel has a holiday theme."

Liz thanked her for her help and hung up the phone. It looked like Travis and the rest of them had gone rogue. She knew one thing: If Travis had dressed in Sgt. McPherson's uniform and brought his gun, that meant he'd known ahead of time about the ball. "Kitty, I think tea and a cranberry-orange muffin might be what I'm craving. What would be your pleasure?"

Brontë slowly opened her eyes, then glanced at her like, *Duh, a fish-shaped salmon treat.*

"Stay there, little one, I'll bring it to you."

She went into her gourmet kitchen, designed by Chef Pierre. The entire beach house had been a welcome-home surprise when she'd moved back to the island after ten years of living in New York. The former Indialantic's bathing pavilion was now her cozy refuge.

Thanks to Minna and Francie, the beach house had been decorated with accessories from the Indialantic's Emporium shop, Home Arts by the Sea. They'd brought in pottery, hand-blown glass vases, pillows, throws, soy candles, and artwork, all sticking to the colors of the ocean panorama outside her window—soft green, teal, aqua, blue, and the palest yellow. From the moment she'd stepped inside, her home environment had echoed the peace and serenity she'd longed for.

Brontë hadn't bothered to follow her into the kitchen, just stretched her tiny body and dug her claws into the tropical-print fabric of the window-seat cushion. "Time to clip your nails, little one," she called out from behind the granite counter. "I can't tell you how upset Betty was when you got hold of that crocheted afghan she was working on. You don't want to be banned from the Indialantic, do you?"

Brontë looked at Liz for a second, yawned, then got up and kneaded a pillow like Grand-Pierre did his bread dough. Aunt Amelia said the act of kneading soft things most likely meant Brontë had left or lost her mother while she was still nursing. One morning last April, an entire litter of kittens had shown up on the Emporium's doorstep. All the kittens found loving homes, except for one. Luckily for Liz, every time someone tried to adopt Brontë, she'd hide. Once, when Liz was in Books & Browsery with Kate, out popped a kitten who'd been sleeping above a stack of Charlotte, Emily, and Anne Brontë's novels. She'd landed on Liz's lap, claws first. It seemed the gray-and-white tiger kitten had decided to come out of hiding, and instead of Liz adopting Brontë, Brontë adopted Liz.

She opened the cupboard next to her restaurant-grade Wolf stove top and got out a tray. On top, she placed a simple white ceramic teapot and filled it with hot water from the electric kettle. Then she dropped in an infuser filled with a special blend of green tea with undernotes of citrus and berries. The mixture had been created especially for Liz by Aunt Amelia. A few months ago, at Liz's suggestion, Aunt Amelia had come up with six signature blends of loose tea she packaged in tins that were designed by Home Art's resident artist, Minna Presley. They now were sold in Deli-casies and were such a hit that Pops had added Amelia's Island Bliss Tea to his coffee bar menu.

Brontë joined her in the kitchen, snaking her little body around Liz's ankles. "I know, I know. As Aunt Amelia says, *Good things come to those who wait*. But now that I think about it, Auntie doesn't wait for anything." She opened a cupboard and got out a container of cat treats, handing Brontë two. She washed her hands and took out a white mug that said WRITER, packets of natural sweetener, and a china teapot, and placed them on the tray.

The teapot had been a housewarming gift from Aunt Amelia. She'd told Liz it had once been used as a prop on *The Andy Griffith Show*. The director had given it to her great-aunt as a souvenir from the set, swiping it off the shelf in Aunt Bee's homey kitchen. Last September, Aunt Amelia took a trip to Mt. Airy, North Carolina, for the Mayberry Days festival and brought back a copy of *Aunt Bee's Mayberry Cookbook*. One night, Chef Pierre made Snappy Lunch's pork chop sandwiches. He'd dipped the boneless chops in a sweet-milk egg-and-flour batter and fried them. On a steamed bun layered with mustard, he'd placed a pork chop, sliced tomato, onions, chili, and coleslaw. When Liz first tasted it, she felt as if there was a carnival in her mouth. She remembered Susannah pooh-poohing the messy, pedestrian-looking thing. But after one bite, she was like a lion snacking on an antelope's carcass, not bothering to wipe away the chili dribbling down her chin, decorum out the window.

Liz smiled at the memory as she picked up the tea tray and carried it toward the small table by the window seat. Glancing out the window, she saw a man with two beasts climbing the steps to her deck—Ryan, his dog Blackbeard, and Captain Netherton's Killer. She put down the tray and said, "Save yourself, Brontë. Go hide in my office." The kitten heard Blackbeard's bark and immediately the fur on her back stood at attention. She took off to hide under Liz's office desk. Killer was a cat lover, but Blackbeard, who was still considered a puppy, hadn't decided if he liked felines or not. For some reason, Blackbeard adored Barnacle Bob. Maybe because the macaw would bark every time the dog came near, a self-preservation tactic on BB's part to keep himself from becoming someone's tasty treat.

On the way to the door, she glanced at her watch. It was an hour before she was supposed to meet Stevenson at the dock to board *Queen of the Seas*. She'd told Ryan about her plans, not that she needed to check in with him, but the way things were going, if she got in trouble, at least he would know where she was.

Liz went and opened the door, "This is a nice surprise. You'd better hurry before that wind blows you off the deck and into the ocean. I hope it's not too rough to go out on *Queen of the Seas*."

Ryan slipped off his muddy sneakers, left them on the deck, kissed her passionately on the lips, and stepped inside. "Oh, yes, your little date."

She glanced at him, ready to get angry. But he winked, and her shoulders relaxed. Blackbeard and Killer followed him inside.

"Thought I'd check up on you," Ryan said, embracing her.

He smelled of soap and had stubble on his chiseled jaw. A lock of hair fell in front of one eye, giving him an appealing roguish look. She grabbed the fabric at the top of his T-shirt and pulled him in for a kiss. Afterward, she pushed him back, like she was done with him.

"Hmmm, I like this spirited, angry side of you, Ms. Holt."

After they separated, she said, "I see you've brought your recruits." She bent down and gave Blackbeard a good scratch behind his large floppy ears. His feet were so large, soon he'd be almost Killer's size. He'd gotten his name because he had a long black goatee like Blackbeard the pirate.

Blackbeard had been one of the ugliest puppies she'd ever seen. Which made him the most adorable puppy she'd ever seen. His calico-colored body was interspersed with long and short tufts of fur. Half of his face was black, the other half a deep russet, like he had some Irish setter in him. His eyebrows grew so fast, Ryan had to clip them weekly.

Killer put his big snout near Liz's hand and gave it a lick. "Brownnoser. Come with me. I'll give you a treat." Killer's unclipped black ears rose at the word "treat." He was a handsome dog and had the same white tuxedo-shirt markings and black fur as his best friend, Betty's feline Carolyn Keene.

Ryan followed her to the kitchen. "You seem way too calm, considering everything that's going on. I'm here if you need to cry or punch something."

"Think I'm past that stage."

Killer stepped into the open kitchen area, then planted his paws in front of the cupboard holding the dog treats. "Okay, okay," Liz said. She went to the cupboard, opened a vintage cookie jar she got from Kate's shop, and handed treats to Killer and Blackbeard. She washed her hands, then turned to Ryan. "Would you like some tea? I just made a pot."

He laughed. "Real men don't drink tea." He went to the fridge and got out a can of local IPA beer.

"And real men don't read *Jane Eyre*. How are you liking it?"

He gave her a sheepish grin.

"You didn't start it, did you?"

Instead of answering, he said, "Did you get a copy of the photo I enlarged and messaged to you?"

"I don't think so. I'm trying to avoid the phone. It seems Sally or someone else gave out my private number to the paparazzi." She walked over to her phone and tapped the screen. "Wow. Paula and Stevenson arguing." The Girl with the Dragon Tattoo and Beast were in the corner of the dining room next to the raffle table. Paula had her right hand raised in a fist that was dangerously close to the Beast's mouth.

"It seems so." Ryan sat on the sofa and Killer sat next to him, resting his huge head on Ryan's lap.

"Come, Blackbeard. You can sit on my lap." The dog happily followed her to a cushioned chair and hopped up.

"If you want, I could stow aboard *Queen of the Seas*, The captain could hide me in the storeroom," he said.

She laughed. "I don't think my life is in danger. Don't you want to know why Stevenson came to Melbourne Beach?"

"Of course."

"Then leave it to me. I just got off with my publicist from Charles and Charles. She told me there was no plan or invitation having to do with the Literary Ball."

"I've been doing some digging. One of the guys from my old firehouse has a daughter who's a best-selling author. Charles and Charles is her publisher. Maybe you've heard of her? Stacy Sorenson."

"Of course I've heard of her. One of the top-selling romance writers, not just in the US but in the world. And the youngest." *And the prettiest*, Liz thought.

"Well, I've got her contact info. I'll call her from the caretaker's cottage while you're on your cruise. Come over later, I'll have a pot of crab chowder, New England style, simmering on my new stove."

"How could a girl refuse an offer like that? Plus, you've been going on about this recipe for a couple of months. I don't understand why you couldn't have whipped it up here, or in the Indialantic's kitchen."

"You know why. It had to be the first thing I made after the renovations."

At one time, Liz and her father had lived in the caretaker's cottage Ryan rented from Aunt Amelia. The renovation on the kitchen had been completed last week and she couldn't wait to see the final product. "I'll bring the wine and bread. I know Pierre just made four loaves of his sourdough rye."

"No dessert?" he said with a pouty face.

"I did see a couple of orange-strawberry swirl cheesecakes on the cooling rack when I was coordinating meals with Pierre and Greta. January is strawberry season in Florida and the oranges, of course, come from our trees. Did you know before the Indialantic was built the land was a...?"

"Orange grove."

"No. A pineapple plantation. There's even folklore that your caretaker's cottage is haunted. Good thing I didn't know that when Dad and I lived there. Kate has the book in her shop. It's not for sale, but Kate lets people borrow it. There are lots of stories transcribed from old-timers who first came to the island when it was covered in palmettos and mosquitoes."

"That explains why I keep waking up to strange moaning and scratching sounds coming from the attic."

"Ha ha. Funny."

"I do know that islanders used to call this the Mosquito Coast until they dropped tons of pesticides to eradicate the little buggers," he said.

They talked for a while about things not connected to Travis's death. When Liz realized Blackbeard was noticeably missing after he'd gone to the kitchen for some water, they went in search and found him chewing on the leg of one of her bamboo barstools.

"Blackbeard! You bad boy!" Ryan called out. The dog didn't look in the least bit sorry.

"Aw, he's still a pup. Hope you don't have any wood furniture in your new kitchen," she said, adding a laugh. "Plus, you know the rule when training: never scold, only praise."

"Tell that to your three-legged stool. Come, Blackbeard, you scallywag. Let's go play some Frisbee before dinner."

Killer's ears shot up at the word "Frisbee."

Liz walked them to the door and opened it. Dark charcoal clouds reflected onto the ocean, making the water seem almost black. "I don't know about Frisbee. You all will be a muddy mess."

Ryan grinned. "That'll make it more fun."

She could see the mischievous little boy in him. And she liked what she saw. "I'll come over after the cruise, unless it's canceled because of the weather."

They kissed good-bye, and Liz watched the trio walk away, happy they were in her life. She thought about Taylor and her love of animals. Then she thought of Taylor's brother, who forbade her to have any. Travis's claim to be allergic to cats and dogs was debatable. Once, she'd caught him holding Paula's Alaskan Malamute, whose dense fur could be found in every corner and on every cushion in her luxury Madison Avenue office. Not a sneeze assailed him.

She was doing it again. Getting mad at a dead man.

Chapter 17

Surprisingly, the sun was shining when Liz boarded *Queen of the Seas.* There wasn't a wisp of a dark cloud—typical island weather. Captain Netherton took her hand to help her over the gap between the gangway and the ship. He looked his old dashing self in his short-sleeved white dress shirt, black tie and pants, and sailor's cap. Dressing the part brought him big tips from the ladies, a reason he had so many repeat passengers on the *Love Boat/Queen of the Seas.*

"Elizabeth Holt, you're looking quite stunning this evening. Your dazzling blue eyes must have every man from here to Key West falling in love with you. I know Ryan is quite enamored."

"Ever the charmer, Captain. You're looking quite dapper yourself." He was in his midseventies, and even though he occasionally relied on a cane, he had perfect posture. Liz wondered if Betty knew about the captain's appeal with the opposite sex. She was sure she did. Only a few months ago, both Betty and Aunt Amelia were vying for the captain's attention. Now that Aunt Amelia and Ziggy were together, Captain Netherton was all Betty's. Plus, Liz knew from day one the captain only had eyes for Betty and had been using Aunt Amelia to make her jealous. It seemed their pets, Caro and Killer, were in a relationship, and so were Betty and Captain Clyde. B. Netherton, as the name on the placard above the pilot's wheel read.

Liz had been ten minutes late boarding the ship. She hadn't been able to decide what to wear to meet one of the Fortune 500, owner of a multinational publishing company, and possible murder suspect. She'd decided on a long gauzy white skirt, white tank top, and a long red linen shirt. Layers were important this time of year, when it could be cool one minute, steaming the next. She'd secured her long wavy hair into a messy chignon and only added a touch of mascara, peach lip gloss, and a dab of concealer with sunscreen to her scar. A long gold-and-turquoise necklace had completed the look.

"Sorry I'm late, Captain," she said as they continued to the main deck.

"No problem, Liz. It gave me time to spruce up the private cabin."

"What private cabin?"

He grinned but didn't answer. "This way, my lady."

She took a few steps and looked around. The boat had ten rows of seating with a center aisle, enough to seat sixty guests. "Where is everyone?"

"The sunset cruise was canceled."

"The weather?" she asked as the captain motioned her forward.

"Not exactly."

"Can I ask a quick question?"

"Of course, my dear."

"I know you know Agent Crowley from the Coast Guard. I'm just wondering if you think he's a good cop. I couldn't tell. And I'm also wondering if you could put in a good word about me. I didn't kill Travis. I swear I didn't know he was coming to the Literary Ball."

"I've already told him plenty about all your redeeming qualities. We worked together years ago. He's bright and quick on his feet. You couldn't be in better hands."

Liz still had some misgivings. She knew it was a strike against her that he'd had to take over the case from Charlotte. "If you learn anything that might help me, can you let me know?" She showed him the photo she'd printed out of Napoleon the pig, and he shook his head in the negative that he hadn't seen him/her on New Year's Eve. "Did you see Travis? He was dressed in a WWII Army sergeant's uniform."

"You know what? I did see him. When I went to freshen Betty's—I mean Miss Marple's drink—he was talking to a woman with tattoos on her arms and a gold nose ring. The nose ring reminded me of a bull. And she seemed as angry as one."

Paula! Liz realized.

"Do you know why she was angry?"

"Something about a movie. If I remember anything more, I'll be sure to tell you."

"You're the best, Captain," she said with a huge smile. "Hope you pass on to Agent Crowley everything you just told me."

"Already done. I try to please my ladies."

"That's for sure."

"Right this way," he said, motioning toward the galley kitchen next to the pilothouse. "Your food is going to get warm."

"Warm? Food?"

"Trust me," he said.

She followed him below to the kitchen. At the end of the cabin was a small open hatch in the floor. Ladder-type steps led downward.

"Beautiful fair maidens before gentlemen," Captain Netherton said, helping her down the first step.

On the bottom step, Liz blinked to adjust to the dim lighting. "Wow. Magical. I didn't know this part of the ship existed."

"It's been used as a storehouse for years. After I found some photos in that cabinet over there," he said, pointing, "and with Amelia's permission, I cleared out the junk. Actually, I gave the junk to Kate, who was very appreciative. Some things Kate refurbished and gave back to me."

Two forties-style sofas flanked the table. On the walls were framed nautical maps, yellowed with age.

He noticed her gaze. "VIPs came on board when they needed a private place to keep under the radar, so to speak."

"But how could they get a tour of the lagoon without being above the water? Down here there's only tiny hatch windows."

"Oh, they didn't come down here for eco/sightseeing tours. Some important meetings went on having to do with WWII and the Cold War. Remind your auntie to show you the photos."

She'd thought she knew everything that had happened at the Indialantic. She envisioned her great-aunt as a spy—Mata Hari wearing lots of makeup. Then Liz remembered Aunt Amelia taking photos—or supposed photos—of Agent Crowley's notebook, and how that had gone awry. Her great-aunt was too young to have helped the effort in WWII—but the Cold War...

Captain Netherton led her to a table big enough to seat eight. It was set for two. Next to the table was a free-standing silver ice bucket touting a magnum of expensive champagne.

The captain pulled out a chair. "Mademoiselle."

After she sat, he said, "I'll leave you to it."

"To what?"

He just smiled and went up the ladder.

She heard a door behind her open. "I hope you like champagne, Ms. Holt?" a deep voice said.

Beast! Liz turned and looked at him. Stevenson was dressed in similar clothing from when she'd seen him at the timeshare—casually elegant.

"Rented the whole shebang; hope you don't mind. I really wanted to see the eco-tour and spend time alone with you," he said.

Should she be afraid? The captain had her back. However, she didn't appreciate being ambushed, even with Cristal champagne on ice. Before she could protest, Captain Netherton came back with one of his part-time crew members following behind. They both carried silver trays piled with seafood. Liz's jaw dropped as they covered the table with platters of crab, oysters, shrimp, clams, mussels, and lobster on chipped ice.

She thought it was overkill for only two people but said, "Wow. You went all out."

Stevenson took a seat. He reached for his napkin, shook it out, then placed it on his lap. "I called ahead of time and the captain arranged everything."

Again, she noticed his gold-and-diamond pinky ring, fashioned into a pair of dice totaling seven. Travis was a big-time craps player in Atlantic City. She never got a handle on the game but knew if she placed a bet on the Pass Line and the person rolling the dice rolled a seven, she'd double her money.

After the captain and his crew returned to the bridge, she said, "Before we continue, I'd like to know why we had to be alone. Why you came to Melbourne Beach. And what you want."

"You don't mince words, do you?"

Stevenson wasn't classically handsome, but there was something about him that was attractive. He had a perpetual smile on his face, and numerous laugh lines by his mischievous blue-green eyes.

"As to why I want you alone, I wanted to talk to you without that barracuda of an agent within earshot."

"Paula?"

"Yes.

Liz could commiserate. Paula had frequently butted into her and Travis's conversations.

"And," he said, as he poured champagne into her glass, "I came to Melbourne Beach to see you. We all did."

"Why?"

"That would be answer three."

"And…"

"Paula and Travis insisted I come along because as I'm your publisher, they were hoping you might be easily swayed into doing something that would benefit us all."

"Doing what? No offense, but wouldn't it make more sense if Debbi, my editor, came, not one of the heads of the company? Or if you talked to *my* agent and she gave me a heads-up?"

"I'll get to that. As you know, or maybe you don't know, *The McAvoy Brothers* movie is scheduled to come out in July."

"I had no idea."

"Our company, Charles and Charles, owns a subsidiary movie production company, Black Angel Films. They're producing *The McAvoy Brothers*. Play your cards right and maybe one day we'll make your novel into an Academy Award–winner," he said, adding a wink.

He was laying it on a little too thick. "Go on."

"First, let me serve you an oyster."

He took an oyster off the shaved ice, tapped a few drops of tabasco sauce on top, reached over, and held it to Liz's lips. She couldn't resist. She opened her mouth, chewed twice, closed her eyes, then swallowed. It was like tasting the best the ocean had to offer.

When she opened her eyes, Stevenson looked pleased with himself.

"I still don't see what it has to do with me." The engines roared and the ship lurched forward. They grabbed their champagne glasses to keep them from spilling.

He tapped his flute against hers. "Cheers."

She tapped back, then took a drink. The bubbles went up her nose, making her cough.

"You okay?"

"Embarrassed but okay. You were saying?"

He continued, "In order to sign Travis on with Charles and Charles, he had to agree to sell all film rights and future film rights to Black Angel Films. I don't know how to put this, but Mr. Osterman's recent book, which he published with his old publisher, has done poorly. Not to speak ill of the dead, but if I would've seen that manuscript prior to signing him, there wouldn't have been a contract for his sequel."

Liz felt a little vindicated. "I didn't read *Blood and Glass*. And don't plan too. That doesn't answer my questions. What does the book have to do with me? Even if I went on a social media blitz, which I would never do, I certainly couldn't change the opinion of the readers and reviewers at this late date."

"Paula and Travis thought that was why I agreed to accompany them. I wasn't completely aboveboard with them. For a good reason. That's not what I'm asking of you."

He sure knew how to drag things out. "What *are* you asking?"

"I want you to sue the production company that's making the deplorable *Blood and Glass* into a made-for-TV movie."

"A what! You want me to sue your company?"

He laughed as he stuck a cocktail fork into a blue-crab claw, removed a good-size chunk, dipped it in a creamy mustard sauce, and shoved it in his mouth. "Heavenly," he murmured, wiping his lips with his napkin. "Black Angel Films isn't producing *Blood and Glass*."

"I don't understand…"

"Travis and Paula sold the rights under the table without our knowledge. They thought by changing the name to *Bloodstained Love*, and saying it was based on a true story, they could pass it off as a docudrama and we wouldn't find out. The industry is small, and our reach is large. Although it did take us a while. *Bloodstained Love* is scheduled to be released the same month as *The McAvoy Brothers*. You see, the production schedule for a television movie is much shorter than for a feature film. So, therein lies the rub."

"Therein lies *your* rub. What do I have to do with it? Isn't it a moot point now that Travis is dead?"

"You can file a lawsuit, sue his estate, and get an injunction. Our team of attorneys will pay for everything."

Even though the seafood in front of her was fit for Neptune, Liz had lost her appetite. "So, if Travis was still alive, you planned to find me and talk me into suing him, like he'd tried to sue me?"

"Exactly. It would be payback, and very cathartic for you."

Liz stood up, feeling the floor sway beneath her. For a moment, she'd forgotten where she was. After she steadied herself, she said, "I'll decide what's cathartic and what isn't. My new life is cathartic. I don't care about television movies or feature films and I don't care about money, if that's the next thing you're suggesting. I have no intention of suing anyone. I'm sorry you made the trip for nothing."

He bit a shrimp in half, swallowed, then said, "You're not afraid that when the television movie airs about the night you were injured, spun the way only Travis Osterman can spin it, your little island paradise will turn into *Jurassic Park*?" Cocktail sauce remained on one corner of his mouth, resembling blood. He followed her gaze and licked it off, Barnabas Collins–style.

Liz began to feel uneasy in the cramped room. There was a cunning look in his eyes. She said, "I have to go tell Captain Netherton to turn the boat around."

He didn't get up and he didn't stop her.

When she reached the ladder, she turned and asked, "Did you all plan to come to the Literary Ball ahead of time?"

He stabbed a razor clam with his fork and took his time in answering. "The original plan was that Travis would come alone, but then Paula insisted on coming in case you weren't easily persuaded. And you know why I came. To get you to stop the airing of *Bloodstained Love*."

It gave her the creeps, knowing they'd all plotted to coerce her into doing something.

He put down the fork. "I'd also like to offer you the services of the criminal division of the Manhattan law firm we use, free of charge. If you get in a little pickle because of the other thing."

"Pickle?"

The clam dangled from his cocktail fork. "I heard everyone, including the police, think you murdered Travis...," He took a gulp of champagne. "And another thing," he said. "How's your next book coming along? Are you going to make your deadline? I wouldn't mind seeing if it's up to snuff. Unfortunately, another book by an author who writes similar women's fiction, recently had to be thrown to the scrap pile. It just wasn't good enough."

Suddenly, the Beast wasn't a prince in hiding.

He was just a beast.

Chapter 18

The words, *Elizabeth Holt, you are under arrest. You have the right to remain silent. Anything you say can and will be used against you in a court of law...* repeated like an anthem when she looked down. They were waiting for her on the dock. Ryan, her father, and Agent Crowley. For a moment, she was frozen in terror. *This is how it happens*, she thought. One minute you're drinking champagne and sucking down oysters, the next you spend your life in jail for a murder you didn't commit.

Her father must have seen the panic in her eyes. He called up, "It's okay, Lizzy. Agent Crowley just wants to talk to you..." He hesitated for a moment before saying, "At the station."

She felt someone standing behind her and hoped it was Captain Netherton, but of course, when she turned, it was Stevenson Charles wearing an I-told-you-so look on his smug face. "You better scooch, and don't forget my offer of representation."

Anger filled her gut. She stuck out her chin and said, "I won't be needing them, Mr. Charles. Now, if you'd be so kind as to get off my family's boat, I'd appreciate it."

Captain Netherton must have heard her last words. He turned the corner and said, "Here, sir. Let me escort you off." He handed Stevenson a piece of paper.

Stevenson glanced at it. His cheeks reddened. "This is an outrageous bill."

"You said you wanted the best. Well, we gave it to you. If there's a problem, you can take it up with your credit card company."

Stevenson threw the credit-card receipt on the deck and stormed off the boat. As he neared Ryan, he shouted, "Out of my way!"

Instead of moving, Ryan stepped into his path. He was about five inches taller than Stevenson, thinner but more muscular. Stevenson elbowed him as he passed by. Ryan remained stationary, and Stevenson lost his balance. His foot got stuck between the planks of wood. He tripped and fell face-first onto a flapping mullet fish dropped by Pearl, the Indialantic's semitame pelican. Pearl glanced down from her piling, and Liz could swear she was smiling.

Crowley went to Stevenson and helped him up. "Mr. Charles, I'm glad you're still in town."

"I didn't think I had a choice," he said, glaring at Crowley, then Ryan.

"Here's my business card if you can think of anything else that might help my investigation." Crowley handed him the card.

Stevenson snatched it from his hand. "Thanks for the address of the station. I might just swing by to file a formal complaint against that guy." He pointed at Ryan.

Ryan remained stoic as Stevenson strode away toward the parking lot.

Liz was still on *Queen of the Seas*, watching the show. After Stevenson disappeared from sight, her anxiety came back. Captain Netherton put his hand on the small of her back and they came down the gangway together.

As they approached Fenton, Ryan, and Crowley, the captain tipped his hat at Crowley and said, "Derek, how's the family?"

Crowley replied, "Crazy as usual. But a good crazy. Meredith graduates from high school in May, then she's off to Vanderbilt on scholarship."

Liz interrupted their small talk. "Am I being arrested, Agent Crowley?" She couldn't take the suspense any longer.

"Not at this time, Ms. Holt. I came looking for you at the Indialantic and ran into your father and this young man, who told me where I'd find you. I suggested your father come along."

That didn't sound good. "What's this about? New evidence?" she asked.

Fenton stopped her questions by saying, "Liz, we'll go in my car and meet Agent Crowley at the station."

She breathed a sigh of relief. She wasn't being arrested. But the words "at this time" echoed in her head.

When they reached the Emporium parking lot, a sheriff's car was idling with an officer inside. Fenton's Jeep was parked next to it.

"Is it okay if I tag along?" Ryan asked Fenton.

"It's up to Liz," he said.

Liz took Ryan's hand and said, "Of course; the more the merrier." She spied Brittany standing next to her SUV with a rack of evening gowns to bring into Sirens by the Sea. Just what she needed, her childhood nemesis witnessing her "almost" arrest.

Ryan and Liz got in the back seat of her father's Jeep. When they pulled away, so did the sheriff's patrol car. As Liz took a last glance toward where Brittany was standing, she saw her take out her cell phone to call someone.

When they got to the station, Crowley was waiting for them on the other side of the metal detectors. "I think the conference room is free," he said. He looked at Ryan and nodded toward a door with the placard WAITING ROOM. "You can wait in there."

Ryan looked torn.

"It's okay. We've got this. Right, Dad?" she said too enthusiastically.

"Right, kitten."

They followed Crowley down the hall, passing Charlotte's office. It was empty. Instead of the last door on the right, like last time, they took another short hallway and were ushered into a room. The windowless space was humid and the air smelled stale, harkening back to when smoking indoors was legal. The only AC vent was positioned behind where Crowley took a seat. Was it a ploy to keep them sweating? They sat across from the detective. Her father placed his portfolio case on the table and took out a notepad and a pen.

Crowley's notebook and a recorder were in front of him. From his jacket pocket, he took out a small recording device. "If it's okay with you and your client, counselor, I'm going to tape this interview."

Liz glanced at Crowley's notebook. It was the same one Aunt Amelia had photographed—or thought she'd photographed. He caught her gaze and did a drumbeat on top of the notebook with his fingers. Liz wasn't sure he knew about her great-aunt's snooping, but it would explain the look in his eyes.

"We have no objection to the recorder. Do we, Liz?"

"None."

"Very well," Crowley said. "Let's get started."

Liz leaned across the table. "What evidence do they have against me besides my prints and someone's statement that Travis and I were arguing?"

"We recently obtained an audio version of your argument with Mr. Osterman on the night he was murdered."

"Impossible. Why would someone wait so long to submit it?" Liz hadn't recalled her exact words to Travis during their confrontation. She could only imagine how guilty it might make her sound if you could hear the anger in her voice.

"We need you to confirm it's your and Mr. Osterman's voices on the recording." Crowley touched a button on the recorder, and Liz relived the entire exchange with Travis, one heated word at a time. She wished Sally had videotaped it instead; then Crowley could see everything in context, including the way she'd pushed back the rifle when Travis shoved it at her and the way he grabbed her arm. He hadn't been the victim. She had.

Her father spoke up. "Is this something new? This audiotape? Why is it just coming to light now?"

Crowley hesitated, then continued. "We got the recording from the producer of a local news show. Someone planned on playing it on the five o'clock news. He didn't want the station to be charged with interfering in a murder investigation."

Liz should have guessed. Sally Beaman would do anything for a story. She was a small-town girl who had big aspirations.

After Crowley stopped the recording, Liz said, "Yes. That's me and Travis Osterman." She stood up. "Is that all? Have you been talking to Travis's agent, publisher, or even his intern about his murder—or only focusing on me? Because I didn't know he was coming to town. Anything more on the person dressed as a pig on New Year's?"

"Rest assured, Ms. Holt, we're exploring every avenue. And you should probably try to stay out of our way. Not like you did with my predecessor." He looked over at Fenton.

"I think it's time to leave, Liz," her father said. He stood, reached across the table, and shook Crowley's hand.

"Please stay nearby for the next couple of days, Ms. Holt."

They left the room and found Ryan leaning outside the waiting room door. "Everything okay?" He wrapped his arm around Liz's shoulders, and they followed Fenton to the car. Ryan helped Liz into the front seat. She didn't protest as he reclined the seat. "You look a little green around the gills, Ms. Holt."

"I feel worse than that," she answered.

Ryan got in the back seat. As they were pulling away, Liz exhaled in relief.

As they got closer to the Indialantic, they saw that the media had already arrived. And Liz knew who to thank. Brittany! "Dad, isn't there any way to get more information about other suspects in Travis's murder? Charlotte must be privy to some insider information."

"I'm sorry, but on this one, I know as much as you."

Ryan leaned forward and said, "You're innocent, and we'll prove it. You and I will be sharing your pink wine up in the bell tower while watching the sunset for the next forty years."

"Only forty?" she said, laughing. "Pink wine. Admit it. You loved the last rosé we had. Pops sure knows his wine."

"And now he knows his craft beer, thanks to me," Ryan said, adding a grin. "Fenton, what did you think of the grapefruit IPA you had yesterday?"

"I'm from the old school of beer, but it was actually pretty good. Refreshing. Charlotte loved it."

She knew what they were doing. And it almost worked. Almost.

Ryan put his hand on her shoulder. "I forgot to tell you. While you were on *Queen of the Seas*, I had a little chat with Brittany. She confirmed what Ashley said, that she'd met with Travis at Deli-casies. He wanted to get the scoop on you. He'd first come into her shop to buy a gift for you. She'd told him she had seahorse earrings to match a necklace you'd bought a while ago."

Ryan knew about her obsession with seahorses. Travis had never paid attention to the way Liz dressed, unless to criticize. In his mind, her taste level was a couple of rungs below his—the key being *in his mind*. She fingered the delicate gold chain around her neck, which held a small 18k-gold seahorse charm. "I'm surprised Brittany would go out of her way for me. I'm sure she's the one who called the press when she saw us in the parking lot with Crowley."

"You don't know that for sure," Fenton said. Like Aunt Amelia, her father always saw the best in people. Liz usually could, but not when it came to Brittany. She'd been burned too many times.

"I saw her take out her phone as we were pulling out of the Indialantic's parking lot. I don't need more evidence than that. Ryan, did she say anything about finding Travis's phone?"

"Yes. When she was with Travis at Deli-casies, he got a phone call. His ringtone played one of her favorite songs, which she recognized when emptying the shop's trash. She fished it out and called the number last dialed and got..."

"Paula," Liz said.

"Yes."

Liz looked over at her father. "If the Sheriff's Department has Travis's phone, is there any chance you can get a copy of his calls?"

He sighed. "Only if they use it as evidence in court. Then I'd get a list of everything. But that won't be happening because you won't be arrested. And even if Charlotte was on the case, she wouldn't give them to me."

"I won't be on his phone records anyway. You can trust me on that" She glanced out the window. Squidly's was packed with their usual crowd. "You can drop me at home. I think I'll make it an early night."

"I'm not taking you to the beach house," her father said as he turned onto the drive leading to the back of the hotel. "You need some hugs from your auntie. It's not up for discussion."

Secretly, she was relieved. She kept thinking of Crowley's words when she'd asked if she was being arrested, *Not this time, Ms. Holt.* "What about Brontë?"

"I'll walk over and get her," Ryan offered.

"You have to…"

"I know, put her in her basket…"

"And can you also bring a small can of food? She's such a light eater, there's only one brand she seems to like. Even though the Indialantic's pantry has more pet food than human food."

Fenton pulled into a spot and parked at the rear of the Hotel, near his office entrance. Liz waited until Ryan came around before getting out of the car, checking to make sure the paparazzi weren't hiding behind the palmettos. Ryan opened her door, took her hand, and the three of them rushed inside. They went into her father's apartment, where Aunt Amelia was waiting for them. She had a hunch Ryan must have called Aunt Amelia from the sheriff's station.

"Oh, Auntie!" Liz cried as she was engulfed in her great-aunt's comforting arms.

"Lizzy, everything will be fine. What did I always do when you were a child and you had a nightmare?" She brushed Liz's bangs out of her eyes and kissed her on the nose.

Liz sniffled. "Sprayed Monster Rid spray?" After her mother's death, when she and her father first moved into the caretaker's cottage, she'd had nightmares that one of the gargoyles on the façade of their Manhattan townhouse had followed her to Melbourne Beach. The howling creature would smash against the glass of her bedroom window, wanting in. Aunt Amelia had taken a can of aerosol room freshener and covered it with a printed label that said MONSTER RID SPRAY with a cartoonlike drawing of an ugly gargoyle type monster being sprayed by Monster Rid. Then, in the next scene on the can, the gargoyle turned into a pile of dust. Years later, Aunt Amelia had told her she got the idea of Monster Rid spray from one of the hotel guests, who was a child psychologist. The woman had said, *If you tell your children to believe in Santa Claus and the Tooth Fairy, why is it so unrealistic that they also believe in monsters? They're as real to them as the Easter Bunny.*

Aunt Amelia laughed, "No, I wasn't thinking of Monster Rid spray. Though I might still have a can somewhere I was saving for my first great-

great-niece or -nephew." She winked at Ryan, and both Liz and Ryan's face reddened.

Liz slapped her knee. "Oh, I know, what I used to recite after you woke me from a nightmare! *Auntie, Dad, and Me make three, then there's God and Mom above, shining down their love.* Then we would make a monster-proof tent in the middle of my room and I would sleep in my *Little Mermaid* sleeping bag."

"Exactly, my love. Now you skedaddle into the kitchen. Greta's been keeping your dinner warm." She looked over at Ryan. "You too, young man."

"I'd love to, Aunt Amelia, but I have something I need to do." He kissed Liz on the lips and Amelia on the forehead, then strode out of the apartment.

Liz told Aunt Amelia, "He's going to collect Brontë. We're worried the press is back there. Sorry you guys are involved in all this."

"Don't be ridiculous, Elizabeth," her father said. "Do what your auntie suggests. Go eat."

She didn't protest and went out the door leading into the interior of the Indialantic. Food was the last thing on her mind. But the thought of the Hotel's welcoming kitchen, where she'd eaten so many happy meals, spurred her on.

A few minutes later, Pierre said, "Mon chérie, have a petite nibble. Greta and I made your favorites." He took her fork, stuck it in the creamy seafood cassoulet, and put a chunk of blue crabmeat to her lips.

She felt a queasiness in her gut. She loved crab, but her mind flashed back to her time on *Queen of the Seas* with Stevenson, reminding her of the seafood spread and his offer of a stable of high-priced criminal attorneys. Stevenson obviously didn't know her father was a lawyer. Was it possible that right after she'd seen Stevenson at the Literary Ball, he'd confronted Travis about the TV movie *Bloodstained Love*? She'd seen him heading outdoors to smoke his cigar only minutes before midnight. He and Travis could have scuffled, the gun could have gone off, hitting the tree, and the next bullet ultimately found Travis's chest. Travis said the rifle wasn't loaded. If that was true, his murder was premeditated. Someone would have had to add the bullets beforehand, or at least brought them with them. Paula, Stevenson, and Hallie were staying in the same house as Travis. They had access to the rifle. Sally...

"Is something wrong? You aren't eating," Greta said.

Liz gave her a soulful look.

"I know, honey," she said, walking over to the table. "Keep the faith."

"I'm trying." She took out her phone and opened to the photo of Napoleon the pig. "Greta, do you remember seeing this person at the Literary Ball?" She held the phone out.

"No. I think I would remember that scary thing."

Pierre glanced at the photo. "Napoleon. Of course. I saw him talking, or should I say shouting at that poor soldier I found unearthed by the storm. It was when I went to my kitchen garden to get some basil leaves for the chef de cuisine. The poor woman was going to used dried. *Une mauvaise* decision."

"Do you know if the pig—Napoleon—was a man or a woman, Grand-Pierre?" Liz asked.

"Why, I don't know, Lizzy. All the words were muffled by its headdress. I just know the soldier wasn't too happy. Wait, how could the soldier be talking to Napoleon? When I found him, he'd been there since the War." Confusion clouded his eyes.

Greta took Pierre's hand and said, "It's okay. It was probably another soldier. In fact, I think I saw him. He was dressed as a character from Hemingway's *A Farewell to Arms*."

His shoulders relaxed, "Of course. If you find out who Napoleon is, Lizzy, I have his book. He dropped it when he saw me. The soldier had already stomped away. I have it in my desk drawer."

Liz jumped up and went through the open door to the pantry. Barnacle Bob was napping. Usually, Liz would tiptoe around him. Not this time. She pulled back the chair and opened the drawer of the desk where Pierre wrote out his daily menus. Inside was the copy of *Animal Farm* the person dressed as Napoleon had been holding in the photo. She took it out and flipped it open, hoping to find someone's initials or a clue to the owner. Nothing. "Darn!"

Barnacle Bob woke and opened his beak. Liz said, "Put a cork in it, BB. I'm not in the mood." Then she apologized. "I'm sorry for snapping at you, my fine feathered friend."

He wasn't big on accepting apologies, especially when his sleep was disturbed, and went through his usual temper tantrum. He'd even added a new curse word to his vocabulary. Someone in the Indialantic was guilty of speaking it. She just didn't know who.

Disappointed about not finding anything in the book, she brought it back to the kitchen and sat down at the table, just as Kate and Betty came charging toward her.

"The captain just told us that Agent Crowley was waiting for you on the Indialantic's dock," Betty said. "I'm happy to see you're here."

"We were worried you were being arrested," Kate said. "Why would they think you killed that jerk!"

"Just some questioning," Liz said in a low voice, pasting on a smile when Pierre glanced her way.

It was too late.

"What jerk?" Pierre asked. "Lizzy is accused of killing someone?"

Liz put her hand on his. "No. No. Grand-Pierre, Kate is talking about an Agatha Christie movie."

"*Mon Dieu*! You gave this old man a scare."

Betty came next to where Liz was sitting and whispered in her ear, "Don't worry, we've got this. I think someone else is going to be charged with his murder. And it will be very soon."

Liz's searched Betty's face. She couldn't help but blurt out, "Who!"

Pierre looked over, and Betty smiled like nothing was wrong.

Kate sat across from Liz and Pierre. "Eat, Elizabeth Amelia Holt. You need all your energy, so we can catch a..." Liz gave her a dirty look and nodded her head toward Pierre. "...fish."

"Now you're a food pusher too?" Liz asked.

"That, plus I'm willing to eat any leftovers and don't want them to get cold. I adore chef's seafood cassoulet," Kate answered.

"Knew you had ulterior motives. Especially when it comes to food," she said, trying to remain upbeat in front of Pierre. She did feel better after Betty's comforting words. "Okay, okay. I'm eating." She ate as much as she could stomach, while everyone looked on like she was a fragile robin's egg ready to crack. Which she was. She handed Kate her dish. "It's all yours."

"You sure?" Kate asked, then didn't wait for an answer as she cleaned the plate. "Magnificent, Chef!"

"Thought you decided to go vegan?" Greta said to Kate.

"I decided. I just haven't gone," Kate said, laughing at her own joke. "Chef, what do you think about veganism?"

Liz could tell everyone was trying to keep things light and airy for both Liz and Pierre. She glanced down at the book she'd placed in front of her. Fingerprints. There could be fingerprints. She got up and went to a drawer next to the sink and retrieved a clear plastic bag. She put *Animal Farm* inside and sealed the bag. She would show it to Betty as soon as she could get away.

Then she had a thought: Maybe she was making too big of a deal of the person dressed as the pig. He or she could have just been a guest at the Ball who had no connection to Travis. But Pierre had said the pig was arguing with Travis. Granted, Travis could get defensive and loud when pushed in a corner. But with his public, he usually had perfect decorum, even projecting a faked sense of humility. She went back to the table and joined the conversation.

"Well, Katie," she heard Pierre say, "I think veganism is a worthwhile way of eating. Vegan diets are higher in vitamin C and fiber and lower in saturated fat. But there's the risk of not getting enough vitamin D, B12, calcium, and omega-3 fatty acids." Pierre's kitchen garden was filled with herbs and vegetables. Some of his herbs he used for medicinal reasons. Unbeknownst to him, Liz had planted some new herbs to help with his memory loss. Aunt Amelia was involved in the conspiracy and mixed them into her tea blends without his knowledge.

When the discussion ended, Liz stood up. "Betty and Kate, let's go do that uh... thing we have to do. Have a great night, Greta and Grand-Pierre." She looked at Pierre. He was reaching for the morning version of the *Melbourne Beachsider*. Its headline: Another Murder at the Indialantic by the Sea. Liz snatched the paper away. "Do you mind if I take this with me, Grand-Pierre? I want to make sure the ad Aunt Amelia put in looks as she planned."

"Of course, ma petite. But don't forget to bring it back later."

"I won't," she said, crossing her fingers as they left the kitchen.

When she reached the lobby, she stuffed the paper in the trash.

Chapter 19

Wednesday morning, Liz was in the kitchen, helping Greta with the breakfast dishes. Instead of sleeping in her beach house, she'd spent the night in one of the Hotel's empty suites. She'd intended to sleep at home, but when she'd walked out of the Indialantic the previous evening, a lone reporter was waiting. He stuck a microphone in her face and asked how it felt to be the lead suspect in her ex-boyfriend's murder. She'd given him a "no comment," then fled back into the safety of the Indialantic. Her father and Aunt Amelia insisted she stay the night.

Before bed, Betty, Aunt Amelia, and Liz had a little powwow in Betty's sitting room. All were dressed in their pjs. Liz had borrowed one of her dad's T-shirts, and Betty wore a flannel nightgown. Aunt Amelia had looked like Doris Day from the old movie with Rock Hudson, *Pillow Talk*, in her short little pink nightie, pink soup-can curlers, and pink heeled slippers affixed with feathered pom-poms. After slathering their faces with deep-sea mineral mud masks, they went down to the screening room to watch an episode of *The Twilight Zone* in which Aunt Amelia had played a psychic who led the army to a spaceship filled with pointy-headed aliens.

Following a cup of Aunt Amelia's version of Sleepytime tea, Liz had had no problem falling asleep. It was when she'd woken in an unfamiliar bed that the panic had set in. If it hadn't been for Brontë snuggling beside her, she would have run to the dock, untethered her father's cabin cruiser, *Serendipity*, and taken off for the Bahamas, only 150 miles away.

She hung the last copper pan on its hook just as the swinging doors from the dining room opened and Ryan walked in. In a serious tone, he said, "Liz, I need to have a word with you." In one of his hands was an overnight bag, in the other, a winter jacket.

She opened her mouth, glanced at Greta, and said, "Okay."

When they were safely in the empty dining room, she asked, "What's with the winter coat?"

"I'm going to New York."

"You're what?"

"We can't do everything from here," he said. "I need to investigate. Everyone on our list lives in Manhattan or nearby. Also, I heard from Stacy Sorenson and she's willing to meet with me this evening before she goes on an international press tour for her upcoming novel. It's a long shot, but she might know more about Stevenson Charles, and maybe even Osterman."

"I'm meeting Sally Beamon tomorrow for breakfast at Deli-casies."

"Be careful." Something deeper than concern showed in his deep brown eyes.

"I'll be fine. Sally's harmless, plus Dad's already given me a pep talk."

"I remember in the past you thought someone else was harmless and they turned out to be a murderer."

"That's why I chose Deli-casies. Thought you'd be there." She stuck out her bottom lip in a pout. "I just need to ask Sally what happened after I left Travis on the terrace New Year's Eve. I'll promise her an exclusive at a later date. That'll be all the bait she'll need."

"I'll tell Gramps to keep his eye on you."

"Isn't it strange that we both lived in New York City at the same time, then ended up on this little island?"

"And we're both happy with small-town life."

"Extremely so," she said, grinning. "Does Dad know about your trip?"

"Yes. It was his idea. I've also lined up some of my contacts at the NYPD. So, if I do get caught doing anything that crosses the line, hopefully they'll give me a free pass. Have you finished looking at the photos Ashley took?"

"I went through them quickly but plan to go through them again."

"Good."

"There's something slightly illegal I need to ask you," he said.

"Slightly?"

"Do you have keys to Osterman's apartment?"

"His penthouse? I think so. But there's a doorman, Pete. Travis always warned him not to let anyone through. The doorman before him got fired for letting in a crazy fan."

Ryan didn't say anything, just looked at her.

"You're right! A crazy fan. Travis said the woman was unstable. I think he even put a restraining order on her."

"A restraining order!" they both said at the same time.

"It could be the same person sending threatening letters," Liz said, excitement in her voice.

"The letters are just a theory," Ryan said, "but worth investigating. In the meantime, while I'm gone, I think you better read *Blood and Glass*." She realized Travis wouldn't be handing out directives anymore, or blackmailing her into promoting it, the opposite of what Stevenson wanted her to do.

She broke his gaze and looked out the window toward the terrace. After a few seconds, she said, "Okay. I'll do it."

"Good."

"You could probably get away with saying you're Travis's cousin or something," she said. "I know he rarely talked about his family to anyone, including me. Can't believe you're leaving me."

"It should just be an overnight. In the meantime, be careful."

"And I can say the same to you. Especially if you get caught in Travis's penthouse and even the NYPD can't save you."

"Okay, Bossy Pants."

"Okay, Snoopy Pants."

"No one bosses you around, Ms. Holt." He got more serious. "I'm determined to clear your name."

Liz felt bereft at the thought of him leaving. He wrapped his arms around her, and for the moment, they were silent. When they drew apart, she glanced into his dark eyes and said, "Thanks. I know this isn't easy because Travis and I had a past and now you must go digging into it. What are you hoping to find?"

"I'm sure the police have his computer hard drive. But if there were actual physical letters, we have a chance of finding them." He brushed his finger across her bottom lip.

"The letters or emails might have even come through his former publishing house, Minton and Castle. I don't remember his editor's name."

"Leave that to me. I already have Minton and Castle on my list."

"Of course you do," she replied.

"By the way, Susannah also gave me an assignment. It seems your buddy, the Beast..."

"He's not my buddy."

"Just kidding. Anyway, Susannah found out that Stevenson... Who goes by the name Stevenson anyway? Shouldn't he be called Steve, Stevie even?"

She laughed. "It *is* a tad pretentious."

"Susannah found out that Stevenson has a major gambling problem. His father is past retirement age but won't let *Stevie* take the reins until he clears up all his debts and attends Gamblers Anonymous meetings."

"That's interesting." She thought about the significance of Stevenson's pinky ring with the three and four dice. "Stevenson plays craps and so did Travis."

"Do you know where?"

"I know where Travis did. Maybe there's a connection? A private club on Fifth-Seventh and Lex. The Diamond Club, or maybe it was the Platinum Club. Something like that." She hadn't had a chance to tell him about her and Stevenson's time on *Queen of the Seas* and gave him the short version.

After she finished explaining, he said, "I wish you would have told me sooner. I would have purposely tripped him on the dock, then pushed him into the lagoon." He balled his fists and clenched his handsome jaw. "Maybe I shouldn't leave you? I have a lot of contacts in New York..."

"Stop. I'll be fine. Plus, you need my key to Travis's penthouse. I'm not scared of Stevenson." She remembered what Betty had just said. "When you come back, someone besides me might be charged with murder. Betty just whispered that she thinks someone will be arrested very soon. Do you know anything about it?"

"No. But if Betty says it's true, I'd believe it. And I'll be on the next plane home." He enunciated the word "home."

"I've been meaning to ask why you had Taylor go see my father. Something to do with her brother's will?" Liz hoped that was the case.

"It was something about a horse."

"A horse?"

"Yes. Some stipulation in her parents' will about what would happen to it after they died."

"Darn. I was hoping it had something to do with Travis's will, not his parents. That would be something good to get hold of, Mr. Investigator."

"I'll do my best. I'll video chat with you once I get inside the penthouse and find out what Ms. Sorenson says about Stevie."

"She's a steamy romance writer, but that's selling her short. She's a wonderful storyteller. And very attractive. You stick to the job at hand; no straying from our path."

He laughed. "There's only one path I intend on following: the one that leads me back to you."

She burst into tears.

"Hey," he said, pulling her to him. "What did I say wrong? I'm not the most articulate when it comes to my feelings. As you've guessed."

"You're very articulate, Ryan Stone," she sniffled.

"Hopefully, when you get to your hotel room, someone else will be charged with Travis's murder." *Please, please let that be true.*

"I'll assign you and Betty the job of continuing to talk to our suspects. Except Stevenson; don't get near the guy. Maybe send Susannah Shay after him. That'll teach him." He picked up his bag and slung his jacket over his shoulder. "You better go get the key to Osterman's penthouse. I'll wait in the lobby and look for the cab."

"I could drive you?"

"No. We don't want the press following you to the airport."

"True. The key's in my purse in the butler's pantry. I'll be right back."

When she entered the kitchen, it was empty. She went into the pantry, where Barnacle Bob greeted her with a medley of '60s commercial jingles, ending with, "'From the valley of the jolly HO HO HO Green Giant!'"

"I know the others, BB, but I never heard Auntie mention the Green Giant. You're certainly in a good mood."

Praising him was a big mistake, because he spewed a string of curses. "You're a lost cause."

"Kiwi. Kiwi! Polly wants a treat. Polly wants a treat!" he shouted.

"Put a muzzle on it. I'm not falling for that one. I'm sure you already had yours."

She took her handbag out of the cupboard and dug inside for her keys. There were so many times she'd meant to take it off her key ring. Why hadn't she? She slipped the key off. Travis had made such a big deal when he'd given it to her. *The key to my kingdom*, he'd said. She suddenly felt sad at the memory. He could be quite charming when he wanted to. When he wasn't drinking.

"Tootles, Barnacle Bob. Catch you later."

When she went into the lobby, Betty and Ryan, who'd been sitting next to each other on a bamboo settee with their heads together, immediately split apart when they saw Liz. Ryan said. "Did you get the key?"

"Yes." She handed it to him.

Ryan stood, grabbed his down jacket off a wicker chair. and said, "Wish me luck."

"I'll text you the address. Sometime around four in the afternoon, Pete takes a smoking break. If Pete's still the doorman. Oh, and you use the same key in the elevator to get to the penthouse."

"Got it." He walked over to Liz and gave her one last kiss.

As he pushed against the revolving door, she called after him, "Call me when you get there."

Then, under her breath, she whispered, "Love ya."

"I heard that," Betty said.

Liz felt her cheeks tingle with heat. "He didn't, so it's our little secret."

"I think you're safe with that one. Ryan reminds me of my husband, Jack."

Over the years, Betty rarely had mentioned her deceased husband. She'd moved into the Indialantic after he passed.

"You never talk about him," Liz said softly, "What was he like?"

"He was wonderful. A genius, and very popular with his students. As a professor of quantum physics at Florida Institute of Technology, you'd think he'd be dry and boring. He was the opposite. I don't know what he saw in me. There was a gaping wound in my soul after he died. It's gotten smaller, but it's still there. Grab what you can in this life and don't be afraid to love. I took a chance. And thank God I did." She swiped a tear from her cheek. "Do you want me to take over your class at St. Benedict's? I just need your lesson plan and I'll coordinate it with mine."

"No. I plan to go. I'm trying to be more positive this morning, and I'm putting a lot of trust in your words that someone else will soon be arrested."

"If you're sure?"

"I am. You're my role model."

"I *am* a tough old bird," she said, laughing.

Liz kissed her on the top of the head. "With a soft heart."

"I have an assignment for you," she said, flustered at the flattery. Betty wasn't good at showing emotion, always blaming it on her staid English forebears.

"I'd welcome any assignment."

"I think you should try to get hold of your old school chum, Ms. Beaman, and ask if she saw Napoleon the pig on New Year's Eve. I've found a photo in which they're standing near each other. Maybe she talked to him or her. And they can corroborate your alibi of being by the pool."

"Great minds think alike. I already have an appointment with her. We're meeting at Deli-casies in the morning. Boy, wait until I fill you in. Hold on one sec." Liz left the lobby, went down the hallway, through the dining room, and into the kitchen. She grabbed *Animal Farm* off the counter, where she'd left it yesterday, and rejoined Betty.

She handed the book to Betty and explained about Pierre finding it.

Betty opened the cover and went to the publication date. "Hmm, 2006" she said, "I wonder if this book wasn't someone's personal copy. Look at the finger smudges and folded corners on the pages. A good psychologist would be able to discern what type of person identified with Napoleon the dictator pig."

"Yeah. We need an analyst from *Criminal Minds*. But then again, we have you. The book also could have come from a used bookstore. I'll ask Kate. If she'd sold a copy, she'd know to whom and when."

"Do you mind if I keep it?" Betty asked. "In case our killer turns out to be a pig?"

"Of course. Sure you can't fess up and tell me who's going to be arrested? I promise not to have any expectations if it doesn't pan out" *Liar.* "Do you think it's possible one of our suspects, Stevenson, Paula, Hallie, or Sally, had two costumes for the ball, so they wouldn't be recognized when it came time to kill Travis?"

"We both know anything is possible. I believe all will be revealed shortly. Patience for now."

"I prefer fortitude. I need to keep pushing forward or I'll sink into an abyss of self-pity." Patience and Fortitude were the names of the stone lions flanking the steps to the New York Public Library on Fifth Avenue. When Liz was small and lived in Manhattan with her parents, she'd thought the lions were magical. But not as magical as all the books that had been waiting for her inside.

"I promise all will be revealed very soon," Betty said, heading toward the revolving door. "I'm meeting Agent Crowley this morning near where the body was found. I'd invite you along, but he might think the thing I'm going to show him was planted."

Liz glanced at what Betty was wearing. It wasn't her usual stylish garb. She had on a navy belted dress with a small floral print. Her shoes were something Eleanor Roosevelt might have worn to a WAC meeting. And she wasn't wearing any makeup. "Where's your knitting bag, Miss Marple?"

"I'm dressed like this in case the detective remembers me from the night your ex was found. I want him to believe I'm just a little old lady living on a pension. Doing my civic duty by turning in possible evidence in a murder investigation."

"Good luck with your recon work. But you'd better fill me in as soon as Crowley leaves."

"Patience and Fortitude, Liz. Patience and Fortitude," Betty repeated, as she left to meet Crowley.

Betty was right. Liz needed to carry on and find a killer. On her way out of the lobby, she checked her cubby for mail. Even though Liz lived in her own separate house, her mail came to the Hotel. The cubbies in the mahogany cabinet at one time were coordinated with the Hotel's guest suites. One of the few chores Aunt Amelia had given Susannah as assistant manager was to put everyone's mail in their assigned cube. Back in the day, there might have been mail for Lauren Bacall or gangster Al Capone.

She pulled out a thin envelope with only LIZ typed on it.

Why did she have a feeling the letter was from a dead man...

Chapter 20

Liz went to open the envelope just as her phone rang. It was Kate, calling from her shop. "Liz, there's someone here who wants to see you. She didn't want to come to the Hotel because she saw a news van parked outside."

"Who is it?" Her first thought was Stevenson. She'd promised Ryan she wouldn't see him.

"Ms. Resnick. The agent."

"Don't say a word. I'll be there in two." She hung up the phone and stuffed the envelope in her pocket. She needed to get to the Emporium as soon as she could. Between Kate's impetuous nature and her life's mission to be Liz's protector, she might scare Paula away.

Liz started toward the revolving door, then changed her mind. She didn't want to bump into anyone from the news or tabloids. She exited the lobby and went to the kitchen and out the door next to the pantry, hurrying to her father's apartment. He wasn't at home. She grabbed a Marlins baseball cap and a pair of her dad's sunglasses on her way outside, keeping her head down as she walked north toward the Emporium. Dark clouds filled the sky to the west, but above her was only the sun. When she reached the Emporium's parking lot, she scanned the area. Thankfully, all was clear. She didn't want to take a chance entering through the main doors, in case she got waylaid by the press in the atrium. Taking her key from her handbag, she unlocked the exterior door to the community storeroom and walked inside. She went out the open door on the other side of the room and into the hallway. As she neared Zig's Surf Shack she saw Ziggy in the midst of selling a board to a mother and her teenage daughter. "Nothing to worry about, Mom," she heard Ziggy say, "girls can surf as well, or better, than boys." Then he ruffled the top of the girl's head, saying, "This board is perfect for a beginner." The mother didn't look convinced. If Liz wasn't in a hurry to see what Paula wanted, she would have gone inside and showed them a video of eighty-year-old Amelia riding the waves. She hurried by. Ziggy looked up but didn't recognize her.

She looked around as she entered Books & Browsery, not seeing anyone around. She hopped over crates overfilled with Kate's estate and flea market finds. Kate often told Liz that her vintage and antique items told just as much of a story as one of her used books. When her elbow knocked a Slinky off a shelf, Kate called out, "We're here. Behind the cash register."

Through the glass window atop the antique brass cash register, she saw Paula's dark hair. She and Kate were sitting on the down-filled magnolia print love seat where Liz and Kate usually shared morning coffee from Deli-cases. The pair looked ill at ease. Unusual for Kate, because she got along with everyone. Then Liz remembered New Year's Day, when Paula had burst into the dining room, accusing Liz of knowing where Travis was.

She continued down the aisle, sneezing as she went. Kate wasn't keen on dusting; she liked to let people think they were in an old curiosity shop from Dickens. As she passed by a skeleton hanging from a brass stand, Liz thought Books & Browsery was becoming more like the shop in Stephen King's *Needful Things*.

Paula stood when Liz reached them. And she wore a smile. "I'm so happy you could meet me on such short notice."

Who the heck was this woman? Liz thought. "What do you want, Paula. Unless it's to confess to Travis's murder. I have nothing to say to you."

Liz saw that it took everything she had not to respond. Her smile remained, and she let out a short laugh through clenched teeth. "I always liked your sense of humor, Liz. I'm here to tell you that I don't believe you killed Travis. I think he must have been recognized at the Literary Ball by someone with an ax to grind; then a misadventure transpired."

Misadventure? "What do you want, Ms. Resnick?"

"I want us to have an understanding. It's important we close ranks. I don't think you murdered anyone. Neither did I. I have a proposition for you?"

Liz felt the letter in her pocket burning a hole in her thigh. "Yes…"

Kate had taken a feather duster as a prop and was nearby, dusting a section of books dedicated to Edgar Allan Poe. The tips of the feathers didn't touch one book.

"I want you to sign with my agency. We've had our differences, but I never doubted your abilities as a writer. No one can stop us now."

Her last sentence hung in the air for a while. Finally, Liz said, "That's it? Sure. Where do I sign?"

Paula stumbled back a step. "Well. Good. Well. Okay," she stuttered.

"Do you have the contract with you?" Liz asked, smiling on the inside.

"Uh, no. But there's one…"

Here it comes, Liz thought.

"There's one other thing I need you to do before you sign with the agency."

Bingo. "Does it involve a release for a television movie deal?"

"Well, yes. How did you know?"

Liz didn't answer, just held Paula's startled gaze.

"It was Travis. Wasn't it?" she asked. "He told you. I should've known."

It was interesting that Paula didn't know Stevenson was privy to her and Travis's undercover deal to make the television movie of *Blood and Glass*. Liz said, "I don't think it's wise for me to sign anything until after Travis's real killer is apprehended."

"Not to worry," Paula said, taking a step closer to Liz, "you can still publish in prison…I mean, we can work things out if God forbid that would happen…which it won't."

"I'll tell you what, Paula. I promise you, with Kate as my witness, I will *never* promote or have anything to do with *Blood and Glass* or any other related project having to do with Travis Osterman."

"My dear, you seem very angry. Angry enough to kill, I might say." Her claws came out Wolverine style, and the true Paula Resnick emerged. "You just wait and see. When you're rotting in a cell with nothing to do but regret this decision, you'll come calling. Why don't you think about someone else besides yourself for a change!"

"That's rich," Liz couldn't help saying. "Oh, by the way. I like your earrings. Aren't they a little sedate for your usual over-the-top style? I'd never pegged you as someone who'd wear something so understated as tiny seahorses."

Paula's face flushed, but she kept her composure. "At least think about your family. Don't you think they could use the extra money for running that old hotel? Or are you too selfish to consider others?"

"I'm not being selfish. I refuse to be blackmailed by you or anyone else."

She thought she saw the corner of Paula's mouth twitch.

"That's enough!" Kate shouted. "Get out of my shop. Pronto! And don't come back."

Surprisingly, Paula started for the door.

"One second," Liz said, holding out her phone. "Do you have any idea who was dressed in this costume on New Year's Eve?"

Paula snatched it from her hand, the tips of her nails leaving marks on Liz's palm. She quickly glanced at it and handed it back. "No. I didn't run into any pigs, just a beast," she said with an angry twist to her mouth before stomping out of the shop.

Kate said, "You aren't mad I kicked her out, are you?"

"Of course not." She squeezed Kate's shoulders. "I'm actually happy Ms. Resnick showed all her cards. She seemed scared, and I bet it has something to do with Travis's death. Did you catch the comment about the 'beast'? I wonder if she was referring to Stevenson Charles?"

Kate patted the open space next to her and Liz slunk into the cushions.

"I think you might be happy about something I did while we were waiting," Kate said. Liz could almost feel the adrenaline coursing through her friend's veins. "Paula was looking at a list of recently missed calls on her phone. I got out my phone and pretended I was texting someone. Instead, I took a photo of the list."

"Why, Kate Fields, there's hope for you yet."

"I sent it to you."

Liz got out her phone and opened her text window. "A lot of these are 212 numbers. I'll forward this to Ryan."

"Do you know Travis's phone number?"

"Only if he didn't change it from when we were together." She made the photo larger. "There it is. From New Year's Eve. But we can't swipe to the right to see the time. And, of course, there's nothing suspicious about an agent and her author talking to each other. Thanks, friend, for trying to save me."

"Anything for you." Kate got up from the love seat and looked down at the floor. "Wait! What's this?" She bent down and reached for a crumpled piece of white paper. "It might be a clue. Do I need to preserve fingerprints?"

"I doubt it." She wanted to slap herself. Why hadn't she put the letter from the mail cubby in a plastic Baggie? The letter must have come today because she'd checked her mail yesterday. She knew one thing: Travis hadn't delivered it.

Kate picked up the slip of paper and handed it to Liz. After smoothing it out, Liz whistled. "Kate, you're on a roll. It's a receipt from Worth Avenue."

"I know that shop. It's where they rent costumes year-round, along with designer eveningwear. I'm sure half of the people from the Literary Ball got their costumes there. Which might include the person dressed as the pig. Beauty and the Beast's costumes were quite elaborate, too. It's the only place within sixty miles you can rent costumes on that scale. If Francie from Home Arts hadn't helped us with our costumes, that's where I would have gone."

"Of course," Liz said. "I know where it is, next to Waldo's restaurant."

"Yay, I found a clue!" Kate said, hopping up and down in excitement. "Do I sense an impending road trip to Worth Avenue?"

"Indeed you do. We'll go tomorrow. I have a morning appointment; then we can leave and be back before my seminar at St. Benedict's."

She had a feeling they might finally identify the mysterious pig.

Chapter 21

After Liz left the Emporium, she ate lunch on her beach house deck. Brontë was in her basket beside her, snuggled under a fleece blanket. The thermometer on the post next to her read fifty degrees. Per last night's weather report, they were in for a cold snap. Liz just hoped it wouldn't affect Pierre's kitchen garden or Aunt Amelia's cutting garden. She reveled in the peace and tranquility of the ocean panorama in front of her. Welcoming the nip in the air with open arms. If it wasn't for the palm trees, she could be back in New York on a fall day. Dark clouds encroached from the south, and the waves crashed against the shore in a loud, steady rhythm.

The envelope was on the beverage cart next to her; unopened and in a plastic bag. She'd called Betty as soon as she'd returned to the beach house and promised to wait before opening it—even though it was killing her. It was like it had a life of its own. It might turn out to be nothing. Then again…

To pass the time, she made a list of what they needed to follow up on to catch a killer. It was a doozy. She might have been willing to leave it to the authorities if her life wasn't on the line. Literally. She'd had a short conversation with Captain Netherton at breakfast, and he'd assured her that Agent Crowley was an excellent homicide detective and had also been a highly decorated US Coast Guard captain before joining the Brevard County Sheriff's Department.

"Knock knock, earth to Liz," Betty said, banging on the wood railing of the deck. "Where is it?"

"What happened to Patience and Fortitude?" She pointed to the envelope, then shivered.

Betty had changed into a black sleeveless cotton shift with black slip-on shoes. She wore a short black-and-white-paisley scarf around her neck, and a white sweater was tied across her shoulders.

"Wow. What a difference a change of clothes makes, Miss Marple," Liz said.

"And a little makeup," Betty added, laughing.

"How did it go with Crowley?"

"We'll see. I'm optimistic. That's all I'm saying for now. Tomorrow, I should be able to fill you in on everything. Now let's look at the task at hand. The letter."

"It could be nothing."

"How many letters with just your first name typed on the front do you get? Ballpark figure..."

"Okay. Okay."

Betty took a seat on the lounge next to her. She dug into her handbag and took out a pair of thin latex gloves and put them on. It seemed only a few months ago, they'd done something similar that required gloves. Oh, wait. They had. Betty reached for the Baggie. Opening it, she withdrew the letter. Liz saw a slight tremor to the hand holding the letter. Betty was just as nervous as Liz about what it might say.

Betty turned it over. "It looks like someone else might have opened this, then resealed it."

Liz looked it over; the seal was puckered in places and off-center.

"Susannah Shay!" they said at the same time.

Betty took out a single sheet of paper from the envelope. The letter was typed and addressed to Mr. Stevenson Charles, at Charles & Charles Publishing. It went on to say that he should investigate the fact that *The McAvoy Brothers* wasn't written by Travis Osterman. And they had proof. Then there was a postscript: *Another letter with instructions will follow. If they aren't adhered to, the press will be contacted.*

Liz was stunned. "I know one thing, Betty. This letter didn't come from Stevenson. But if he received it and thought Travis had plagiarized *The McAvoy Brothers*, it sure gives him motive for murder."

"Not only does it give Mr. Charles a motive, but someone else, if they knew about it and tried to exhort money from Mr. Osterman."

"How about Paula? What if she was privy to his plagiarism? Even encouraged it. It would explain why all his other works were subpar compared to *The McAvoy Brothers*. And why *Blood and Glass* was such a bomb. Hallie told me that Travis wouldn't let her see the manuscript for the sequel, *The McAvoy Legacy*. Pretty strange not to let your intern help you with your novel. Hallie also told me Paula had had a hissy fit Monday morning in Travis's office at the timeshare. Throwing pages of *The McAvoy Legacy* on the floor."

"His agent killed him because she didn't want him exposed as a fake?"

"Well, it does sound far-fetched. But I bet some of her money is riding on the made-for-TV movie. And remember, if she found out that he'd plagiarized *The McAvoy Brothers*, he couldn't write the sequel, and she would lose out on the commission."

"Sally's another possibility," Betty said. "She's a reporter; maybe she dug up something pointing to Travis being a phony."

"An interesting angle. But wouldn't Travis want to kill Sally, not vice versa?"

"You'd better turn this over to Crowley," Betty said. "You can drop it on the way to St. Benedict's. Perhaps with what I gave him, he'll be able to zero in on the real killer."

Liz stood. "We'd better leave now if we're stopping to drop off the letter. I'll settle Brontë, then be right out. Sure you don't want to wait inside? It's chilly out here."

"I don't mind. I love being outdoors on days like this. We have our seasons on the island; they just don't involve snow, sleet, and below-zero temps."

"True. We also have hundred-degree summers and, of course, hurricanes."

"Bah, those little ol' hurricanes never bothered me."

"Knock on wood, Betty. Knock on wood," she said as she picked up Brontë in her basket and carried it inside.

Betty called after her, "You coddle that kitten. I'd hate to see you with a baby."

A baby. First Aunt Amelia, now Betty. Liz was only twenty-eight and lately felt like fifteen. A baby was out of the question.

"And what about you and Carolyn Keene, Ms. Lawson? I rest my case," Liz called back. Maybe she was a coddler. Weren't most pet owners? Brontë had added so much to her life, just like Ryan's pup Blackbeard added to his. While in New York, he'd left Blackbeard in Aunt Amelia's capable hands. As long as her great-aunt kept Blackbeard and Barnacle Bob separated, everything would be fine.

After Liz collected her things for the workshop and put on some classical music for Brontë, Liz and Betty left for the sheriff's station in the blue bomber. When they reached the station, Betty waited in the car, while Liz ran inside.

Liz handed the letter to Agent Crowley, who just happened to be walking out as she was walking in. She filled him in on Stevenson trying to get her to stop the production of *Bloodstained Love* and Paula's connection with the movie. Crowley seemed very appreciative, until she mentioned Napoleon the pig. Then she saw his eyes glaze over.

When she got back in the car, Betty asked, "How did it go with Crowley?"

"He seemed receptive to the idea that perhaps I'm not the only one with a reason to kill Travis," she said, putting the car in Drive and heading south on A1A toward St. Benedict's.

On the twenty-minute drive, Liz told Betty about her impromptu meeting with Paula in Kate's shop, and about the receipt Kate had found from Worth Avenue. Betty didn't hesitate about joining Liz and Kate for a trip to Vero Beach.

"I think you're right," Betty said. "Paula's scared. If what Stevenson Charles told you is true, Paula is the only one stopping him from getting the TV movie canceled before *The McAvoy Brothers* hits the theaters."

Liz hadn't thought of that angle. What little she knew about Paula, Liz knew she would have a backup plan. "Betty, can you text Ryan to check into the production company of *Bloodstained Love*?"

"No need, my dear. It's already done." She rifled through her ginormous handbag and pulled out her iPad. She turned it on, then tapped the screen a couple of times. "WK Pictures is the name of the company."

"What does WK stand for?"

"Women's Kaleidoscope. It seems they make thrillers that a certain audience of women adore. Usually there's an ex out to get them or vice versa."

"Ouch. How apropos. I don't even want to think about how Travis portrayed me in the TV movie. I started *Blood and Glass* last night. What a bunch of lies and ego-stroking. I'm treating it as a farce and happy it's not on anyone's best-seller list."

Betty glanced at her, began to say something, then closed her mouth because they were pulling through the gates of the monastery. Up ahead, Hallie was getting out of a cab. She wore the same dress she'd worn on the first day of the workshop. And from a distance, she really did resemble Liz.

Liz parked and put her hand on the door handle.

"Hallie," Betty said.

"What about Hallie?"

"Why is she here?"

"You know why. Agent Crowley told everyone to stay put until he says they're free to leave."

"No." Betty said. "What I mean is, why is she here at the monastery? You shared her first writing class assignment with me. Certainly it isn't the end product of a serious writer."

"There's always hope. Look at all the people you've helped by teaching your creative writing class at the Barrier Island Community Center. Plus, Hallie's mother is very sick. Dying, I think. She might not have been in the best frame of mind. Then there's her boss's death the night before."

"Was Travis her boss or Stevenson?"

"Technically, she's an intern for Charles and Charles, assigned to Travis. I'm sure they wouldn't hire her without proof she's a competent writer. But I see where you're going. Maybe Stevenson and Hallie are in it together. They were Beauty and the Beast at the Literary Ball."

Hallie was waiting for them. She looked over and waved.

Liz waved back.

"It's amazing how much she looks like you," Betty said.

"That's easy to explain. Travis has a type. Hallie and I were his type. That reminds me. I never read hers or the rest of the classes in-class writing assignments from yesterday. Maybe she redeemed herself. I should have had you take over the class. My mind's all over the place."

"Understandable. You have a lot on your plate. I'm not taking over. You'll be fine. We need to find out who put the letter in your box. I'll ask Susannah; she might not be so forthcoming with you. Maybe you could pull Hallie aside and ask about any letters, threatening or otherwise, she might have seen come across Travis's desk."

"Okay, Nancy Drew, I'm on it. And hopefully, Ryan will find something when he searches Travis's penthouse."

"Make up your mind," she said with a smile. "Am I Miss Marple or Nancy Drew?"

"You're both rolled into one."

Chapter 22

Thursday morning, Liz got up, showered, and put on minimal makeup. Dark smudges remained under her eyes. The person looking back at her in the mirror told of all the nightmares she'd had last night. All having to do with Travis. She dressed in capri jeans, an aqua cotton long-sleeved shirt, and black flats. Liz's melancholy matched the panorama outside her bedroom window. The sea was as turbulent as her thoughts. Once again, if it wasn't for Brontë, she wouldn't have felt the need to get up, preferring to snuggle under the covers and come out when Travis's murder was solved. "Come, little one, let's go see Dad, then get breakfast at Deli-casies. I need to talk to a certain newscaster."

Soon after, she walked into the Indialantic's library and found, as she suspected, her father in front of a roaring fire. What she didn't expect was who was with him. His fiancée, Agent Charlotte Pearson, and Betty. "Did someone forget to invite me to the party?" she asked.

"Well," Charlotte said, getting up from a leather armchair, "we certainly didn't forget. And now that you're here, I must leave." Smiling, she touched Liz's arm as she passed and called out, "Fenton, please explain it to her."

After Charlotte left the room, Liz took her still-warm vacated seat. "Dad, what's all that about?" Next to her on a small bamboo table was a coffee service. She turned one of the cups right-side up and poured herself some coffee, inhaling the aroma before taking a gulp.

"You're not adding natural sweetener or milk?" Betty asked from the love seat.

"Didn't sleep last night. Horrific nightmares."

Her father looked concerned.

"I'm good. I needed this fire. And you guys. Dad, what did Charlotte mean?"

"As you've probably noticed, she hasn't come around to the Indialantic lately. Doesn't want to interfere with the investigation. She snuck in my office door, parked in Squidly's, and wore a hooded sweatshirt. She doesn't want you to take her departure personally."

"Charlotte, wearing a hoodie. That, I would like to see." Charlotte Pearson came from a moneyed Orchid Island family and dressed liked she shopped in Palm Beach. Her clothing choices mirrored her confidently reserved manner. With her blond hair and classic beauty, Aunt Amelia said she was the spitting image of Grace Kelly from the old Hitchcock film *To Catch a Thief.* Liz agreed, and liked to think of her father as a doppelganger for Cary Grant. They were the perfect couple.

Liz turned to Betty, "So, was Charlotte here because this is the part where you tell me they've arrested someone for Travis's murder?"

Betty kept quiet and her father spoke. "We're getting close to that scenario. But you must be patient."

"Ugh. Patience again!" she said, then winked at Betty. "I read the rest of *Blood and Glass* last night. You were right, Dad, a fifth grader could've written it. It was disturbing how he twisted everything to make it look like he was the winner of the Jilted-Lover-of-the-Year Award. I read the part about the threatening letters, but other than that, everything having to do with the night I called 911 was pure fabrication. If it wasn't written so poorly, I'd be upset. His depiction of me was more like a cartoon character. While he came off as a put-upon artistic genius, comparing himself to Hemingway and F. Scott Fitzgerald. I don't care what threats Travis came up with. I never would have promoted that book."

"Didn't you think it was interesting, the way he talked about the main character's literary agent. She was too perfect," Betty said.

"Betty! You read the book too?"

"I got an eBook version for ninety-nine cents last night. And I also met with Susannah. I don't know what Amelia promised her, but she's like a dog with a bone about finding dirt on Travis Osterman."

Liz sighed. "Bet most of the dirt has to do with me. A year ago, I was buried in it."

"Don't sell the woman short," Betty said.

"Should I be rethinking my original theory that she went to the police after she heard us talking about Travis on New Year's Eve?"

"I asked her about that." Betty got up and topped off her coffee, then sat back down.

Liz leaned in closer. "And?"

"The reason she went to the police was because of another conversation she overheard. One between Mr. Osterman and Paula Resnick or *the girl with all the awful tattoos and the disgusting nose ring,* as Susannah put it. Paula was threatening Mr. Osterman about dropping him as a client if he couldn't get you to endorse *Blood and Glass* and sign a nondisclosure agreement promising not to sue because of a certain television project."

Liz moved to the edge of her seat. "*Bloodstained Love,* the made-for-TV movie Stevenson told me about."

"How did Travis react?" Fenton asked.

"Apparently, he was quite confident he'd get Liz to do whatever he wanted."

"Paula is good at making threats, but that doesn't prove she was his killer," Liz said. Then she told them about the seahorse earrings she was wearing, which were meant to be a gift for Liz.

"I'm not finished," Betty said, excitement in her eyes. "Mr. Osterman threatened her in return."

"With what?" Liz's mind went to what Travis could have used against his agent.

"Susannah said Mr. Osterman promised to tell the world about their collaboration on a certain matter, and he had proof she was just as dirty as he was."

"What a lovely couple. We have motive. Now we need opportunity." Then Liz told her father about yesterday's impromptu meeting with Paula at Kate's shop. "Did Betty fill you in on the letter I got yesterday?"

"Yes. She did. I assume you took a photo of it."

"Of course we did," Liz replied. "Betty, did Susannah tell you if she saw the letter and put it in my cubby?"

"Said she knew nothing about it. But she did say she saw Taylor snooping around the area yesterday morning."

"Taylor?"

"Your auntie and I have been doing a little investigative work ourselves," Fenton said. "We got the list from the Literary Ball and called everyone on it. We put the people we didn't know into a public records search site and didn't see anyone who had ties to Mr. Osterman. Ryan has the list, just in case."

"Any chance I could have it?" Liz asked. "Maybe there's someone on there I knew from when I lived in Manhattan."

"I don't see a problem with that. I know Crowley has it too."

"Shall I tell her, Fenton?" Betty wore a Mona Lisa smile.

He nodded his head in the affirmative, then reached over and placed his hand on top of his daughter's.

"Spill," Liz demanded.

"Remember I told you I found something near the bench besides the button from Mr. Osterman's uniform?"

"Of course I remember," Liz said. "It's been driving me crazy twenty-four-seven."

"Before I tell you more, I want you to know I've just hired your father as my attorney. That's why I couldn't tell you about it yesterday. This way, Fenton can't spill to his law-enforcement fiancée about our privileged conversation."

"Wise move," Liz said.

"Here it is," Betty lowered her voice to just above a whisper, "I found a small gold-hoop earring. Or what I thought was an earring until I saw a photo of Paula dressed in costume on New Year's Eve wearing the same gold hoop as a nose ring."

"That's fantastic," Liz said, clapping her hands. "But why didn't you show it to me right away? I would have been able to recognize it as part of her costume because I'm the only one of us who saw her."

"Because I thought it was an earring, not a nose ring. And I had to make sure it wasn't yours. I know you wear similar earrings. What if you'd lost it before Travis was murdered, and the police found out it was yours and put you at the scene of the crime? I grabbed it and put it in a tissue, just in case, knowing I could put it back later."

"Which she did yesterday, then called Agent Crowley," her father said. "I'm happy Betty hired me before telling me what happened. Tampering with evidence in a murder investigation is a felony. But I know what she did was to protect you, Daughter."

"Betty, you never thought I killed Travis, did you?"

"Never. But there's something I haven't told you. When I got up to my rooms and looked at the earring, or what I thought was an earring, there was blood on it. I was concerned that perhaps during your confrontation with him, he'd ripped it off your earlobe."

Liz understood why Betty had to keep it from her. Betty was nothing if not thorough, as proven in the way she plotted her mysteries. "So, you put the nose ring back under the bench…"

"I told Crowley I discovered it while sitting in Amelia's garden. I was out getting some fresh air, bent to tie my shoelace and voilà! There it was."

Betty had thought of everything. Liz remembered the clunky shoes she'd been wearing yesterday to come off as a sweet little old lady. "Crowley believed you?"

"Of course he did," her father said. "Look at that innocent face. I'd believe her, and I know the real story."

"How long until they can get DNA off the blood on the nose ring?" she asked her father. She remembered Paula holding tissues to her red nose the day they found the body. Ripping out a nose ring would be painful and cause the area to be swollen and raw. "Is there enough to charge her? We have Susannah's testimony about Paula and Travis's fight, what I learned from Stevenson about the television movie, the letter about the plagiarism, and now the earring with her blood found in the location where he was murdered. Paula's alibi that she had a headache is weak at best."

"We'll have to wait and see. I can't ask Charlotte or anyone else about this. It might jeopardize the case. If I was a betting man, I'd say the chances are good all eyes will transfer to Ms. Resnick."

Liz's phone rang. She took it out of her pocket and glanced at the screen. "It's Ryan."

She got up, grabbed a pad of paper and a pen off the library table, then went to the other side of the huge room. They talked for five minutes. After she hung up, she went back and told her father and Betty what Ryan had learned so far.

"Ryan met with Stacy Sorenson. Interestingly enough, she had some very disparaging comments to share about Stevenson Charles. Apparently, after her success in the literary world, Stevenson became interested in her. They started dating. In the beginning, he would bring her gifts. Expensive jewelry from Cartier and Tiffany. They took trips together. It took a while before she realized that everywhere they went, there was gambling. When she sold a million copies of her book *Thorns and Roses*, Stevenson started asking her for money. Usually, she didn't stand next to him at the craps table, but one day she watched him from a distance, hidden in the crowd. He lost fifty thousand dollars in the space of ten minutes. The next time he asked for a loan, she told him no. He threatened to smear her name on social media. She wasn't intimidated by him and went immediately to his father and told him about Stevenson's gambling and got a restraining order against him. Thankfully, he left her alone."

"Susannah already told us there were rumors of his gambling. But the fact that he wasn't above blackmailing people, especially women, says a lot about his character," Betty said.

"There's more," Liz said. "Guess who Stevenson started hanging out with after they broke it off?"

"Travis's agent. Paula Resnick?" Fenton asked.

"No. Travis," Liz said. "Maybe Travis had also lost money gambling, which is why he and Paula sold the rights to *Blood and Glass* without Charles and Charles's permission. It would also explain why Travis switched publishing houses. Maybe he owed Stevenson money or vice versa. Stevenson told me when we were on *Queen of the Seas* that when Travis came to Charles and Charles, they'd bought the film rights from Minton and Castle to *The McAvoy Brothers*. That's why he was so upset about the *Bloodstained Love* television movie coming out at the same time as the feature film of *The McAvoy Brothers*. Ryan also told me Ms. Sorenson said a couple of weeks ago she was waiting in Travis's father's outer office at Charles and Charles and overheard Travis's father saying it was all his son's fault they brought the albatross Travis Osterman to the company. Then he went on to warn his son that he'd better clean up the whole mess or he'd find himself working in the mail room."

They were silent for a few minutes, digesting everything they'd heard. Liz sat back down and glanced over at a tray of croissants, a dish with tabs of honey butter, and a jar of orange-mango jam. "Oh dear!" She stood up. "I forgot, I'm meeting Sally Beaman for breakfast at Deli-cases." She looked at her watch. "I'm fifteen minutes late."

"Don't worry," Betty said. "I'm sure she'll wait hours for the scandal of the century."

Chapter 23

The scent of bacon, coffee, and something sweet hung in the air as Liz stepped inside. She already knew what she was going to order. Sally was sitting at the barista bar, chatting up Ashley. Liz could only imagine the questions she was asking the poor girl. Sally saw her and waved her over with a smile. When she reached Sally, there were no words of recrimination because she was tardy. Betty was right. Sally would wait hours for a chance to talk to Liz about the murder. She said, "Hi, Ash," then, to Sally, "Why don't we snag that table in the corner? I'm going to order breakfast. You want anything?"

"No. I'll just bring my coffee with me. I don't see anything on this menu that's gluten-free."

Ashley wordlessly flipped over the menu. On the back was a complete list of gluten-free dishes. While Sally decided, Liz ordered a Belgian Waffle Melt.

"What's in a waffle melt?" Sally asked.

Ashley handed Sally a refill on her latte, then said, "Scrambled eggs, cheddar cheese, and honey ham between two Belgian waffles."

"I guess I'll try it."

Ashley looked over Sally's head, and Liz shrugged her shoulders. It looked like Sally was as gluten-free as Kate was a dyed-in-the-wool vegan.

"You ladies take a seat. I'll give the order to Pops and bring it over," Ashley said.

"Thanks, Ashley," Liz replied.

Sally got up from her stool and spoke to Ashley in a loud voice, obviously wanting everyone to know who she was, "Tell your pops, if I find the food here to be exceptional, I'll pass it on to my producer, and he might invite your grandfather to make a dish or two on the premier of my news show, *Melbourne Mornings*."

Ashley nodded her head in excitement and scurried to the back to give Pops the order, not bothering to correct Sally that Pops was Ryan's grandfather, not hers.

As they walked to the table, Liz said, "That's something new, Sally. Your very own morning news show. Congrats." It was funny how Sally came across as tall as Charlotte's five-foot-ten on the television screen, but in real life was only about five-two. "When did that happen?"

Sally didn't meet Liz's gaze and mumbled, "A few days ago. It's in the works; it'll be announced soon."

Liz knew what "in the works" meant. If Sally caught a killer, namely Liz, using her recording of Travis and their fight, she would get the show.

After they sat, Liz said, "Let's get on with it. I'm not going to ask you any questions about what you gave to the police, but I would like to ask about what happened after I left Travis on the terrace on New Year's Eve."

Sally raised a perfect eyebrow that looked stenciled on. As she opened her mouth to respond, Liz pushed the palm of her hand toward her to stifle her next question. "I know what you're going to ask and I'm willing to give you an exclusive on-camera interview. Just not today."

"Whether you're behind bars or not? And who said I gave anything to the Sheriff's Department?" Sally got a notepad and pen out of her bag and put them on top of the table.

Liz pointed, "No, Sally. Please put those away. After they find the person who killed Travis, I'll give you an on-air interview."

"I don't know. What if you're convicted? I insist you agree either way. If not, I have other people to talk to. She pushed back her chair, ready to stand.

"Okay. Okay. It's a moot point. I won't be convicted because I haven't been arrested."

"Yet." Sally put the pen and paper back in her bag.

Liz watched her dig around for something, but her hands came up empty. "Can I see your phone?" she asked.

"Whatever for? You're being ridiculous."

"Let me see it, Sally. Or no deal."

Reluctantly she fished it out of her handbag and passed it quickly in front of Liz's face. As Liz suspected, there was a red blinking light on the screen. Sally planned on recording their conversation. "Let me see you turn off your phone. We'll leave it on the table in full view. Whatever we say is strictly off the books. I need to know if you saw Travis or anyone else near the area after I left the terrace."

"Between you and me, I was pretty wasted that night. I really shouldn't be talking to you, but seeing we've been friends since high school, I'll tell you that after Mr. Osterman went to look for you, someone came to look for him. Or should I say two someones."

They'd never been friends in high school, but Liz went along with Sally's warped memory of the good old days. "Let me guess. Stevenson and Paula?"

"You got one right. Paula and Hallie."

"Paula said she went home with a headache," Liz said, more to herself than to Sally.

"I vaguely remember pointing her in the direction of where Mr. Osterman went. I was pretty soused. The Hemingway champagne fountain, followed by a few French 75s, did me in. I thought if I stuck with champagne as a base, I'd be okay mixing drinks."

"Did both Paula and Hallie go looking for him?"

"Like I said, it's all fuzzy. But, no, Paula went in search of him and Hallie got me a cab.

"Do you know what time that was?"

"What's this about?"

"What do you think it's about? Can you just answer? What time was it when Paula went looking for Travis?"

"I have no idea."

"Were the fireworks going off?"

While she was searching her alcohol-fractured memory, Ashley brought over their food. "Oh my gosh, that looks amazing," Sally said, putting her napkin in her lap and grabbing her fork and knife.

"It's better if you eat it like a sandwich." She couldn't spend another second on the niceties, so she got down to it. "Sally, were you and Travis trying to set up a little sting operation on New Year's Eve? The reason for taping our conversation?"

"Of course not. I just came prepared; where there's smoke, there's usually fire."

"How original."

Liz wanted to say she heard Sally wanted to put their argument on the nightly news. But kept quiet. "Can you please answer my other question? Were the fireworks going off?"

Sally put down her fork and knife. "I don't know if I should even be talking to you. I'll be called in as a witness when—I mean if—you're arrested." She stuck out her chest a little farther. "But if you promise me an exclusive, I can tell you this: The fireworks had just started when Ms.

Resnick went in search of Mr. Osterman. Honestly, that's all I remember. Am I allowed to take a bite?" She didn't wait for Liz's assent and brought the waffle sandwich to her mouth.

Deli-casies was busier than usual for a Thursday morning. Soon, Liz saw why. People were looking at her, and then whispering. She was used to people staring at her scar, but this was different. And it wasn't because she had dandruff, like in Aunt Amelia's Head & Shoulders commercial. They were staring because she just might be the murderer of the Pulitzer Prize–winning author of the best war novel of the century, as one critic put it.

"Did you call to invite Travis to the Literary Ball?"

Sally kept her focus on her plate.

"Sally?"

"I didn't invite him per se. But when I called to interview him about *Blood and Glass*, I might have mentioned it. And my assistant may have sent a copy of my invitation."

"Wow. Thanks for that one."

"Well, you wouldn't talk about the book or your relationship with me."

"Did you ever think I had my reasons, Sally?"

"Your scar?"

"That's only part of it."

"I would have told your side. I'm as unbiased as possible."

"See, it's the *as possible* that bothers me when it comes to the media."

They were silent while they ate. It was hard for Liz not to choke on her food. She was so angry that the reason Travis had come to her island oasis was because of Sally Beaman. He'd be alive right now and Liz would be continuing to live her blissful island life. She stood up, then thought of something. She opened her handbag and took out a photo. "Do you remember seeing this person wearing this costume on New Year's Eve?"

Sally took the photo out of Liz's hand and examined it. "I don't remember the pig. But I do remember the ring."

Liz snatched the photo back and looked at Napoleon's hands. There it was. On her right hand. The ring Taylor said was her mother's. She stowed the photo back in her purse. "I didn't know you knew Taylor."

"Ms. Osterman gave me a short interview yesterday. That aquamarine is one of a kind. Plus, it's my birthstone."

Liz was speechless. She tried to remain coolheaded, not wanting Sally to put two and two together. She stood. "I have to go, Sally. I'll be in touch."

"You didn't finish your food," Sally said, licking her fingertips. Hers was gone.

"It's all yours, Sal. Make sure you invite Pops on your new morning show." *Not that you'll get a show, because I'm innocent*, she thought, as she headed for the exit.

While walking back to her father's office, she rehashed what she'd just heard. Taylor was dressed as Napoleon, hence, she was at the Literary Ball the night her brother was killed. Paula went to find Travis when the fireworks started, hence, she lied about going back to the timeshare with a headache. Paula didn't have an alibi, hence, Liz was one step closer to being taken off the suspect list. All she needed to do was wait for the DNA match to the blood on the nose ring. But where did Taylor fit into all this? And what about Stevenson and the letter?

She hurried her steps, excited about all the new developments. Nearing the Indialantic's dock, she saw Taylor feeding Pearl, the pelican. Taylor had some explaining to do. She just hoped Aunt Amelia was right, that Taylor hadn't killed her brother. Liz didn't see anything nearby that Taylor could use as a weapon against her, unless you counted the bucket of baitfish she was serving Pearl.

Taylor noticed her and called out, "You have so much amazing wildlife on the island. It's like paradise for someone like me."

"I see you've met Pearl," she said, walking toward the dock. Then, following in Sally's footsteps, she fumbled in her handbag, found her phone, and turned on the recording feature.

Time to take things into her own hands…

Chapter 24

As Liz got closer to Taylor, she saw she wasn't wearing the aquamarine ring. What if Sally was wrong, and it was someone else wearing a similar ring? "Taylor. Great to see you. I know Auntie's been keeping you busy. Hello, Pearl, how's it goin'?" The pelican gave Liz a sideways glance, the only one she could give. Something squirmed in the pouch under her beak.

"Isn't she fabulous?" Taylor's red hair had been French braided. No doubt by Aunt Amelia. Freckles covered her face and shoulders and her nose was sunburned and starting to peel.

"She is."

"Did you know the pouch under her bill is called the gular and that pelicans have air pockets in their skeleton and under their skin to help them float?"

Liz did know a lot about birdlife on the barrier island; she'd grown up taking school trips and going on nature walks. "That's so interesting. Looks like you've been getting a lot of sun."

"I was on *Queen of the Seas* for an eco-tour. Did you know thirty-five percent of loggerhead and green turtles in the United States nest on your island's beaches?"

"I did know that, actually."

"I forgot, you grew up here," Taylor said with a laugh. "Captain Netherton is a goldmine of information."

"He certainly is." Liz wanted to shake her and ask, *Why did you lie about when you arrived on the island? What were you doing arguing with your brother? And, most importantly, did you kill Travis and let everyone think I'd done it?* But she kept quiet. They needed more proof; as in plane tickets and a receipt from the costume shop, just to name two.

"How are the plans for your brother's funeral coming? Do you need me to do anything?"

"Thanks, Liz, but Aunt Amelia is taking care of everything. They're releasing the body tomorrow and I'll be flying home with it the next day."

Now that there was good reason to believe she'd dressed as Napoleon the pig on New Year's Eve, Liz had to find a way to keep her from going back to Connecticut. "Glad Auntie was able to help you. Why don't you stop over at the beach house later? I'll fix us some dinner and we can chat."

"I'd love that. You're the best home chef I've ever met. How about your boyfriend, Ryan? Will he be joining us?"

"No, he's in New York."

Taylor looked like someone had slapped her. All the freckles on her cheeks fused into two red patches. "Uh, why is he there?" She bent down, took another fish from the bucket, and threw it up in the air to Pearl. The pelican smoothly caught it and swallowed.

"Some family business. He used to live in Brooklyn," she lied. "Let me take a photo of you and Pearl. It's such a gorgeous day."

Liz saw immediate relief in her stance. Why should she be nervous Ryan was in New York? Unless she had something to hide. Liz took the photo, then showed it to her for her approval.

"Can I have a copy? Can't wait to show it to some of my friends at the animal shelter."

"Give me your cell number and I'll send it to you."

Taylor did, then asked, "What time should I come over?"

"Six? I have the writers' retreat workshop until four thirty, so it'll have to be something easy."

"I know your version of easy; it's Michelin-star easy." She laughed. "I never learned to cook. Spoiled by Mrs. Sullivan all my life. She's a great cook, but not as good as you."

"Mrs. Sullivan is still with you?" She'd met the cook/housekeeper the one and only time Travis had brought her to meet-the-parents at their house in Connecticut.

"Oh, yes. She's still there. Not as young-hearted as Aunt Amelia, and not as agile, even though they're a similar age. Now the roles are reversed. I take care of her more than she takes care of me." Taylor had always shown a kind heart to animals and humans. Even with the odds stacked against her, Liz wanted to believe Taylor was innocent. Just like Aunt Amelia did.

"I'd better get going. See you at six."

"My appetite and I will be there!"

Liz turned to go.

"And Liz..."

She turned toward Taylor.

"Thank you for everything you've done. Agent Crowley was just here asking a lot of questions about Paula. Do you think she killed my brother? If she did, I hope she gets the death penalty. Do you know anything? Is she going to be arrested?"

"I'm not sure, Taylor. I just know there are still a lot of unanswered questions." *And a lot of them have to do with you*, she thought. "See you at six."

Chapter 25

After she left the dock, Liz went in search of her great-aunt and father. Neither were home. Hoping to find another letter, she made her way to the lobby to check her mail cubby. When she entered the room, Susannah was standing under the chandelier with a long-handled duster in her hand. She didn't notice Liz and let out one of Barnacle Bob's favorite curse words when a cobweb floated down and landed on her upturned face.

"Miss Shay!" Liz admonished. "I didn't know you knew that word. That's probably the reason French maids wear white caps, to keep all the spiders out of their hair."

At the word "spider," Susannah dropped the duster and flailed away at the top of her head.

"Any mail for me?"

With a "Humph!" Susannah picked up the duster and walked behind the check-in counter. "There's no mail for you. Especially not one *without* a postmark. Agent Crowley already phoned. I didn't see it and I certainly didn't put it in your mail slot."

"Can you just be honest? I'd really like to become friends. Equals even." Liz meant it. She didn't like holding grudges. Her feud with Brittany caused enough discord. Maybe it was time to bury the hatchet, or throw it in the lagoon.

"We come from different generations, Elizabeth. That is an impossibility."

"Okay. Then at least be honest with me as a favor to Auntie. Are you the one who opened the letter and resealed it?"

"No. I didn't open any letter...."

"If you see anyone suspicious around my cubby, will you let me know?"

"Of course."

Trying to get on her good side, if she had one, Liz asked, "How are you and Bastian getting on?"

"Do *not* mention that man's name," Susannah said in a shrill tone.

She remembered Aunt Amelia saying Bastian had a girlfriend in California. Liz knew what it was like to feel betrayed. "If there's anything…"

"And while we're on the subject of cheaters…" She removed her phone from her pocket, tapped the screen, and then turned it toward Liz.

It was a Page Six photo from the *Post* showing Stacy Sorenson and Ryan chatting at a black-tie fund-raiser for the FDNY. They were both dressed in elegant eveningwear and seemed in a deep conversation. Ryan looked so handsome, it took her a minute to tear her eyes away. Apparently, by the look in Ms. Sorenson's eyes, she felt the same way. She wore a gold-sequined floor-length evening dress with a large slit showing a long, shapely leg. Around her neck was a yellow-diamond choker that set off her long raven hair and almost-amber eyes.

"They look pretty cozy together, don't you agree?" Susannah said, snatching her phone back.

Was she jealous of Stacy? No. Just envious she hadn't spent the evening with Ryan.

"Have you ever read any of Stacy Sorenson's romance novels?" Susannah asked. "They can be quite descriptive, from what I've been told. Though that's not the type of literature I keep by my bedside."

I bet, Liz thought. "I've read a few. They're wonderful reading. You can't always judge a book by its cover, Miss Shay. I would think you would know that after what happened with Bastian."

"Well, I never!" she said, then stomped away toward the dining room.

So much for trying to be friendly and compassionate, as Aunt Amelia had urged her to do.

At eleven, Kate and Betty were waiting in the parking lot at the rear of the Hotel, Kate's aqua junkin' van sounding like it needed a major tune-up. Liz opened the rear passenger door and moved a pile of cigarette-smelling used books to the other seat. She got in and sneezed. "Kate Fields, what are you going to do with those stinky books?"

Kate pulled away from the Hotel and made eye contact with Liz in the rearview mirror. "What I always do: save them. Then they can once again be shared with the world. One of them might be a first printing of Hemingway's *The Sun Also Rises*."

"Well, the smell also rises," Liz said, taking out a tissue from her handbag and blowing her nose.

"Hardy-har-har. Next hot sunny day, I'm going to lay them out. I guarantee ninety percent of the odor will disappear."

"And what about the remaining ten percent?"

"Well, we'll just have to pretend someone who liked to smoke a pipe, like Papa Hemingway, had been the previous owner."

Betty turned to Liz. "Did I see you talking to Travis's sister from my window?"

Liz explained to them about her conversation with Taylor and what Sally had said about the aquamarine ring.

"Wow!" Kate said. "Taylor lied about when she came to Melbourne Beach?"

"Seems so," Liz answered. "But it doesn't mean she killed him."

"You know better than that," Betty said.

"Yes, Liz. Be careful," Kate scolded.

"That's rich, coming from the most impetuous person I know!"

"I'm just saying…"

"Ryan's calling. I'll put him on speaker."

Ryan was waiting for a subway car, and the reception was spotty at best. She'd updated him on everything she could, then he'd done the same. He'd received the photo Kate took of Paula's last-called numbers. The most important result of his sleuthing was that he'd found a few pages torn from Sgt. McPherson's journal. Unfortunately, he hadn't found any threatening emails or letters. There was a lot of static and the line went dead. Liz sent a text, asking if he could contact Mrs. Sullivan at Taylor and Travis's family home in Connecticut for any info on Travis's stalker and Taylor's alibi for New Year's Eve.

Twenty minutes later, Kate pulled to the curb in front of Worth Avenue. Betty said, "Last March, Amelia and I went into Worth Avenue for our Mardi Gras costumes. I chose a simple harlequin mask, but you know Amelia; if it's not over the top, she's not wearing it. Anyway, they had all these huge heads displayed on a shelf in a back room. I don't remember a pig, but then again, why would I?"

"We could've just called the shop and asked about the costume," Kate said, "but this makes me feel like we're doing something."

"This is why we had to come in person." Liz showed them the photo she'd just taken of Taylor and Pearl. "I figured the salesclerk might remember better if we had a photo of Taylor."

"Great thinking," Betty said. "Hand me your phone. Maybe I should handle this, just in case they recognize you."

"I'm coming with you," Kate said.

"Okay. But let me do the talking," Betty said.

Betty and Kate got out of the van. Kate's cheeks were flushed with excitement. There was a reason Liz, Ryan, and Betty kept their unofficial detecting within ranks—Kate and Aunt Amelia were too impulsive and excitable. Liz was dying to go inside but knew her face was plastered all over the media.

Twenty minutes later, they were sitting at Waldo's at an outdoor table overlooking the ocean. The temperature had risen to sixty-five and there was a gentle breeze, making it perfect for lunch outdoors.

Liz said, "Well, what happened?"

Betty opened her mouth to speak just as a server came up to take their orders. Kate ordered something vegan and Betty a shrimp po'boy. Liz didn't have much of an appetite. She ordered a cup of crab chowder, which reminded her that Ryan would be home soon, and they'd be sampling his chowder in his new kitchen. If she wasn't arrested first.

When the server left, Liz turned to Betty. "Miss Marple?"

"You were right. Taylor is Napoleon the pig. And this is where Paula got her Girl with the Dragon Tattoo costume and Hallie and Stevenson, Beauty and the Beast. The owner was extremely upset about the Napoleon costume and pig head; actually, she said it was a boar head. Anyway, neither the Napoleonic uniform nor the boar head have been returned."

"Did Taylor come into the shop at the same time the others did?" Liz asked. "The receipt said the twenty-ninth."

"No, she rented the costume on the thirtieth."

"When I first saw Taylor on Monday, she said Paula had called her to tell her about her brother's death. Do you think there's any way they could be in on it together?"

"Of course there's a chance," Betty said. "Duh."

"Granted, that was a stupid question," Liz replied.

"Even I know that," Kate said, laughing, then took a sip of her lemon water. "Between the two of you and your Agatha Christies, Sherlock Holmeses, and the like, I'm surprised you haven't already put this one to bed."

"I think we'll have a resolution soon. We'd better eat fast," Betty said. "Someone has to pass all this on to Agent Crowley."

Liz wasn't sure. "How about a compromise? I'll have my dad tell Crowley, but first, I want to talk to Taylor alone."

"Are you crazy?" Kate shouted. The couple at the next table glanced over at them.

"Taylor won't hurt me. Plus, I think Paula's the guilty one," Liz whispered, her voice barely audible over the crashing surf. "Don't you agree, Betty?"

"Seventy percent Paula, twenty percent Taylor, and the last ten percent Stevenson, Sally, or Hallie."

Liz took a sip of water and said, "I bet Sherlock, Marple and Poirot would go after the ten-percenters,"

"You can't be that naïve about being alone with Taylor," Kate said sternly. "After everything we just found out."

Betty leaned in. "Maybe we should get the food to go? Liz, you talk to Taylor, but we'll be waiting in the wings."

"If it makes you feel better."

"It does," Kate answered for Betty.

They paid for their food and headed north on A1A. The plan was to reconvene at the beach house at five thirty, after Liz and Betty returned from St. Benedict's.

When they were less than a mile from the Indialantic, Liz yelled, "Stop!"

Kate slammed on the brake and they swerved to a stop, the scent of burning rubber assailing them through the open windows. "What is it?" Kate asked. "A turtle? Good thing no one's behind me."

"No. Look through those gates to your right," Liz said.

"Cop cars." Kate said. "So?"

"So, that's the beach house Stevenson, Paula, and Hallie are staying at," Betty said. "Kate, pull over and inch up to the beginning of the driveway."

Kate did as she was told. They looked through the gates just as Agent Crowley and two officers came out the front door. In front of them was Paula Resnick. Her hands were behind her back in handcuffs.

"Looks like the blood on the nose ring matched Ms. Resnick's," Betty said.

Chapter 26

Betty and Liz were once again on the road. Now that Paula was arrested, there was a definite weight lifted from her shoulders: *dead weight*. It was doubtful Paula would make bail in a murder case, but there were still a lot of unanswered questions. She'd called Ryan as soon as they returned, and he'd told her he'd done all he could on his end and would put a call into Crowley. The good news was, he'd be catching a plane out of LaGuardia and flying into Melbourne in the early evening. Betty, Liz, and Ryan arranged to meet at eight in the gazebo—the three detectiveteers reunited for another murder case. Liz would stick to her plan of having Taylor over for dinner. And, in case she needed them, Betty and Kate would be hiding down on the beach. Not necessary, but comforting all the same.

Her father couldn't share any info about the details of Paula's arrest. Until Paula was formally arraigned, he had to stay out of it. Hopefully, Charlotte would be back hanging out at the Indialantic, and Liz would find relief from her guilty conscience. If it wasn't for her, the newly engaged couple wouldn't have had to meet in clandestine locations for the past couple of days. It was hard to believe Christmas had been less than two weeks ago. Thankfully, it appeared Liz would attend another family Christmas at the Indialantic. Not spend it eating Pierre's büche de Noël behind bars.

Chapter 27

As they passed the McLarty Treasure Museum on their way to St. Benedict's, Liz had a thought. "Betty, I don't know if I told you. But the first *supposed* day Taylor was here, Ryan took her to see my dad."

"About what?"

"Ryan said it was something about a horse. I think I know which horse. I just don't know what the legal problem was. Travis and Taylor's parents owned a racehorse who'd won the Preakness two years in a row. I think Silver Lightning was its name. The horse is now retired."

"I'll research it." Betty took out her iPad and tapped away on the screen. A few minutes later, she said, "Looks like Silver Lightning was sold to Mrs. Clayton Pendergrass of the Kentucky Pendergrasses. The sale went through last week. You should see the photo of Mrs. Pendergrass standing next to the horse with a mint julep in her hand. They share the same teeth and long face. See." She tilted the iPad toward Liz.

Liz laughed. "It's like people who resemble their pets. Do you think I look like Brontë?"

"No, *I* look more like Brontë because I have gray hair."

"And you're thin and petite," Liz added, "Petite, but you pack a punch."

When they were close to the entrance to St. Benedict's, Liz said, "I hope I can get Hallie alone."

"What do you plan on talking to her about?"

"I never asked her if any letters or email threats came to Travis recently. She said she oversaw all his correspondence. And of course, I want to get all the gory details on what went down with Paula's arrest."

"Of course. And you might want to ask if she ever saw Taylor and Paula together."

"You really think so?"

"Indubitably. That's why I think you should wait to meet with Taylor until after we go over what Ryan's uncovered."

"I don't know. I'm still on Auntie's side about Taylor's innocence. I'm banking it was Paula. If anyone is evil enough to partner with Paula, I'd pick Stevenson. Now, let's distract ourselves for three hours. I'm not even bringing in my phone."

"Well, I'm taking mine. And you might want to bring yours to record whatever Hallie tells you," Betty said.

"Sally tried to pull that on me this morning at Deli-casies. Seems the en vogue thing to do," she said, changing her mind and stowing her phone in her handbag.

A few minutes later, when Liz walked into the classroom, there was one empty desk. Hallie's. It had been hard to hide her disappointment, but she still managed to engage everyone in the day's assignment. After the class was dismissed, Liz went outside and saw someone sitting on the blue bomber's hood.

Hallie.

She bounded toward Liz, grabbed her arm, and said, "I wanted to talk to you before we left."

"Left for where?"

"New York. Stevenson and I have no reason to stay. I need to collect my last paycheck, then get home. I just wanted to thank you."

"For what?"

"You just seem like a good person. I'm glad to have met you. Even with all the stuff you had to go through with Mr. Osterman, including your scar, you never gave in to him. Paula deserves to be charged with his murder. She's mean and manipulative, and I'm happy to be rid of her."

"Do you know anything about what evidence they have against her? Were you there when Agent Crowley came?"

"Oh, I was there all right. I let them in when they showed me the search warrant. I also witnessed her walk of shame from the lanai straight into the sheriff's car. One of the officers had a clear plastic bag with brass rifle bullets in his hand. Something they found in her room."

"If you want to keep in touch, we could exchange cell numbers." Liz didn't want her to run away until she talked to Taylor and they knew for sure that Paula was guilty. It wasn't hard to plant evidence.

"I already have your number," Hallie said. "It was on the email I received after signing up for the retreat. I'll be sure to keep in touch."

Liz took out her phone. She opened her contacts and pressed the plus sign to add a new number. "Okay, shoot," Liz said, her finger poised about the phone screen.

Hallie hesitated, then finally recited her number. "Even though it's something Pastor Mullins at First Redeemer would say is unchristianlike, I'm glad Mr. Osterman's dead and won't be bothering you or anyone else anymore."

Liz held her gaze. "What did he do to hurt you, Hallie?"

She looked away. "Just the usual chauvinistic advances. Typical of his kind. He wasn't that bad, just self-absorbed." She turned to go.

"Wait. I have a quick question for you. Do you remember seeing any correspondence addressed to Trav...Mr. Osterman that was threatening in nature?"

Hallie paused for a moment and glanced up at the sun before answering. "No, I don't remember anything. I was in charge of all his mail, 'e' or otherwise." Then she turned and walked to beyond the gates to where a taxi waited.

Liz closed her open mouth. She felt like she'd been the victim of a drive-by farewell. Something was bothering her, and it took her a minute before she figured out what. Hallie's style of clothing was the opposite of what Liz had seen the past couple of days. She was dressed in ripped jeans and a low-cut tank top with the words TALBOT STREET ART FAIR printed over a skull with flowers coming out of its eye sockets.

She heard Betty call her name at the same time her phone rang. She answered.

"Elizabeth, it's Paula. I need you to meet me at county jail. I didn't do it. But I think I know who did..."

Chapter 28

The line went dead at the same time someone tapped Liz on the shoulder. She jumped.

"Betty! You won't believe this one!" Liz explained about the call from Paula, then hit Redial. All she got was a recording saying no incoming calls would be accepted.

They hurried to the car and got in, then Liz pulled through the open gates. The car's tires spit stones and seashells as they sped away. Then Liz told Betty about Hallie's exodus.

They were silent for a while, each trying to process the last few minutes.

Finally, Betty said, "Until you get a chance to talk to Paula, we have to keep looking at everyone as suspects."

She dropped Betty at the lobby entrance of the Indialantic. As she pulled away, she saw Aunt Amelia and Taylor in her great-aunt's cutting garden, each with a basket on their arm. They waved as she passed. For a second, Liz panicked. What if Taylor *was* her brother's killer? She didn't usually go with her gut, because her gut had betrayed her in the past. But this time she was trusting it. If Taylor had killed her brother, she hoped it was an accident.

Liz pulled into the Emporium's parking lot. She had to run into Delicasies and buy the ingredients needed to make a quick meal for her and Taylor's dinner. The wind was so strong, it rocked the caddy. The blue bomber felt like a boat on rough seas. It was already five thirty.

Originally, she'd planned to take off for Sharpes Correctional Facility in Cocoa, where Paula was being held, but her father had told her that prisoners in the county jail weren't allowed visitors. Only lawyers. He'd promised he'd see if he could arrange a visit. Paula might have been all those things on Hallie's nasty list, but as her father had taught her, everyone was presumed innocent until proven otherwise.

Once inside Deli-casies, she scored some fresh sea scallops, heavy cream, and a slab of Parmesan/Reggiano cheese. When Pops handed her the bag, he said, "You must take a container of strawberry/rhubarb crumble. Pierre sent over enough for the week. Although I sampled some and it might not last through tomorrow. It's that good."

"Crumble à la rhubarbe et aux fraises, one of my favs from Grand-Pierre," she said, "especially good because it's strawberry season." She told Pops that his grandson was due home soon. He'd raised a gray eyebrow but left whatever else he had on his mind unsaid. Liz had no idea how much Ryan had shared with his grandfather about his current girlfriend's ex-boyfriend's murder—even thinking it was a mouthful.

A half hour later, the table was set. Liz had the fettucine in the water, the sea scallops rinsed and seasoned with salt and pepper, just waiting on a clean paper towel to be put into sizzling butter and oil for their searing. Her partners in crime, Betty and Kate, were already down on the beach, dressed in sweatshirts. Kate had a fire permit in her pocket and kindling and logs ready for the strike of a match. All they had to do was wait for Liz to call after Taylor arrived.

The plan was to leave the phone on the counter so her two bodyguards could hear her and Taylor's conversation.

After waiting thirty minutes for Taylor to show up, Liz called her. It went straight to voice mail. Next, she called Aunt Amelia.

"I know she had a headache after we were in the garden. Stay on the phone and I'll go check."

She heard shuffling and a slight panting that told her Aunt Amelia was climbing the circular staircase. She refused to take the service elevator off the kitchen, not even after she'd sprained an ankle last fall kickboxing.

Liz turned off the gas burner, reconsidered, and threw the scallops in the pan. She continued to make the dish while waiting for Aunt Amelia to locate Taylor. After she drained the pasta, Aunt Amelia spoke into the phone. "She's in her room with the lights off. Sleeping. I think we should let her be. I'll tell her you called when she gets up."

"Thanks, Auntie." So much for their little mousetrap. She called Betty, and they came up from the beach toting blankets, bags of marshmallows, chocolate bars, and graham crackers.

After dropping their coats on the chair by the door, Kate sniffed the air. "I didn't have time for dinner. Looks like Taylor's loss is our gain."

"That's another way of looking at it," Liz said. "There's more than enough."

Betty took a seat on a barstool at the counter. "Until we talk to Ryan about what he found on Taylor, we should look at this as divine intervention."

Kate joined Betty at the counter. Liz piled creamy alfredo-coated linguine topped with five seared sea scallops on top of two plates, finishing them off with freshly grated cheese and snipped parsley. Then placed a plate in front of each of them. Grabbing two prepared bowls of mixed green salads from the fridge, she brought them to the counter. "Would you prefer to eat at the table?"

"No, this is fine," Betty said. "More than fine."

"Where's your plate?" Kate asked.

"I can't eat. Too much angst in my belly."

"Everything happens for a reason," wise Betty said. "Fix a small plate and join us. You need your energy. I think after we talk to Ryan, we should go seek out Taylor. You told me her brother's body will be released tomorrow. Time is of the essence."

Liz fixed a plate and joined them. Then she told them about how she wasn't allowed to visit Paula at Sharpes Correctional Facility

"Maybe it's for the best," Kate mused. "I only met her twice, but I don't trust her. Did that photo of her most recent phone calls pan out to anything?"

"I turned that over to Betty and Ryan," Liz said.

Betty turned to Kate. "There were a couple of calls from Paula to Mr. Osterman on New Year's Eve and New Year's Day. Liz had given me Stevenson's and Taylor's numbers; they weren't on the list."

"Why would Paula call Travis on New Year's Day if she killed him New Year's Eve? Maybe his sister did kill him," Kate groaned.

"Paula could have called his number as a cover-up. Knowing the Sheriff's Department would check her phone," Betty answered.

"I just texted Hallie's number to Ryan, but we can also check it." Liz took her plate to the sink, grabbed her phone, and recited Hallie's phone number."

Betty tapped her phone screen. "Nope, Hallie's number isn't on Paula's recent call list. Kate, you mind giving me a lift to the Indialantic? It's getting pretty blustery out there. I need to change before we meet Ryan. It seems we have a lot to discuss."

"Of course," Kate said, glancing at her watch. "I have a date with Alex anyway. But I expect lots of updates." Alex was a world-class international surfer. When he wasn't a volunteer firefighter for Barrier Island Fire and Rescue, he taught surfing down at the Sebastian Inlet Beach. With firefighting in their blood, Ryan and Alex had hit it off immediately.

After walking Betty and Kate to the door, barely able to close it because of the wind, she turned to Brontë, who was still licking her lips from one of Kate's scallops. Liz had been surprised the finicky kitten had eaten from Kate's hand. Kate had a way with animals. Like she did with children. Treating them as equals. She put the dinner dishes in the dishwasher and hung the frying pan on its hook. It was an hour until they were supposed to meet in the gazebo. She glanced out the window at the huge waves buffeting the shore. The tide was high, and she knew there was a full moon somewhere, hiding behind sooty clouds. The thought of the full moon brought her back to New Year's Eve. How easily things could change in an instant. Something she knew better than anyone, she thought, tracing the scar on her cheek. "Buck up, Elizabeth Holt," she said out loud.

Brontë gave her a questioning glance.

She needed to be proactive and marched to her office, glancing longingly at the open laptop. She was so close to finishing her novel. Only one more day at the monastery; then she could get back to it. She removed a pad of paper and a pen from the desk drawer and wrote down a list of things that were bothering her. She'd agreed with Betty: They had to confront Taylor before she left the island—headache or not. She checked her phone for any collect calls from Sharpes Correctional Facility Nothing. Why had Paula called her of all people? Because Liz knew the person Paula was accusing? Or was it just a desperate woman's plea for help?

The wind chimes on the deck smashed against one another, making for a less-than- soothing melody as she wrote down all the loose ends they needed to address at the gazebo. It wasn't a long list. Was it a moot point anyway? Should they just stroll over to Squidly's for karaoke night instead of meeting at the gazebo? After all, Paula was behind bars.

She had an uneasy feeling they'd missed something. And she just couldn't shake it off.

Chapter 29

The wind was fierce. Walking toward the gazebo, Liz's long wild hair escaped its clip, blocking her vision. She held a lantern, not to help her navigate, because she knew the way blindfolded, but more as a beacon in case the bogeyman or a mischievous spriggan came calling. Near the Native American gravesite, she startled at the sight of a dozen stargazer lilies in the area where Travis's body had lain. It made her wonder what the historical society thought about the recent happenings at the Indialantic by the Sea Hotel. Newly deemed a historical landmark, she prayed they wouldn't rescind their approval.

"Liz-z-z-z."

Was she hallucinating? Had someone just whispered her name? She held up the lantern and twirled around in a circle, swiping the bangs from her eyes with her free hand. No one was there. A ghost? Travis's ghost? A Native American ghost? She propelled herself forward toward the direction of the gazebo. A figure came toward her.

"Ryan!" she called out.

He ran to her and they embraced. When they parted, he said, "You're shaking."

"It's chilly, Mr. Stone. In case you haven't noticed."

"A jacket might help."

"Mine are still packed away from when I moved from New York."

He grabbed her to him, then led her up the gazebo steps. "Betty's here. Don't you think we should reconvene somewhere warmer? The library in front of a fire, for instance?"

"Not a good idea," she shouted over the wind. "Taylor's there. We could go to your place, the caretaker's cottage?"

"No way. Then you'd see my kitchen, and I told you, no viewing pleasure until after I make my chowder."

She hadn't realized how much she'd missed him until she saw his solid six-foot-three frame and handsome face in the light of the lantern. She didn't have butterflies in her stomach, more like hummingbirds. "Let's get to it!" she said as they stepped inside the gazebo.

After last October's hurricane that wasn't, Aunt Amelia had restored the white wrought-iron-framed gazebo to its former glory by adding hurricane-resistant panes of glass. Her great-aunt had built the gazebo, which to Liz was more like a summer house, to replicate the one in *The Sound of Music*. White wooden benches with white cushions followed the perimeter of the space. Potted orchids and palms were arranged in each corner. The center of the gazebo was left bare in case a pair of lovestruck kids or seniors wanted to dance under the glass ceiling in the moonlight. There was no moon tonight.

Betty was seated on the bench with her iPad on her lap. Ryan flipped the light switch, and the gazebo glowed with soft light coming from four outside lampposts.

"I don't know if we want to illuminate the fact we're inside," Liz said. "We're sitting ducks for anyone looking out the windows from the Indialantic." She sat next to Betty, pulled out her phone, and opened a photo of the notes she'd written filled with their loose ends.

Ryan sat next to her. "It's not like you to be so sissyish. What gives?"

"I swear, someone called my name when I was close to where Travis was found."

"Probably just Athena, or the wind," Betty said.

"I know the difference between Athena's screech and a human's," Liz said. Twenty years ago, she'd named the great-horned owl, who'd lived on the Indialantic's property, Athena after Grand-Pierre told her the story in Greek mythology about the wise goddess and her love of owls.

"And someone's putting flowers on the Ais chief's grave," Liz added.

"Okay," Betty said. "To be on the safe side, let's turn off the streetlamps and use our electronic devices instead. We can email or text what we have after we're done touching base. I don't think Paula's going anywhere soon."

"But Taylor might be," Liz said.

Liz and Betty told Ryan about their trip to Vero Beach and their confirmation that Taylor had been the one dressed as Napoleon the pig on New Year's Eve.

"Oh, and Hallie told me she's leaving Melbourne Beach," Liz added. "And she said as far as she knew, Travis never received any threats by phone, email, or text."

"I assume that means Stevenson is free to leave the island also," Betty said.

"Ah, Mr. Charles," Ryan interjected. "You were spot-on, Liz, about *Stevie* and Osterman frequenting the Platinum Club. Unfortunately, I was kicked out before I could get more info or place a bet." Liz's lantern illuminated his roughish grin. "However," he said, continuing, "I did pass the gambling angle on to my friend, and there's a small team from the NYPD coordinating with Agent Crowley. The only problem is, now that they have their lady, I doubt there'll be more investigating by the authorities. I was also able to visit with Taylor's housekeeper on the way to the airport," Ryan said. "If Mrs. Sullivan wasn't in Connecticut on the night of the murder, I'd list her as a suspect. She's not too fond of Osterman. But very protective of Taylor. Mrs. Sullivan confirmed that Taylor got everything in their parents' will. She also told me that the horse, Silver Lightning, had recently been sold illegally without Taylor's knowledge. Taylor was furious when she found out and told Mrs. Sullivan she was going to seek out her brother and sue him if she had to. The housekeeper thought Taylor was in Kentucky in an attempt to buy back Silver Lightning, not at the Indialantic."

Liz leaned in closer to Ryan's warm body. "Anything on the older woman who showed up at the Connecticut house who Taylor said her parents talked to?"

"Or a restraining order filed by Mr. Osterman?" Betty added.

"As for the visit to the Ostermans' home, Mrs. Sullivan collaborated the woman's appearance. Said she was in her fifties, looked very down and out, and was screaming and carrying on. The interesting thing was, when she left, the woman had a smile on her face." Ryan looked down at his phone. "Osterman did have a restraining order on someone, but as of yet, I can't access police files to get a name. I have your father working on it. I sent him a report on everything I found out in New York and he's going to pass it on to Crowley. So far, they haven't found Osterman's will. A contact at the NYPD said they're not sure he even had one."

"Probably thought he'd live forever," Liz said, shivering. "No doubt if a will isn't found, Taylor will be the recipient."

Ryan had already given Liz his jacket. Now he wrapped his arm around her and said, "I know you told me Hallie said they found bullets to the rifle in Paula's room. If they come back with her prints, I'd say her goose is cooked."

"And if they don't..." Liz said.

"Another reason we need to confront Taylor," Betty said. "I found something interesting before I came here." Betty tilted her iPad screen toward them. "Liz, what's Travis's middle initial? And how old was he when he died?"

"His middle initial was P for Peter. Travis Peter Osterman. And he was..." It was a good thing she couldn't remember what year he'd been born, especially when she noticed Ryan's scowl. She was sure he'd had enough of Travis Osterman to last a lifetime. "I think he was thirty-nine or forty. Why?"

"Look." Betty brought the screen closer to them, and they saw the initials TPO magnified, looking like they'd been written in the sand. "The frontispiece of the book had been ripped off, but I could make out the indentation of someone's initials that transferred onto the top of the title page." Betty swiped to another photo, showing *Animal Farm*'s copyright page. "The publication dates jive with when Travis would have been about thirteen years old. The age most kids read the book in school."

Liz thought about the book. It was written by George Orwell as a parody on the Russian Revolution, Communism, and Stalin. Also, in the book, was a tragic tale of a lovable, mistreated workhorse. "What are we waiting for? I say we should all go and confront Taylor together. There's still no concrete proof she killed her brother. But she did lie."

"Ryan, what about Hallie? Anything on her before coming to Charles and Charles?" Betty asked.

"I had Stacy talk to the receptionist who covers for both Stevenson and his father about her hiring. She said they'd had open interviews, with Osterman giving his final approval. Hallie went in, and the receptionist was told immediately to tell everyone in the waiting room to go home. Like you said, Liz, Hallie must have reminded him of you. She'd only been an intern for about a month and had recently moved to Manhattan. I know you just sent me her phone number. I'll check it out when I get back to the caretaker's cottage."

Betty stood and said to Liz, "I think before any more digging, you and Ryan should go find Taylor. I don't know her enough to be confronting her. It doesn't mean I won't be in the other room, listening to your conversation with a glass held to the wall."

"Oh, Betty," Liz said, "that's teenage mystery detecting. I'm sure you'd rather I leave an open phone line."

"That would work, too. And Nancy Drew detecting is what I used to discern the book belonged to Mr. Osterman because of the imprint of his initials transferring to the next page," Betty added, sticking out her tongue.

"Touché, Miss Lawson," Liz said.

Chapter 30

"I think we should leave her be," Aunt Amelia said. "I've given her some tea to relieve the stress and we can always talk about things in the morning."

"But Auntie," Liz groaned, "Taylor might have killed her brother. We have proof she was here on New Year's Eve, rented that disturbing pig costume, and was seen arguing with Travis before he was murdered."

"I know, my darling. She told me all about it after Susannah found the costume in the bathtub of the Oceana Suite."

"She did?" Ryan said. "What was Taylor's explanation?"

"Hush, now. Let's move away from the door and go down to the lobby. I'll tell you everything." Aunt Amelia looked to the end of the hallway and said, "And you can come out, Betty. And join us."

Betty sheepishly popped her head into view, then came to meet them at the top of the staircase.

Aunt Amelia wore one of her colorful caftans and had a turban covering her hair. Her face was covered in thick white cold cream. It looked like someone had thrown a pie in her face, like they did daily on the old children's show from the '60s she'd had a guest appearance on, *Lunch with Soupy Sales*.

"What did Taylor tell you?" Ryan asked.

"It's something of a tragic tale," Amelia said. "But there's no cause for alarm because, as I said before, Taylor is an innocent. Her brother," she glanced at Liz, "not so much. Where to begin…" she said a tad dramatically.

Her cold-cream-slathered face made it hard for Liz to keep her focus. "Auntie, let's start with the book *Animal Farm* and Napoleon; then you can tell us what her reason was for lying."

"*Animal Farm* was her brother's favorite book. Remember, there was a big age gap between them. It seems Travis relished reading it to Taylor over and over again, knowing Taylor's love of animals, especially horses. Well, years passed, and their parents died in a car crash. Taylor was left their estate, which included a horse named Silver Lightning."

"Yes, we know all about the horse," Betty said, trying to move things along.

"Well, Silver Lightning was Taylor's favorite pet. She went to Travis's penthouse to tell him she was filing a lawsuit against him if he didn't buy back the horse immediately. He'd told her that would happen when hell freezes over, then pushed her toward the door. As she was leaving, she saw luggage in the vestibule. He told her a cab was waiting and he was on his way to convince you of something, Lizzy. Taylor said she came here to warn you."

"I'm sorry, Auntie, but that gives her more of a motive," Liz said. "Someone needs to guard her door."

"That's not necessary, Liz," Taylor said.

She'd appeared like an apparition. How long had she been standing there?

"There's more," Taylor said, collapsing onto a wicker peacock chair. Dark circles ringed her eyes, similar to Aunt Amelia's Miss Havisham at the Literary Ball. "I got a call from one of my mother's friends saying she saw a piece of my mother's jewelry at an estate jewelry store on Madison Avenue. I went to the safe and found her jewelry gone. All I had left was this ring, because I'd been wearing it." She held up her right hand and showed the aquamarine. Then she burst into tears.

Aunt Amelia rushed to her side, and they waited until she quieted.

"After I saw the jewelry was gone, I went into Travis's childhood room. His favorite copy of *Animal Farm* was there. I hated that book, so I grabbed it. I wanted to confront him about all the nasty things he'd done to me in the past. But selling Silver Lightning was the worst. Saying he was going after you, Liz, just added to my anger." Taylor looked in Liz's direction. "You know how he forbade me to have a pet. I wanted him to take the money from Mother's jewelry and buy back my horse. When I got here the day before New Year's Eve, I heard about the Literary Ball. I found a costume shop, the only one around, and combined two costumes into one. Napoleon Bonaparte and a Mardi Gras pig to make the character from *Animal Farm*. I thought I'd scare Travis as much as he'd scared me.

"I confronted him in the garden on New Year's Eve. We had words and were supposed to meet for lunch on New Year's Day for a compromise. But he never showed, so I left Melbourne Beach. Then I found out he was dead from a call by his agent. I was scared they'd think I'd done it, so I came back pretending I'd been in Connecticut. You have to believe me." She looked at them with pleading in her eyes. "My grief is real. If I hadn't left him in the garden, he'd be alive today."

"Didn't you realize the police would check your alibi and flight info?" Liz asked.

"I didn't fly out of New York. I originally flew to Kentucky to see Silver Lightning when I found out about Mother's jewelry, I rented a car and drove down here. When Travis didn't show up on New Year's Day, I drove back to my hotel in Kentucky. Then I got a call from Paula and took a flight from Louisville to Orlando. I told Aunt Amelia earlier that I'd go to the police in the morning. I didn't kill him. I could never kill him."

Aunt Amelia pulled her up from the chair, saying, "Come. Come. Let's get back to bed. I'll top off your tea and you'll be asleep in no time."

As they walked toward the staircase, Taylor turned and said, "I'm sorry, Liz, for everything he did to you. But you must know I had nothing to do with his death."

Did she know that?

Chapter 31

After Taylor and Aunt Amelia left the room, the consensus was to leave everything until the morning because there was no real proof Taylor killed her brother. Ryan was exhausted from his day of travel and left for the caretaker's cottage. Betty went up to her rooms to analyze all the latest findings. Before leaving for home, Liz sought out Susannah to ask her about discovering the costume in Taylor's suite. Susannah confirmed what Aunt Amelia had told her about it being in the bathtub. Liz only had one problem with the story: Why had Susannah been in the Oceana Suite's bathroom? Surely not to clean it? That chore was always left for Greta. Or, in a pinch, Liz. After questioning her, Susannah had stuck out her pointy chin and said, "As assistant manager, it is my job to check my employee's work."

"Wouldn't Greta have found the costume days ago when she cleaned the bathtub? Fess up, Miss Shay. Where'd you really find it?"

"Well, I never!" she'd said, turning away from Liz.

"Find anything else in Taylor's room you want to share?"

"If I had," she had said, choosing her words carefully, "I would have reported it to Amelia, like I did that disgusting costume. Something's not right with someone who would choose something so garish and disturbing to wear to a charity ball. After I told Amelia about the pig head, she said I shouldn't tell anyone else. Now she owes me." Then she'd walked away.

Now, rehashing the scene, Liz couldn't believe the gall behind Susannah's last comment. Aunt Amelia owed *her*? Susannah owed Aunt Amelia. Big-time.

Back at the beach house, Liz tried to fall asleep but couldn't. She moved to the sofa dragging a snoozing Brontë with her. With everything going on, she'd forgotten about the reading assignments from the writers' retreat. She rifled through the papers until she came to Hallie's. The assignment was to choose a room that had a lot of meaning in your life and use all five senses in describing it. Hallie had used them all. She'd chosen her grandfather's bedroom after he'd passed away.

The writing was raw, and Liz could feel the loss Hallie experienced with each memory assigned to the objects in the room. The last object sent Liz's own senses reeling. She jumped up, catapulting Brontë from her lap to the rug. Brontë landed on her feet and looked up at Liz in worry. "It's okay, little one. Sorry I startled you, but Mommy's got something she has to do."

She padded in bare feet to her office. The wind had picked up a notch, bringing with it sand that scratched at her windows like a banshee wanting to get in. After turning on her laptop, she immediately searched the internet using a few keywords. Ten minutes later, she texted Ryan she was on her way to the caretaker's cottage. She put on a hooded sweatshirt and grabbed a flashlight.

Brontë looked confused as to why her mother would ever want to go out in the middle of the night in such weather.

Liz wondered herself.

Chapter 32

Liz jogged along the path that followed the south side of the Indialantic. As she neared Aunt Amelia's cutting garden, she saw a light. And it wasn't from a firefly. Switching off her flashlight, she moved toward it. Then paused, took out her phone, and shared her location with Ryan.

Just in case.

The wind sent palm fronds and leaves hurtling in all directions. She crept closer to the bobbing light. Standing on the spot where Travis's body had been found was a woman dressed in a long dark raincoat. As if she knew Liz was nearby, she glanced in her way. The flashlight in the woman's hand was pointed up, illuminating her face. The woman's hair and eyes were dark.

Liz knew when to approach a murderer and when to retreat. She backed up until she was near the garden wall, then passed through the trellised opening, increasing her pace with each step. She turned toward the lagoon and the path that would lead to Ryan's. Light glowed from inside the caretaker's cottage. She broke into a run, tripped on an exposed tree root, and screamed one of Barnacle Bob's curses on the way down.

After getting into a sitting position, she felt her left ankle. The pain was unbearable. She knew she'd broken it. Whimpering, she pulled out her cell phone.

"I wouldn't do that, Liz," a dark-haired, brown-eyed Hallie said.

"I'm injured, Hallie. Have some compassion." Liz took out her flashlight and aimed it up at her face. It was the same person she'd found online in a photo standing next to Sgt. McPherson's daughter at a church picnic.

Hallie shielded her eyes and said, "Where was Travis Osterman's compassion for my mother? I'll give him credit, he came through in the end. If he would've come through sooner, he'd still be alive. And I wouldn't have to do what you're going to witness in the next few minutes." Hallie aimed her flashlight to the bank of the lagoon and took a step toward it. Liz tried to open the messaging feature on her phone just as Hallie glanced back. "I'll take that."

She came back and wrenched the phone out of Liz's hand.

"What do you mean, if Travis could have come through sooner?"

Hallie ignored her and walked fifty feet to the edge of the shore. Liz followed her movement with her flashlight. Once she reached the bank, Hallie bent down and started filling her raincoat pockets with large river rocks. Liz felt the panic rise. Hallie planned on forcing Liz into the lagoon wearing the rock-filled coat. "Why did you kill Travis, Hallie? Because he'd plagiarized your grandfather's journals?"

"That was only part of it. He wouldn't give back my grandfather's things to my mother. She had to beg for them. He refused, then put a restraining order on her. After his novel came out—or should I say my grandfather's— Mother went to Travis's family home and asked his parents to convince him to do the right thing. She'd read all her father's, my grandfather's, journals and knew that in some places, he'd stolen passages word-for-word. She tried to get them to force their son to do the right thing. Instead, the Ostermans made a deal and sent her a check every month. Then, after they died in a car crash, the money stopped. Mother went to Travis's apartment and told him about the deal his parents had made. He pushed her. Physically pushed her into the elevator and sent her on her way. He never even mentioned my grandfather in his acknowledgments. After that, I read everything I could about Travis Osterman. Which included your story. When I found a photo of you, my friend said we had similar features. That's when I got the idea to try to look like you, work myself into his confidence, and find proof he'd plagiarized Grandpa's work.

"When I overheard him talking to Paula about my mother's visit, that's when I lost it. One morning when I was at his penthouse going over his itinerary, he mentioned going to Melbourne Beach. He even had me help pack Grandpa's uniform and rifle. I couldn't believe he planned on wearing it, including all his medals of honor. Later, I searched his penthouse and found the box of bullets and brought them with me. I didn't have a concrete plan then...." She stopped for a moment, staring across the dark waters of the lagoon, then turned back to Liz. "New Year's Eve morning I put a few bullets in the rifle when I saw it leaning against his dresser at the timeshare. My plan was to fire the rifle near enough to scare him, knowing the fireworks would mask the sound. Grandpa taught me how to shoot when I was a kid. I knew how to miss.

"At the ball, after I put Sally in a cab, I doubled back and saw Travis and Paula fighting. She slapped him. He slapped her back, then she stormed off. I waited to see what he planned to do. He called Paula on the phone and apologized for getting out of hand, promising to take care of you, just as they'd planned. The rest of the story is irrelevant now. Let's just say we had words. The rifle was leaning on the back of the garden bench; I grabbed it and fired into the oak tree. He lunged. We struggled. It went off. And the rest is history."

"So, it was an accident," Liz said, the pain in her ankle almost rendering her mute. "Then why do you have to kill me?"

"Kill you? I'm not going to kill you. I'm going to kill myself. I just heard from my mother that a bank account had been opened in her name with a deposit from a Travis Osterman. I can't live with myself. And now that I know she'll have money to cover her hospice bills, I won't have to worry about her final days." She bent and picked up another rock, more like a boulder, and cradled it in her arms like a newborn. Then she slowly took steps backward toward the inky water.

"You don't have to do this, Hallie. You said it was an accident. You and Travis struggled. I'll help you. My dad will help you."

"You're a caring person, Liz. I enjoyed trying to be like you for a while. Travis picked me as his intern even though I didn't have any credentials. All because I looked like you. He must've realized what he'd lost."

Liz didn't know what to do with that statement.

Hallie continued, "Even Pastor Mullins wouldn't hold out much hope for my soul now." She deliberately stepped into the water, the bottom of the raincoat disappearing from the weight of the rocks.

Liz had figured out it had been Hallie who'd killed Travis after she'd read Hallie's paper about a room that meant a lot to her. She'd described her grandfather's room, which included WWII photos, medals of honor, and, most importantly, a Garand M1 rifle. Maybe Hallie had wanted to be caught? Liz also remembered what had been written on Hallie's T-shirt when she saw her earlier at St. Benedict's. She'd looked up the Talbot Street Art Fair and seen it took place in Indianapolis. Then she'd searched a Pastor Mullins at First Redeemer Church in Indianapolis and found a photo of Hallie with her mother at the funeral of Sgt. Michael McPherson. A brunette Hallie with brown eyes.

After she saw the photo, Liz thought back to the letter she'd seen on Travis's desk in Manhattan from Sgt. McPherson's daughter with an

Indiana postmark, and the name Margaret Elliot. After an easy public record's search, she'd found that Elliot was Hallie's mother's last name from a second marriage. Margaret's last name from her first marriage was Corman, and she had a child named Hallie.

Liz aimed her light at Hallie. All that was visible was her head crowning the water. Holding the flashlight in one hand, Liz started a slow crawl toward the lagoon. "Hallie, please come back," she shouted.

Hallie's voice was barely audible over the wind, "Liz, find the journals. Show the world what a hero my grandfather was."

"We'll find them together," Liz screamed. But it was too late, Hallie slowly disappeared from her flashlight's beam.

Suddenly, Ryan came galloping into view. Liz shouted, "Hallie! She killed Travis! She's in the lagoon. Save her!" She aimed her light on where she'd seen Hallie disappear. Another flashlight's beam also swept the area. Ryan jumped in, disappeared for too long, then reemerged.

In his arms was Hallie. Without her raincoat.

Susannah came over to Liz. She moved her flashlight over Liz's body, stopping at her ankle. "Come," she said. "Let me help you up. The Sheriff's Department will be here any second."

Chapter 33

It was the last week in January, and the night of the final performance of *The Mousetrap* at the Melbourne Beach Theatre. The play had ended, and the spotlight found the real star of Agatha Christie's play—the actress who'd played the irritating Mrs. Boyle. She bowed to thunderous applause, and Liz and her father tossed a couple of dozen roses onto the stage.

When the curtain first rose at the opening of the play, Liz had nearly fallen off her front-row-center seat. She'd looked to her right and seen a twinkle in her father's and Grand-Pierre's eyes. They'd known. Then she'd glanced at Ryan, Betty, and Kate to her left and seen they were as surprised as she. On stage, sitting on the sofa, had been the play's lead, Mrs. Rolston, but she wasn't being played by Amelia Eden Holt. Instead, they saw Susannah Shay. Liz had looked down at her playbill, and sure enough, it said her great-aunt was playing Mrs. Rolston, with Bastian Caruthers as Mr. Rolston.

At the end of the first act, when Aunt Amelia made her entrance as Mrs. Boyle, the play picked up, and her great-aunt not too subtly stole the limelight from Susannah. Liz almost felt sorry for the woman. It appeared Aunt Amelia had turned over the lead role as penance.

And Liz thought she knew why.

The night Hallie had tried to kill herself, Susannah had seen the lights from her suite and decided to investigate. Susannah met up with Ryan, who, after wondering what was taking Liz so long, had checked Liz's GPS and was on his way to track her down.

While Ryan waited with Hallie for the police and an ambulance, Susannah had whisked Liz off to the closest hospital in her Ford Escort.

After Liz's broken ankle was set, Susannah appointed herself Liz's Florence Nightingale, waiting on her hand-to-ankle until she was able to hobble along on crutches. Even on the way to the hospital, Susannah had shown her concern by traveling a *whole* five miles over the speed limit. "In rare occasions," she'd said, nervously glancing in the rearview mirror, "rules are made to be broken, Elizabeth. The keyword being *rare*." Susannah even provisioned a queen-size bed to be moved to Aunt Amelia's Enlightenment Parlor because it was on the first floor. She didn't want Liz to climb any bothersome steps. On the first night in the Enlightenment Parlor, Liz woke and found Susannah snoring in the chair next to her.

Now that Liz's ankle had healed, she had a new, somewhat-cloying friend—Susannah Shay. Over the course of her convalescence, Liz had learned the reason Susannah was the wounded bird her great-aunt alluded to. When Susannah had first been married, she and her husband adopted an infant daughter. They named her Amy, after Susannah's distant cousin, the queen of etiquette Amy Vanderbilt. When Amy was only two months old, her birth mother came looking for her. The court ruled in the birth mother's favor, and mother and child left the US to live in Canada. From then on, Susannah had locked up her emotions, only turning to the pages of an etiquette book for guidance. No one had been allowed to see the chink in her shiny armor until she confided in Aunt Amelia, and then, in a weak moment, to Liz.

Recently, to Liz's relief, Bastian Caruthers had been consuming most of Susannah's time. He'd dumped his girlfriend in California and won back Susannah's heart, albeit a very guarded heart. Liz was sure Susannah got weekly reports on Bastian from one of her undercover sources. Once Susannah had said to Liz, "I want to apologize for my behavior at Squidly's when you caught Bastian and me in a delicate situation."

Liz had said, "It's okay, Sue. I'll let that one slide."

Susannah had ratcheted her head toward Liz and burst out laughing. "You are a fresh young thing. Aren't you?"

Chapter 34

"No excuses about your poor ankle," Ryan said as he doggy paddled up to her. "The doctor said you're completely healed. Look perky, and let's try to remember everything the Big Kahuna taught you."

The Big Kahuna was the nickname given to Alex, Kate's new love interest, because of his status as a world-class surfer and his resemblance to the actor who'd played the Big Kahuna in one of Aunt Amelia's and Liz's favorite old movies, *Gidget*.

"But I won the bet. Why do I have to do this? Can't I hop on your board like Gidget did with Moondoggie? You know, the part where she almost drowned. Which I'm likely to do in this rough surf." Saltwater filled her mouth at her last word.

"Look over yonder," he said, pointing. "Your eighty-year-old auntie just found the perfect swell."

Ziggy's board was close to Aunt Amelia's, most likely to keep an eye on her. Or maybe she was keeping an eye on him.

"You do know I used to surf before I went to college? Every islander knows how," she said, splashing him. What she didn't say was that that was a long time ago, and she wasn't the same daredevil teen she'd once been.

A hundred feet out, Kate and Alex seemed perfectly matched as they rode the waves. Wiping out at the same time, then emerging from the foam with huge smiles on their faces.

Betty waited on shore under a cabana, proofreading the first book in her London Chimney Sweep mystery series. Pierre sat next to her reading a Sherlock Holmes tale. It seemed Betty was expanding his palette to include other detective novels.

It was the end of February and the case was closed on the murder of Travis Osterman. Hallie had confessed to killing him, and that it was she who'd sent the letter to Stevenson and put it in Liz's mail slot. She'd set her own mousetrap. Travis had played into it, but she'd also gotten caught.

Paula had been released from Sharpes, and Taylor exonerated. Sally Beaman had had nothing to do with Travis's death. But if it wasn't for her, he'd never have come to the island, nor would Hallie. But who's to say Hallie wouldn't have confronted him at some other opportune time?

Liz was sure Stevenson Charles was guilty of something; she just didn't know what.

They'd found Travis's will, and Taylor had been the beneficiary. He must have had some feelings for his sister. All the old copies of *The McAvoy Brothers* were pulled off the shelves in bookstores and cyberspace, then reissued as *Written by Travis Osterman, Based on the Journals of Sgt. Michael "Mickey" McPherson.*

Per Stacy Sorenson, Stevenson was no longer at Charles & Charles after his father found out about his attempt to blackmail Liz into filing a lawsuit against the airing of the television movie *Bloodstained Love*. Stevenson was the one who owed Travis money from gambling. Which was also the reason Stevenson couldn't sue Travis for breaking his contract about the TV movie after Travis threatened to tell Stevenson's father about the gambling. Travis and Stevenson were two blackmailing peas in a pod.

Paula admitted to penning half of *Blood and Glass* after she saw Travis's poor attempts at writing. Whether Paula knew he'd plagiarized *The McAvoy Brothers*, no one knew. But Liz would bet she did. Paula's literary agency was in foreclosure because of her lost investment in *Bloodstained Love*. Most of Paula's authors had moved to Liz's small literary agency. Liz knew they were in good hands.

Liz hadn't needed to file any lawsuit to stop the movie from airing because Travis's heir and sister, Taylor, pulled the project and paid back all his creditors with money from her parents' estate. Agent Crowley had shown Taylor the photo Liz had found of Hallie and her mother, and Taylor confirmed it was the same woman who had come to her home in Connecticut. Taylor also bought back Silver Lightning and agreed that a certain percentage of all future copies sold of *The McAvoy Brothers* would go to a veteran's charity in Sgt. McPherson's name.

After Liz managed to stand on the surfboard for three quarters of a millisecond, they called it quits. A second pot of Ryan's chowder was waiting in his new kitchen, and they had to go over the plans for the upcoming wedding at the Indialantic between a psychic and a warlock.

The chowder was a recipe for delight, the wedding a recipe for disaster.

"So, how's your life going, Ms. Holt?"

"Pretty darn fine, Mr. Stone. Thanks in large part to you."

"Congrats on mailing in your final manuscript of *An American in Cornwall.*"

"Thank you, kind sir."

"Love you," he said with one of his mischievous grins.

"Love you," she answered.

Because she did.

Acknowledgments

I'd like to once again acknowledge how lucky I am to have Dawn Dowdle at Blue Ridge Literary Agency as my agent and friend. Martin Brio, my editor at Lyrical Press, thanks for all your input and encouragement. And to Chef Lon Ontremba for his wonderful recipes under the guise of Chef Pierre Montague. Once again, I'd like to thank Karen M. Owen for her help and friendship. As always none of this would be possible without my family, friends, and loyal readers.

About the Author

Kathleen Bridge is the author of the By the Sea Mystery series and the Hamptons Home and Garden Mystery series, published by Berkley. She started her writing career working at *The Michigan State University News* in East Lansing, Michigan. A member of Sisters in Crime and Mystery Writers of America, she is also the author and photographer of an antiques reference guide, *Lithographed Paper Toys, Books, and Games*. She teaches creative writing in addition to working as an antiques and vintage dealer in Melbourne, Florida. Kathleen blissfully lives on a barrier island. Readers can visit her on the web at www.kathleenbridge.com

Classic Desserts with a French Twist from the Chef Pierre Montague Cookbook

Crème Brûlée

Serves 8
Preheat oven to 350.

> 8 egg yolks
> 1 c. sugar
> 1 tsp. vanilla
> 1 qt. whipping cream
> ¼ c. Amaretto (or to taste) or 1 tsp. almond extract

Combine yolks, sugar, and vanilla. Beat until light. Fold in cream and Amaretto.

Pour into 8 greased ramekins. Place ramekins in a large roasting pan filled with ½ inch of hot water.

Bake 45–50 minutes. Chill. Before serving, heat oven to broil or high, sprinkle crème brûlée liberally with brown sugar. Place back in roasting pan and broil until sugar is caramelized—3– 5 minutes (get as close to the heat as you can get).

Optional: Top with berries of your choice.

Chocolate Mousse

Serves 8

8 oz. semisweet chocolate, chopped
1 tsp. instant espresso or instant coffee
2 c. chilled heavy cream

Put chocolate and espresso in a bowl that fits into a saucepan. Take a water-filled pan and put bowl inside it. Bowl cannot touch the water. Over medium heat, melt the chocolate/espresso, about 5 minutes (water should simmer, not boil). Remove from heat and set aside. In large bowl, beat cream on medium speed until slightly thickened (30 seconds). Add chocolate mixture, beat another minute until soft peaks form. Spoon mixture into 8 serving cups or glasses (I prefer sundae glasses). Chill until ready to serve.

Alternatively, chill in 1 bowl, pass at table, and have guests serve themselves.

Optional: Top with whipped cream.

Crêpes Suzette

Makes 9–12 crepes. Serves 4–6, 2 crepes per person.

Crêpes
¼ c. pancake mix (Krusteaz Buttermilk pancake mix is Chef's favorite)
¼ c. all-purpose flour
½ c. plus 2 Tbs. water
1 egg, beaten
1 Tbs. butter, melted
1 Tbs. Grand Marnier* (orange-flavored liquor or orange juice)
1 Tbs. orange zest
2 dashes of vanilla extract, optional

Sauce
1½ c. orange juice, freshly squeezed, not from concentrate (or use Natalie's Orchid Island Juice Company brand)
2 Tbs. sugar
2 tsp. orange zest
2 Tbs. Grand Marnier
3 oranges, peeled, sectioned
Powdered sugar

*Can substitute orange juice concentrate for the Grand Marnier, if desired.

Crêpes
Preheat a lightly greased 8-in. frying pan or skillet over medium-high heat.

Stir together pancake mix and flour. Gradually add water, stirring until smooth. Add eggs, butter, Grand Marnier, orange zest and stir or whisk until smooth.

Spoon 2–3 Tbs. of batter into center of pan, tilt, and swirl to coat bottom of pan evenly. Cook until delicately brown, flip, and cook other side lightly. Remove and set crêpes aside.

Sauce

In a large skillet over high heat, bring orange juice to a boil. Add sugar, zest, and reduce heat to a simmer until sugar is melted (4–5 minutes). Remove from heat and stir in Grand Marnier and orange sections.

To assemble:

Gently place a crêpe in the pan holding the sauce mixture. Leave for a minute to absorb the juice. Remove and place sauce side up on a warm serving plate. Repeat with remaining crêpes.

To serve:

Roll up crêpes. Spoon remaining mixture and orange sections over the top. Sprinkle with powdered sugar and serve.

Be sure not to miss the first book in Kathleen Bridge's By the Sea Mystery series,

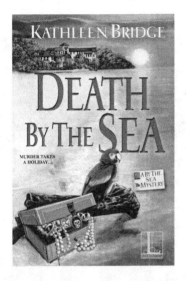

The Indialantic by the Sea Hotel has a hundred-year-old history on beautiful Melbourne Beach, Florida, and more than a few guests seem to have been there from the start. When Liz Holt returns home after an intense decade in New York, she's happy to be surrounded by the eccentric clientele and loving relatives who populate her family-run inn, and doubly pleased to see the business is staying afloat thanks to its vibrant shopping emporium and a few very wealthy patrons.

But that patronage decreases by one when a filthy-rich guest is discovered dead in her oceanfront suite. Maybe this is simply a jewel theft gone wrong, but maybe someone—or many people—wanted the hotel's prosperous guest dead. Only one thing is sure: There's a killer at the Indialantic, and if Liz lets herself be distracted—by her troubled past or the tempting man who seems eager to dredge it back up—the next reservation she'll book could be at the cemetery...

A Lyrical Underground e-book on sale now!

And don't forget the second book in the series,
A Killing by the Sea, also on sale now!

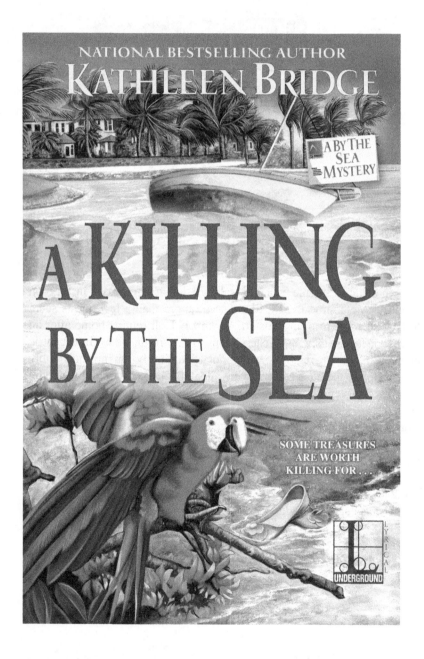

NATIONAL BESTSELLING AUTHOR

KATHLEEN BRIDGE

A BY THE SEA MYSTERY

A KILLING BY THE SEA

SOME TREASURES
ARE WORTH
KILLING FOR . . .

LYRICAL
UNDERGROUND

Printed in the United States
by Baker & Taylor Publisher Services